DESTINY FULFILLED

For Tracie
with love & best wishes
Joanne
xxx
(Joanna Beckley)

DESTINY FULFILLED

JOANNA BECKLEY

JANUS PUBLISHING COMPANY
London, England

First published in Great Britain 1996
by Janus Publishing Company
Edinburgh House, 19 Nassau Street
London W1N 7RE

British Library Cataloguing-in-Publication Data.
A catalogue record for this book is available from the British Library.

ISBN 1 85756 340 9

Cover design Harold King

Photosetting by Keyboard Services, Luton, Beds
Printed and bound in Great Britain by
Antony Rowe Ltd, Chippenham, Wiltshire

BOOK I

DESTINY DECREES

CHAPTER ONE

The First Year 1972

Sarah E. Mannering turned her small car through the wide gates, past the lodge on the left and along the drive flanked by tall beech trees that led to the imposing house of 'Heronshurst' which she hoped would become her home at least long enough for her to sort out her future life. She had broken with her unhappy past and reached out for a new beginning by answering an advertisement in a prestigious magazine aimed at providing personnel for discriminating people.

She was contemplating the beautiful façade of the house she was approaching, when her attention was distracted by the sound of a jingling harness and she was further disconcerted by the feeling as if the little car swayed and jolted like a horse-drawn vehicle. It was only momentary and she gave a small shrug, thinking that the past years must have affected her more than she had considered. Reaching the house, she parked a short way from the main entrance and walked towards the big double doors.

Ringing the bell, she glanced briefly at her small car and was startled again by the illusion that she was looking at an elegant carriage bearing a crest on the door. She shook her head, feeling utterly confused. Really, I must pull myself together she thought, as the door opened.

The butler, on her announcing her identity and business, replied, 'Yes, madam, his Lordship is expecting you. Please come this way,' and with a strange sense of *déjà vu*, she followed him into the wide hall and along a passage to the left of the magnificent double staircase of carved oak, that curved up both sides of the hall, reaching either end of a galleried landing.

Passing several doors, they arrived eventually at one at the end of the passage. The butler knocked and opened the door, standing to one side to let her in whilst announcing her arrival.

Sarah's first impression was of a very comfortable study with a book-lined wall between windows behind a wide desk opposite her, at which sat a man. Beside him was the biggest, handsomest Alsatian dog she had ever seen, which, having regarded her intently, stood up suddenly and with easy loping strides, crossed the room to her and reared up, resting his paws on her shoulders while keeping his weight on his hind legs.

He was very nearly as tall as she and she could look straight into his face. If he had wanted to do so, he could have knocked her flying, but she had never been afraid of dogs and the expression on his handsome face held nothing but intense interest and an obvious desire to be friends.

The man at the desk rose and speaking sharply to the dog, he apologised to Sarah for what might have been a frightening experience.

She lifted the huge paws gently from her shoulders and lowered them to the floor, realising that, yet again, she seemed to have encouraged what was obviously a normally well-trained animal to behave out of character. She had lost count of the number of times she had been followed by dogs when she was out walking and had needed to retrace her steps to return them to their owner.

His master spoke to him again, ordering him to return to his original place, but although he looked over his shoulder almost apologetically, the dog stayed where he was and turned back to gaze at Sarah adoringly.

She spoke very softly, telling him to return to his rightful place and after considering her for a moment, he obeyed and went back to his spot beside the desk.

Realising that Sarah was neither hurt nor frightened, the man laughed somewhat ruefully, saying, 'You have obviously made a conquest. I have never known him to behave like that before.' He held out his hand, adding, 'I am Robert Falconbridge, by the way. How do you do.'

Sarah took his hand. 'How do you do, sir,' and because she was feeling confused and guilty, as she always did when causing other people's normally well-trained dogs to misbehave, she blurted out, 'I've fallen in love – and I don't even know his name!' Then instantly, 'Yes, I do – it must be Merlin to embody so much magic,' wondering, as usual, how she could be so sure the moment the words left her mouth.

4

Lord Falconbridge looked surprised and studying her closely, asked, 'That is clever of you. How could you possibly know that?' adding, 'By the way, please call me Robert and may I call you Sarah as this reprobate has already presumed on your friendship?'

'Please do,' Sarah replied, already feeling very much more comfortable. She registered in her mind that the man was as handsome in his way as the dog. His thick brown hair was touched slightly with grey at the temples and at close quarters she could see the fascinating green and gold flecks in his hazel eyes above a strong, straight nose. His mouth was firm, with well-shaped lips and seemed to smile easily. It was a face to inspire loyalty and trust – and love? an unbidden voice asked at the back of her mind. That would be very unwise, she thought. Too many women fell in love with their employers – that way trouble lay.

In his turn, Robert was regarding the woman who had suddenly invaded his existence. As far as he knew, he could not possibly have met her before, so why did her face seem so familiar to him – almost dearly familiar.

The deep blue/grey eyes under well-marked brows that curved like wings, the small, straight nose and generous curling mouth. Her silver hair – premature surely? he thought – was well-cut and fitted closely round her neat head.

She looked about thirty-five but he knew from her application that she was fifty, two years younger than he and he thought approvingly that her honesty in stating her exact age was endearing. So many women whom he had met would have claimed 'forty-nine', or if they looked as well as she did, something considerably less.

He realised that neither had spoken for a while and to avoid any likelihood of an embarrassing silence, he said easily, 'I am curious to see what Merlin would do, if you went away. Would you mind going out of the room and walking back to the front door?'

Sarah turned and approached the door with her easy, graceful steps, turning the handle and pulling open the heavy door. Passing through, she had half closed it behind her, when a form squeezed by her and she almost shut Merlin's tail in the door. He stood looking at her with an expression very like a grin on his handsome face and she looked back with something like despair on hers.

'You,' she told him, 'are likely to lose me this job before we have even had time to discuss it. However, I had better do as I was requested this time,' and she walked back along the whole length of the passage until she reached the main door, Merlin staying firmly beside her.

What do I do now? she thought. He is determined to come, too, and turning, she returned to the room from which she had come, opened the door and approached the desk.

'He would have followed you without a backward glance,' Robert remarked, incredulously. 'It seems to me that the only way to keep him here is to kidnap you.' He laughed, 'I'll ring for some tea and we can drink it on the terrace. It is very pleasant at this time of the day in autumn. We will forget about business until then,' and so saying, he reached for the bell-pull. When the butler appeared he said, 'Tea for two, please, Bates, and perhaps some of Mrs Briggs' excellent little cakes?'

He showed Sarah onto the terrace and they settled either side of one of the tables in comfortable, chintz-cushioned chairs.

Sarah's attention was taken by the sheer beauty and tranquillity of the scene, bathed in the late afternoon September sunshine. Beyond the terrace, lawns and flower beds sloped down to where an ornamental fountain splashed and sparkled, then more lawns that reached a large lake, almost mirror-like in its stillness. At four points round the lake were small jetties, two of which had a punt moored to them, one nearest to them and one on the opposite side. To the left of the lake, broadleafed woodland stretched from beyond the front of the house and down beside the lake, to fields of corn and pasture to the horizon.

Robert studied the still, clear-cut profile. He sensed that she had been very unhappy – why else would she set out at fifty years of age to start a new life where accommodation was necessary?

The job that had caused her to be here now – that was a problem he had not yet solved. One thing of which he was certain, he considered that she was worthy of more than the rather mundane post of helping to catalogue his special collection of books and another thing, he was adamant to himself that he did not now want to put them on an employer/employee basis.

A nebulous thought was stirring at the back of his mind that needed very careful consideration. On the face of it, it was a little unconventional but to him it seemed such a natural solution that he realised he must be very, very careful how to present it to

Sarah. What his friends and the rest of the world made of it did not worry him unduly. He had always made his own decisions, regardless of outside opinion.

He was well aware that many people could not understand why he had not married – if only to provide an heir – but he had never met the woman who could satisfy all his requirements for a person with whom he wanted to spend the whole of his life. He had wanted something more than a decorative, intelligent wife who would grace his name and provide suitable issue.

Good heavens, man! he thought, what do you want? But in his heart of hearts, he was aware that Destiny held something special for him and that when the time came he would know. So far Destiny had deferred but he had a feeling that at long last, he was going to be shown the way.

Robert's thoughts were interrupted by the arrival of tea. Bates took the tray from the maid and with a little bob, she returned to the house. He settled the tea-things on the table, enquiring, 'Shall I pour, my lord?'

'No, Bates, thank you, that will be fine. Mrs Mannering will do me the honour, I am sure,' smiling gently at Sarah in a way that set her completely at ease and gave her the feeling of having arrived in a safe harbour after a storm. 'You will probably find that there is Earl Grey in the silver pot and Lapsang Souchong in the porcelain one,' he mentioned casually, adding, 'Earl Grey for me, please.'

For the next few moments, Sarah busied herself pouring the tea, Earl Grey for Robert and Lapsang Souchong for herself. She passed Robert his cup, ignoring the sugar bowl and he was intrigued by her absolute certainty that he did not take sugar. It was as if she had been pouring tea for him all her life. Sarah offered a plate in either hand, one containing petit fours and the other, tiny macaroons. He took one of each saying, 'Where cakes are concerned, I have a sweet tooth,' and smiled like a small boy. Sarah smiled back and picked up her cup, drinking her tea the way Robert liked his China tea – no milk, no sugar.

It was a measure of her faith in his understanding, that she told him of her experience while driving up to the house and the illusion of seeing the coach. Normally, nothing would have induced her to mention it to an outsider.

Robert listened with close interest, then said, 'When we have had tea, I will show you some of the house and family portraits.'

They sat in companionable silence for a while and Merlin lay on the terrace, watching them carefully. Sarah did not make the mistake of offering him titbits and Robert silently approved.

Presently, he rose to his feet and helped Sarah back with her chair and they walked into the house and through the long passage that led into the main hall. This time, Sarah was able to take in more detail and noticed that the newel posts bore coats of arms.

At the head of the stairs was a portrait of a young man in hussar uniform. In spite of the fact that it was painted probably in the late seventeenth or early eighteenth century, there was a remarkable likeness to Robert and Sarah was not surprised when he said, 'That was my seven times great grandfather.'

A matching portrait of a young woman in a gold satin dress took her attention. Her luxuriant brown hair was piled on top of her head at the front and sides, falling in glossy ringlets behind her delicate ears. One hand rested on the neck of a borzoi sitting beside her and the other held a small fan. The garden and lake formed the background.

'Why, that is Estelle!' Sarah said in a faraway voice, 'she was a duchess in her own right and both her parents died when she was very young. She arrived here in a coach to meet her future mother-in-law, who was very fond of her and very glad when she became engaged to her son, Robert. Not only was it a very suitable match for them both, they were extremely in love.' Her voice died away and, trying to conceal his astonishment, Robert asked softly, 'Do you know what happened to them?'

Sarah seemed to come back to him from a distance and he watched the effort she made to resume normal conversation.

'No,' she said, at last, 'That is as much as I—' she was going to say 'remember' but after a moment's hesitation said, 'know.'

Robert forbore to enquire how she knew. As far as he was aware himself, there was no written history available to anyone other than close family. More and more the feeling was over-taking him of being carried along on a tide of events that was inevitable and beyond his control. He was very content that it should be so. He said as casually as he could manage, 'Estelle was expecting their first child when Robert had to go to war and he was one of the casualties of the battle of Blenheim. Tallard, the French commander, had taken a strong position along the west bank of the Nebel, thinking that no one would dare to attack while he was protected by the Nebel, Danube and the fortified village of Blenheim, but he reckoned without the Duke of Marlborough and his ally, Prince Eugene of Savoy and was

8

astonished one morning to find the allied army of English, Dutch, German and Danish soldiers under the Duke's command, preparing to cross the river.

'Tallard had mistakenly positioned his troops too far back, allowing the allied army to re-group after crossing the river. Marlborough had to hold off the attack until Prince Eugene's forces had reached its place on the flank.

'For five hours the French guns pounded unremittingly at the waiting troops. Marlborough himself narrowly missed being hit by a cannon ball as he rode round reviewing the situation, but my ancestor, who was near him, was not so lucky. He was only twenty-four years old. The shock caused Estelle to go into premature labour, the baby survived but Estelle died. She had appeared to be quite well. The nurse thought she heard her speaking and went in to see her but she was dead. Robert's parents brought up the baby, a boy, and he grew strong and healthy and was a great comfort to them, helping them to recover from the loss of their beloved son and also of Estelle, whom they had loved dearly.'

Sarah's face reflected her sadness and she appeared to be trying to remember something.

'There is a legend,' continued Robert, 'that before she died, the words the nurse overheard was a vow that she would find her adored husband, where he had fallen on foreign soil and she was reputed to have said, "Some day, Robert, we will return to earth again and bring up our son together." But there has never been anyone like her since,' concluded Robert, adding to himself, until now.

The likeness that he had been trying to place ever since Sarah's arrival, which had escaped him, suddenly became obvious. Allowing for the difference in ages, Sarah and Estelle were very much alike. The same proud carriage of the head and shoulders, the beautiful, expressive eyes of deep blue/grey under the same winged brows, even the mouth – especially the mouth – and the delicate well-shaped hands. Looking at Sarah, Robert thought, so might Estelle have looked had she lived longer.

He continued to show Sarah around the main part of the house, trying to control the turmoil in his mind. Somehow soon, they had to resolve the problem of the reason why she was here. It seemed a lifetime since she arrived – what was it? Less than two hours ago!

Playing for time, Robert said as casually as he could manage, 'You are not in a hurry to get back, are you? Will you stay for dinner, please? It will be only the two of us, so quite informal,' he added, realising that she had no luggage with her. 'I have been thinking about the post for which you applied and I do not think it is really suitable for you.' He hurried on, 'I have another one in mind which I think will be much more amenable to you but I do not want to rush you into a decision until we have had plenty of time to discuss it. Would it be presumptuous of me to ask if you could stay overnight? Frazer, my chauffeur, could drive you to collect your belongings and, if you find, after all, that your future is not here, you can return in the morning.' He regarded Sarah anxiously, willing her to understand that her welfare was his sole concern.

She returned his look steadily, sensing his solicitude and, like him, carried away on the tide of events. Good heavens, she thought, I am a grown woman, I should be able to make a decision.

It seemed a very long time to Robert, waiting for her answer, but was in fact only a few moments.

'Yes,' she replied gravely, 'I would like to stay for dinner and there is no reason why I cannot stay overnight.' Her trust in him showed in her eyes and he breathed a sigh of relief.

'I will not let you regret it,' he promised. 'You seem so at home here it would be a shame if you had to rush away.'

Merlin had joined them downstairs and his enthusiastic tail-wagging approved the arrangement.

'Have you been listening to our conversation?' Robert chided him, but the dog looked completely unrepentant.

'We have dinner at seven when I am alone,' Robert informed Sarah. 'It gives the staff time to clear earlier. Would you like Frazer to drive you to get your things before dinner?' He would have liked to suggest that he drove her himself – anything rather than letting her out of his sight now that he had found her, but refrained for fear of being too importunate.

'First of all, I will get Mrs Bates, the housekeeper, to show you to your room and you can freshen up after your long drive,' and so saying, he rang for Mrs Bates.

When she appeared, Robert said, 'Please show Mrs Mannering to the Rose room. She will be staying the night – possibly longer,' he added.

He noticed Mrs Bates' slight start as she looked at Sarah and wondered whether she too, had recognised her likeness to Estelle. Staff could be very possessive and protective where 'family' was concerned, he'd found.

Sarah followed Mrs Bates up the main stairs and noticed this time that the two coats of arms on the newel posts were different and supposed, rightly, that one belonged to Robert's family and the other to Estelle's, which had been cleverly replaced over the original when Estelle married into the family.

Having arrived at the gallery landing, they walked along until another corridor led off to the left over the downstairs passage that she had first traversed on her arrival, thence to another one running along the front of the house.

Mrs Bates opened an ornately carved door and ushered Sarah into one of the most appealing rooms she had ever seen. It was utterly feminine and very restful, the walls of palest shell pink with the pattern of a single perfect rose repeated at intervals, the carpet was a deep rose, which was echoed in the silk bed cover. The wardrobe, dressing-table, stool, small bedroom chair and luggage rack were a delicate, almost silver-grey wood. The whole effect was charming and tranquil.

Mrs Bates was busy opening wardrobe doors and drawers to show her, then she walked to a door at the far side of the room and said, 'This is your bathroom.' She left the bathroom and opened another door on the same side of the room. 'This is your sitting room,' she said, standing back to allow Sarah to enter. Sarah was enchanted. A Sheraton desk topped by a bookcase, with its delicate and graceful lines, stood beside the window, which she realised faced south along the side of the house. The whole suite must be on the corner, she realised, getting her bearings.

As well as the desk, there was another generous-sized book-case and a chintz-covered suite of chairs and a small sofa. The carpet was a pale, soft sage green and the curtains repeated the colour in a slightly deeper shade.

'I hope you will find everything to your satisfaction and be comfortable here, madam. If there is anything more you need, just ring.'

'Thank you, Mrs Bates, I am sure I will. Everything is delight-ful.' Sarah was intrigued that the bathroom and sitting room seemed to exist in their own right and had not been adapted to mar the beautiful proportions of the huge bedroom. When the house was built in the late seventeenth century, during the reign of William and Mary, it could not have had bathrooms. She ventured to put the point to Mrs Bates, who explained that the bathroom had been a dressing room and the sitting room was already there. All the main bedrooms had similar facilities. The master bedroom had had a dressing room either side, one of which had been adapted to a bathroom, leaving the other still as a dressing room for the head of the house.

When Mrs Bates had gone, Sarah walked to the bedroom window and noticed that it was at the front of the house looking down the long beech-lined drive and to the other end of the woodland that ran past the house down to the cornfields at the back. It was facing east and she would get the morning sun, which pleased her. As a child, she had always been able to tell the time within reason, at any time of the year, by where the sunlight fell on the walls of her bedroom. She wandered into the bathroom, which was predominantly white – another plus, as far as she was concerned – with the rosebud motif echoed on all the accoutrements. There was everything anyone could possibly need in the way of toiletries and after a quick freshen up, she returned downstairs, prepared to return to fetch her belongings.

Robert was awaiting her in the hall and told her that Frazer and the Rolls were at her disposal and they walked out to the car together. Robert helped her in, saying, 'Take all the time you need, but come back as soon as you can.' He stood back and waved briefly as the car purred away down the drive. He watched it until it turned on to the road and disappeared out of sight and with a feeling of being bereft, sighed gently and returned to the house to await Sarah's homecoming. He smiled wryly at himself for his spontaneous choice of the last word and hoped that Sarah, too, would find it apposite.

CHAPTER TWO

As the car glided along the drive, Sarah sat back and tried to collect her thoughts. When life, so far, had been so uneventful, though difficult and, finally, impossible to tolerate, how could so much happen in such a short space of time?

Arriving at Heronshurst had felt so incredibly like coming home after a long and stormy journey and being there such a little while made her feel very reluctant to leave it behind, even for an hour or two, in case she awoke to find that she had been only dreaming.

Sarah reviewed the circumstances and blessed them for prompting her to take the actions that had led her to Heronshurst. In her anxiety to escape and shake off the trammels of the past, she realised the need for a post that would include accommodation, as she would be left with only her personal possessions. Any assets that she had owned previously had long since been annexed on some pretext or other, on the excuse that it was mutual property or she had needed to convert them for everyday living. It was strange how, if she a wanted something they 'couldn't afford it' however necessary it was, even using money that had been left to her as a child.

She recalled the first position for which she had applied as a housekeeper at a manor house in a little Cotswold village. The husband had been very anxious for her to take it, but the wife's reluctance seemed to be in direct ratio to her husband's enthusiasm.

The second post for which she had applied, it was the wife who was very anxious for her to start immediately, but although her husband was charming and kind, he was reluctant to commit himself to employing her, but his last words to her gave her the courage to continue her search and aim for the post at Heronshurst.

'Please don't be disheartened,' the man had said, 'I am not rejecting you. You have a lot to offer but I don't think this post is entirely for you. You could do much better and I wouldn't feel at all comfortable giving you orders.' He shook her hand and appeared so anxious that she should not be made to feel inadequate or personally rejected by his refusal to employ her, that she felt more encouraged than discouraged.

As events had transpired, he had done her a favour as, thinking over his words and the sincerity with which they were uttered, she took heart and decided to act on his advice, after all, she did have a lot to offer in the way of honesty, integrity, adaptability and loyalty. She blessed him in her heart for giving her confidence in herself and the courage to apply for the job that Robert had advertised. How the years and circumstances had taken toll of her once sublime self-confidence!

Remembering the second interview, she wondered if it would have made any difference if, when the man told her he had taken up farming after years of serving in the 'Blues', she had not blurted out, 'Oh, really? My grandfather was in the "Blues". He rode in Queen Victoria's funeral cortège and having seen an old newsreel shot of it on television, I realised I could be looking at him. It seemed very strange as he died before I was born.'

Coming back to the present, Sarah glanced out of the window to establish where they were and was surprised at how quickly they had covered the distance. Frazer seemed to be well-acquainted with the road and she thought he would probably be able to drive straight to anywhere in the British Isles if one asked him to do so.

Glancing in the rearview mirror, Frazer noticed the shadow that had passed over her face and wondered what was bothering her. Mr and Mrs Bates were very tight-lipped about discussing his Lordship's guests, but he gathered that there was some suggestion that she could be someone he had known a long time ago and with whom he had lost touch. Perhaps remotely related? One thing of which Frazer was sure, he had never seen his Lordship look so quietly happy as he was today. Oh, well! Whatever happened he hoped Mrs Mannering would be happy, too. He did not like her looking sad, her face was made for smiling.

Sarah had left her belongings – all her personal possessions – several boxes of books, silver, china and special ornaments that had belonged to her childhood home, with a removal firm, intending to have them moved when her address was finally settled. She must remember to cancel her overnight booking at the hotel and pick up her cases containing her clothes, hoping desperately that she would not see anyone she knew.

As they neared the town of Elkesbury for which they were heading, the traffic thickened and Frazer had to forget his speculation about his passenger and concentrate more on his driving. With a word or two from her, he found the removal firm and went in to enquire about Mrs Mannering's possessions. They were about to close but quickly helped him to stack the boxes neatly in the boot, kindly waiving any charge for their brief storage.

Finding the hotel, Frazer waited while Mrs Mannering went into reception and returned with a porter carrying two large suitcases, while she had a square overnight bag. He fitted the cases into the space he had left for them in the boot and soon they were on their way back to Heronshurst.

Sarah leaned back and tried to relax. Well! she had burned her boats now and ahead of her lay a completely new, unknown life. The thought should have terrified her, but somehow it didn't – she had not felt so calm and at peace for a very long time. It would be pleasant to have dinner with Robert in that lovely house and sleep in that restful, tranquil room.

Robert had said he wanted to offer her a job that she would find more amenable and she was sure she could rely on his judgement. She was not unduly curious to know what it was – she felt she could trust him with her life – and it would have to be very unreasonable to make living at Heronshurst intolerable.

The miles slid by and Sarah was surprised to find how near home they were – how easily that word slipped into her mind! She glanced at her watch and found it was after six-thirty. Dinner was at seven so she must not waste too much time getting ready when they returned. She noticed that her own little car had been moved but could not remember whether it was there when they left earlier.

Getting out to help her alight, Frazer caught her glancing toward where the car had stood and said, 'His Lordship asked me to put your car in one of the garages as he was sure you would not want it again tonight.'

'Thank you, Frazer, and also for taking me to get my things.'

Robert had seen the Rolls return and had to resist the impulse to rush out like an excited schoolboy to meet it. He smiled warmly at Sarah as they met on the drive and walked into the house together.

'Frazer will take care of your luggage and see that it is put in your room. Dinner can be served as soon as you are ready, but there is no rush. I expect you are hungry?'

Sarah was surprised to find that she was indeed very hungry and ran lightly up the stairs to her room to freshen up for dinner. She showered quickly and changed into a simple dress that she had in her overnight bag originally for dining in the hotel. It just happened that it was almost the same sage green as the curtains in her sitting room and she grinned, thinking that if she stood in front of them, she would be nearly invisible.

There was still the trace of the smile on her face as she hurried down to join Robert in the dining room and it was reflected on his as he helped her to her place at table.

The dinner was simple but delicious and they talked generalities for the most part. Sarah was surprised and comforted by the ease with which they both conversed. It was very relaxing – something that had been all too rare for longer than she cared to think about.

Robert asked, 'Do you ride?'

'Yes,' she replied. 'I haven't been able to do so for more than two years, but I still have my riding clothes.'

'Will you come riding with me tomorrow morning after breakfast, please? I have to visit several of my tenant farmers. The countryside is pleasant, but it is more enjoyable with agreeable company. We will go to the stables after dinner and you can make the acquaintance of all the horses and choose your mount if you are kind enough to say "Yes".'

'That would be very pleasant, I will look forward to it,' Sarah replied.

'While we are between farms, we can discuss the project that I have in mind, which I hope you will feel able to accept. There is no need to rush into a decision. Take two or three days to think about it, if you find it necessary. I want you to be very sure and happy in your own mind before you commit yourself.'

Sarah had almost forgotten that anyone could be as kind and reasonable as Robert was being. In other circumstances, she might have felt uneasy, but her instincts were very sure and she was certain that there was no ulterior motive as far as Robert was concerned, she could take his offer on face value.

They finished their coffee and left the table, going out to the stables. It was almost dark but the stables were well lit and Sarah was in her element making friends with all the horses. A magnificent palomino took her eye, its gleaming coat shining like gold satin, contrasting with the pale cream mane and tail. She stroked his nose, murmuring admiring remarks to him, judging him to be nearly seventeen hands.

'May I ride this one please?' she asked Robert.

'Yes, of course you may,' he replied, 'That is a good choice, he has a wonderful temperament.'

The name above the stall indicated that he was called 'Apollo'. What a very apt name, Sarah thought. 'God of Light'.

Returning to the house, they sat for a while in the small green drawing room and Robert asked Sarah about her life and family so gently that it did not seem like probing and she answered easily without restraint in a way that she would never have dreamed of with most comparative strangers. 'Stranger' seemed an odd word to apply to Robert. It was as though she had known him well before in another, happier time. But not in another place – the thought came unbidden into her head, taking her by surprise.

Because she felt Robert was entitled to know her present status, she mentioned briefly how a combination of circumstances had led her, at eighteen, into a marriage which had proved disastrous from the start, but that she had always believed in the permanence of the vows and felt that one could give up too easily, until, for the sake of her physical and mental health and on the advice of her doctor, she had to break free. 'There was no one else involved as far as I was concerned, though the same was not true of my husband,' she added. 'It was that the situation had become intolerable and I could not face spending the rest of my life like it and further effort seemed pointless finally. After the prescribed time apart, it can be legally finished. Until then, I shall just take each day as it comes.'

Robert felt that he could not bear to watch her dwelling on her unhappiness – it was over now, thankfully, and he would do his best to make up to her for it.

Although he had not been married himself, he had seen enough of couples to know that, sometimes, one or other partner seemed to go out of their way to destroy the harmony that could exist between them. It seemed to him, on the outside looking in, a form of jealousy, a metaphorical death wish to their relationship.

Robert marvelled that the only effect Sarah's traumas seemed to have had on her looks, was to give her an air of inner strength that he sensed would always sustain her. She was the stuff of which survivors are made. As a red-blooded male, he felt the urge to comfort and shelter her from any more hurt, but realised it would probably be a long time before she could trust another man fully and would be reluctant to rely on anyone other than herself.

To distract her from unpleasant memories, he told her of his own life and family, that his younger brother, Richard, was his heir. 'The house was first built at the beginning of the reign of William and Mary for the parents of the Robert in the portrait at the head of the stairs, when he was about ten years old. When he first met Estelle, her parents were already dead, although she was only six or seven at the time, living with her great uncle, who was her guardian. They were like brother and sister while they were children and Estelle hero-worshipped Robert, while he was her protector and staunch ally. It was fairly inevitable that they should fall in love as they grew up and when they became engaged, the celebration was held at Heronshurst as her guardian was not really able to cope with such a demanding event. Robert's parents adored Estelle and already felt that she was their daughter, so it was a very happy occasion for them.

'Robert and Estelle were married in 1701, when he was twenty-one and she was eighteen and they lived at Heronshurst until such time as Robert's parents should move into the dower house. As you know, Robert tragically lost his life at the battle of Blenheim and his son was brought up by his parents after Estelle died also – some think of a broken heart. The birth was quite straightforward and Estelle had seemed to be blooming.' Robert paused for a while, but realising that Sarah was hanging on his words he continued. 'Legends have a tendency to grow with time. The people who believe in these things say that the reason Heronshurst is not haunted by Estelle is because her spirit is still searching where Robert fell. It was not always possible to bring home soldiers for burial then and they often did not have a proper grave on foreign soil, but it is said that if ever Estelle is seen at Heronshurst, it will be because she has come home with Robert and her spirit is at peace.'

Watching his face, Sarah arrived at the conclusion that the only reason Robert had not married was because, as a young man, he had been more than half in love with the legend of Estelle and, as he said earlier, 'There hasn't been anyone like her since.' She wondered if he believed the legend, but it was not the sort of question to ask. She herself, from personal experience, knew as Shakespeare wrote in *Hamlet*, 'There are more things in heaven and earth, Horatio, than are dreamt of in your philosophy.'

Glancing at the clock, Robert said, 'You must be tired, I'll see you to your room. There is all tomorrow and tomorrow untouched.' He smiled, rising to his feet and Sarah stood up. They went up the stairs together and when they reached her room, Robert said, 'My room is the third door along, so if you have any bad dreams or need me, I'll be there.'

It was said in a very matter-of-fact tone and she knew it was merely to comfort and reassure her that she was not alone in a strange house.

Robert took her hand, saying, 'Goodnight, Sarah, sleep well. I'll see you at breakfast.'

She replied, 'I'm sure I will, thank you. You, too.'

He held her hand for a moment longer, asking, 'When you signed your name it was "Sarah E Mannering". What does the "E" stand for?' But he knew before she answered quietly,

'Estelle.'

CHAPTER THREE

When Sarah went into her room, she found that her cases had been unpacked and everything neatly put away in the drawers and wardrobe. She marvelled that they had been arranged almost exactly the way she would have done it herself.

The curtains had been closed and her bed turned back invitingly. Wandering into the bathroom, she ran a deep, warm bath and having shed her clothes, wallowed luxuriously in the warm, scented water, letting the events of the day drift slowly through her mind.

It seemed incredible that it was such a short time since she had set out this morning. She closed her eyes, letting a kaleidoscope of pictures float gently before her mental vision. The moment she had turned through the gates of Heronshurst, the odd illusions she had experienced, the feeling of *déjà vu* as she followed Bates into the house and how Merlin had monopolised the attention when she first arrived, breaking any constraint she might have felt.

Then Robert's kindness, care and consideration – over the years, she had almost forgotten that such people like him existed. She remembered the look in his eyes when she had answered his question about her second name.

Sarah felt herself drifting and realised that if she was not careful, she would fall asleep in the bath. Standing up, she released the water, wrapped herself in one of the huge bath towels and padded into her bedroom. Picking up the nightie that had thoughtfully been left out for her, she donned it, slipped into bed and instantly fell asleep.

As she came out of the depths of sleep, the morning sun was

pouring through the opened curtains and a soft sound made her turn her head. A young maid had placed a tray of tea for her on the bedside table.

Sarah smiled at her and asked, 'What do I call you?'

The girl smiled back and replied, 'My name is Elizabeth but everyone calls me Lizzie.'

'Do you mind that?' Sarah asked intuitively.

'Well, madam, I didn't mind when I was little but now I'm grown up, I think it would be nice to be called "Elizabeth".'

Sarah suppressed the smile that wanted to come at the words 'now I'm grown up' – Good heavens! she could not be a day over seventeen. Lizzie was actually sixteen and a half. Sarah said conspiratorially, 'From now on I'll call you Elizabeth.'

The girl blushed slightly and said, 'I'd like that, madam, but not in front of Mu ... Mrs Bates.'

Sarah noticed the slight slip of the tongue and asked, 'Are Mr and Mrs Bates your parents?' and was amused that it was Mrs Bates of whom Lizzie/Elizabeth was in awe, but merely said, 'I'll remember that. Thank you for the tea.'

'I hope it is to your taste, madam. His Lordship gave orders that it should be Lapsang Sou ... China tea.' She could not quite manage the name. 'Shall I pour it out for you?'

'Thank you, but I can manage,' Sarah replied and as Lizzie/ Elizabeth went out, she poured some tea, drank it, jumped out of bed and hurried into the bathroom to shower, dressed in her riding clothes and ran down the stairs for breakfast.

She met Robert in the hall and they went into the breakfast room together.

'There are various kinds of eggs, sausages, bacon and all the usual trimmings on the hot trolley,' Robert announced, 'Jolly good things, these trolleys, much better than in the old days when everything had to be rushed up from the kitchen, even after the lift was installed. May I help you to anything or would you rather serve yourself?'

'Thank you, I can manage,' Sarah answered, helping herself to scrambled eggs, crispy bacon, tomatoes and mushrooms.

'Good girl!' Robert said approvingly, eyeing her plate. 'I like to see people eat a good breakfast.'

Sarah grinned, 'What is it they say? "Breakfast like a king, lunch like a lord and dine like a pauper." I haven't seen you eat lunch yet, so I don't know what that entails, but judging by last night's dinner, there must be many a pauper who would like to dine like that.'

21

Robert laughed and they sat down to enjoy their meal – the second together, thought Robert, not counting afternoon tea.

How well she looks in her riding clothes, he mused, but then whatever she wears she looks as if it has been made especially for her. He was aware that could not have been true and contributed it to her discrimination.

He glimpsed Merlin regarding them through the open door, 'Yes, you may come in,' Robert invited him, 'but behave yourself.'

Merlin walked in and lay down watching them, looking as if butter wouldn't melt in his mouth.

Sarah smiled at him and he gave a brief wag with the tip of his tail, content to wait patiently. He knew that riding kit meant going through the woods and fields a nice long way and he hoped he was going to be allowed to join them. There were such interesting smells in the woods and when the horses went into a fast canter Merlin could really stretch his legs.

When breakfast was finished, Robert and Sarah went out to the stables where Apollo and Robert's magnificent chestnut, Flame, were already saddled and waiting. Sarah mounted the way she always did, disdaining the mounting block and feeling thankful that she could still manage it after two years. I'll know I am getting old when I can no longer do that, she pondered.

The groom came and checked the girth and moved on to do the same for Robert.

How well he looks on a horse, Sarah thought, as if they were part of the same entity. She was entirely unaware that Robert was considering the identical thing about her. She was seldom self-conscious and never wondered what people thought of her, just content that not many of them found it necessary to be rude or unkind to her, except one and his ghastly mother, but that was his problem, not hers.

Robert and Sarah moved out of the stable yard and Robert took a path that led round some pasture land, towards the dense broad-leaved wood, Merlin trotting happily behind Apollo. In the wood, they struck off at an angle where the path forked and presently came out on to open land.

In the distance, a cottage of rose-red brick stood out in the morning sunlight and they headed towards it. Robert checked his horse slightly so that Sarah could come alongside him and as she drew level, he said, 'This is a wonderful place to have a private conversation and be really sure you can't be overheard.'

Sarah said, 'Except by Merlin!' and they both laughed.

'Oh, he knows how to keep a secret, don't you, boy?' Robert continued more seriously, 'This is the plan that I want to put to you. I'll explain it as clearly as I can and when you have had plenty of time to consider it and have asked all the questions that may occur to you, you can give me your answer, yes or no and we can take things from there.'

They kept their mounts to a slow walk and Robert expounded his thoughts.

'I am well aware that what I am about to propose might be open to question by ordinary, everyday standards, but you know and I know that the last few hours have been anything but everyday. To put it as succinctly as possible, what I want is that you should be here to help me in my day-to-day life and all that it entails. Today it will be visiting the tenants and helping me to decide, from a woman's point of view, what is best to be done to solve the many questions with which we may be faced. Fixing roofs, plumbing etc. is no problem. The bailiff takes care of that, but you would be surprised what dilemmas my tenants think I can solve for them and often, that is when I think a sympathetic and understanding woman would be able to help a lot more than I can, however I might sympathise with their predicament.' Robert paused to glance at Sarah, wondering if she had any idea of what he meant. They had met only yesterday but he would have staked his life on her understanding.

Sarah had obviously been listening intently and she said slowly, 'Yes, I can see how that might be so, in certain given circumstances.'

Robert heaved an inward sigh of relief, so far, so good. He continued, 'I would also like you to be there when I entertain, go to the theatre or opera and supervise the arrangements for the local periodic celebrations that the tenants have always been accustomed to expect – Halloween, Guy Fawkes night, Christmas, the Hunt Ball—' he stopped, catching sight of the expression on Sarah's face, then, with the instant rapport that had existed between them from the start, he hastened to say, 'Not that I hunt and I will not allow it on my land, but the Hunt Ball is one of those hypocrisies I have to tolerate. I cannot dictate to other people what they should believe – a lot of them belong to families that have been friends with my family for decades, even centuries. In the old days, my ancestors joined in, many were M.F.H., but personally I am with Oscar Wilde, "the English country gentleman galloping after a fox – the unspeakable in full pursuit of the uneatable." '

Sarah remembered the quotation as coming from *A Woman of No Importance*, thinking, that is apt as far as I am concerned.

Seeing Sarah's relieved expression, Robert asked, 'What do you think of drag hunting?'

'Oh, that is all right as long as no wild creatures are hunted and die agonising deaths,' Sarah replied.

'Going back to the problem in hand,' Robert continued, 'what it amounts to is that I can count on you as family. I will probably make impossible demands on your time but I think it will be well within your capabilities and you will possibly enjoy most of it. How does the "job" appeal to you so far?'

Sarah looked into his handsome face and realised it was already too late to warn herself of falling in love with her employer. When someone who looked like him, possessed so much charisma blended with kindness and consideration, it was difficult not to succumb, especially since they were just the qualities that had been absent from her life for so long. Just to be in the same world and to know that he was there, she would be happy to help Lizzie/Elizabeth make the tea and do whatever duties Mrs Bates gave her. She hoped nothing of what she was thinking showed in her face, he would be so embarrassed and that would be the end of a promising future. She said carefully, 'It sounds more than reasonable and, like you, I am not particularly concerned about speculation as long as I know the situation.'

Robert said, picking his words with great care, 'Of course, as a member of the family, you will naturally have an allowance and whatever you need for yourself or your family, you can charge to my accounts.' This was the hardest thing to say without making it seem as if he were employing her or worse, buying her time. 'Somehow you seem to belong to Heronshurst and you will be such a help to me.'

They looked steadily at each other, trying to assess the other's thoughts.

In Robert's eyes Sarah saw sincerity, integrity and something surprisingly like anxiety.

In hers, he saw trust, but a faintly veiled expression as though she were unwilling to reveal her true feelings. It was only to be expected, he thought, bearing in mind what she had been through. She had really said very little, but somehow he sensed it intuitively in a way he had never empathised with anyone before.

'Well, I have stated my case,' he said. 'Now you must have plenty of time to consider it. See how it goes for a day or two at least, before turning it down. Now let us leave the future to take care of itself for today and enjoy our ride, which will give you an inkling of the matters about which I am concerned.' He smiled. 'Don't look worried. If you turn it down, it won't be quite the end of the world.' But in his heart he thought, it will be for me, which was echoed in Sarah's mind.

They were nearing the cottage and both were very quiet, immersed in their thoughts. As they approached, the tenant came out to meet them. He held Apollo's head as Sarah slid from the saddle and took Flame as Robert did the same, leading the horses to the side of the cottage where they could be tethered by a trough of water.

Robert introduced the man to Sarah. 'This is Rogers, one of my farmers. Rogers, Mrs Mannering will be at Heronshurst for a while. She is one of the family,' he added firmly, setting the precedent.

Rogers touched his forehead, 'How-de-do ma'am, pleased to meet you.'

Robert chatted to him for a few moments, asking how things were going. Mrs Rogers came out and was introduced, apologising profusely for, as far as Sarah could see, absolutely nothing at all.

Sarah smiled gently at her and admired her cottage garden. They made their farewells, Rogers fetched the horses, they mounted and with a final 'Goodbye' continued on their way.

'I like to keep in touch once in a while,' Robert told Sarah. 'These people and their forefathers have farmed this land for my family for generations and they like to know that we care for them.'

After they left, Mr and Mrs Rogers looked at each other. 'What do you think?' he asked.

'I don't know,' his wife replied. 'She seems a nice lady, do you think she's his intended?' They turned from watching the departing riders and went about their daily chores.

After visiting two or three more scattered farms, Robert and Sarah turned for home. They reached a wide field that sloped very slightly uphill. Sarah could not resist it and softly urging Apollo, he broke into a trot, then a canter and finally a full gallop.

Behind her, she could hear Flame's hoof beats as well and as she reached the crest of the slope, Robert drew level with her and they reined in their horses. Sarah's eyes were shining and her cheeks flushed.

Robert thought how well she fitted into the whole scene, but all he said was, 'If you haven't ridden for two years I hope you won't be too stiff when we get back.'

Sarah laughed, 'If I am, I can fall off the horse and stagger into a hot bath for a couple of hours.'

'You will miss lunch!' Robert said, laughing with her, as they headed for home.

After lunch, he offered to show Sarah round the rose garden and conservatories. A wonderful black Hamburg grapevine spread through three of the conservatories, while others held colourful tropical plants and more mundane tomatoes, cucumbers and courgettes, which were coming to the end of their season.

On a south wall in the kitchen garden were espaliered peaches, pears and apples. Stretching along the edge of one path was a positive wall of sweet peas, hiding the rows of vegetables – carrots, onions, lettuces, cabbages, brussel sprouts and an asparagus bed. The sweet peas were coming to an end but were still beautiful. Sarah considered that, in their prime, they were probably the most spectacular she had ever seen. The flowers were huge in shades of light and deep pink, blue and mauve with many bi-coloured varieties. 'How lovely!' Sarah exclaimed, 'and their scent is exquisite.'

'They are fine, aren't they?' Robert agreed. 'Old Marlow, the gardener, has a weakness for them. They are his pride and joy and compensate for the more mundane vegetables, which are necessary but not so spectacular or rewarding. I understand that they were his wife's favourite flower,' he added.

Having finally wandered around to the west terrace, Robert remarked, 'It is such a beautiful afternoon, would you like to go on the lake?'

'That would be very pleasant,' Sarah agreed, looking across the smooth shining surface of the water reflecting the banks and trees almost as clearly as the real thing and still feeling as if she were in a dream and afraid that she might wake up. Could she really be in this lovely place that felt more like home than any other place she had lived – even her childhood home – with someone who seemed anything but a stranger, even though they had met such a short time ago? Truly, this sort of sensation only happened in dreams, almost as a consolation for the less pleasant waking hours. It had happened to her before – then she had awakened to the real world. Sarah concentrated hard on holding on to the dream as she had done many times before, while they strolled down past the fountain, between the lawns and on to the jetty where a punt was moored, that she had noticed from the terrace when she first arrived.

Robert helped her in and as she was getting comfortable at one end, Merlin arrived and wanted to join her. She needed to move over to balance his considerable weight and he lay down, contentedly resting his head in her lap.

'You are a fine one,' Robert rebuked him, 'to come uninvited.'

Sarah looked down at Merlin's handsome head and was certain he winked.

Robert took his place at the other end, released the painter and slowly and skilfully paddled the punt out on to the lake, privately thinking that the dog had the best of the deal.

As they drifted slowly towards the middle, Sarah looked sideways at the broad-leaved woodland, it was so peaceful and quiet. She said dreamily, 'The woods are a lot thicker than they used to be, now you cannot see the Temple of Diana, Hermes and old Neptune by the stream that feeds the lake,' unaware of the reaction she caused Robert.

He started violently, nearly dropping the paddle in his surprise. It really was extraordinary, but that was becoming ordinary in the last couple of days. He said as calmly as he could manage, 'We will go over to the jetty near the woods and follow the stream along through the trees and back to the house.'

They reached the landing and he moored the boat, helping Sarah out after Merlin had eagerly abandoned his place at the prospect of a run in the woods. They followed the path, slightly overgrown now, along the stream until they reached the statue of Neptune, sitting by the water. Sarah touched it lightly on the head, saying, 'The poor old boy looks rather more the worse for wear than he used to do.'

Robert was feeling utterly bemused and by this time he was not altogether surprised when Sarah naturally took the left fork of the path and they came upon first, Hermes and then Diana.

As Sarah had remarked, the woods were quite thick now and the leaves had not yet started to change, so apart from the occasional shaft of sunlight, there was a cool, green twilight.

'It will be lovely in the spring, when the primroses are out again, followed by the bluebells,' Sarah commented conversationally.

Robert was trying to adjust to these sudden, unexpected statements and let his mind drift. It was pleasant walking through this quiet, almost enchanted place with Sarah and feeling that this had all happened before.

Eventually they arrived back at the house and settled on the terrace, ready for afternoon tea. This *has* happened before, he thought, marvelling that it was only twenty-four hours since Sarah had walked into his life.

After dinner that night, they played three games of chess. Robert found that, after a fairly conventional opening, Sarah had her own ideas of moves. The first game she checkmated him in about eight moves and he was never quite sure how she did it. The second was stalemate and the third went on for quite a long time until she finally checkmated him again.

Robert laughed good-humouredly, 'You are too good for me,' he said, 'I think you have someone helping you!'

Sarah smiled, 'I would not insult you by not playing to the best of my ability,' she told him. 'Next time you will probably beat me easily.'

They decided it was late and retired for the night. As she drifted off to sleep, Sarah thought, with so much that is old and beautiful in this house, I am glad that the beds have modern comfort.

CHAPTER FOUR

As the days went by, each one showed Sarah another facet of Robert's life. One morning, soon after Sarah's arrival, he announced, 'I monopolise so much of your time, that you must need to spend what little time you have to yourself, doing your personal chores.'

His perception amazed Sarah, used as she was to years of living with someone who was utterly selfish and self-centred.

'What I propose is that we get you a personal maid,' he hurried on before Sarah could demur, 'Mr and Mrs Bates' elder daughter, Charlotte, is two years older than her sister, Lizzie. By the way, you did know that Lizzie was the Bates' daughter?'

'Yes,' said Sarah, with a little smile that made Robert wonder about the circumstances in which she first learned of it.

Robert continued, 'Charlotte was the first member of the family to decide she wanted to be "free".'

Sarah could hear the inverted commas.

'She thought it would be very glamorous to work in a beauty parlour and was apprenticed for two years at a salon in the town, afterwards doing another six months at what I believe is called "an improver". Mrs Bates, of course, was very distressed, especially when Charlotte decided to share a flat with two other girls close to where they worked. She thought her daughter was much too young and had lived too sheltered a life, but young people are much more independent and in spite of a great deal of parental opposition, Charlotte persisted in having her own way. At first everything was fine, Charlotte revelled in her newly-acquired freedom, but gradually the novelty wore off. Although most of the customers were reasonable, there were one or two whom she detested. She was not used to being subjected to rudeness and abuse and what she found was worse, the unfairness of their complaints and being in the position of "the customer is always right". Even dancing every night at the local dance hall gradually palled and she did not like finding that she was just another one of a crowd of young people with no special identity. More and more she yearned to come back to Heronshurst, where everyone has their special niche and is important in their own right. She missed the calm, ordered existence to which she had been used with her family and the flat became a rather slovenly prison.' Robert paused, wondering if, in his anxiety to clarify the situation, he was boring Sarah, but she was listening enrapt, following his every word and understanding just how it might have been for a young girl in Charlotte's position.

Robert when on to explain, 'I learned all this from Mrs Bates a little while ago – I am paraphrasing, but that is the gist. Now Charlotte would like to return to Heronshurst and Mrs Bates asked me if there was a position for her. She and Bates would be so happy for her to return to the bosom of the family until she is a little older, at least. What I propose is this, Charlotte shall come here as your personal maid and be solely responsible to you for her duties. Under Mrs Bates' guidance and with you to train her in your ways, I think she will be an excellent choice. She has spread her wings and found that she would be happier where she will be with people she loves, who love and understand her. During her free time, she can still see her friends and do all the things they like to do, but she will no longer be part of an anonymous crowd, but someone with her own special niche and I think she will be eager to fulfill her role here. Mrs Bates tells me that the sisters get on very well together, so Lizzie will be happy about it, too. There was some suggestion that, as the younger sister, Lizzie was feeling pleasantly superior that she had not gone rushing off and then have to eat, what she thinks of as "humble pie". Lizzie has always known where she wants to belong, but it is as well if Charlotte had to find out for herself by leaving, she has done so.'

Robert was watching Sarah's expressive face as he was talking and he was fairly confident of her answer. You, my darling, he thought, using the endearment in his mind that he would not have dared to voice at this stage, have all the wisdom of centuries. Your spirit got lost somewhere and has travelled a long, hard journey to get back to where you belong, but you are home at last, please God, to stay and you will recognise your way now.

Sarah's first reaction was to say she did not need a maid, but was aware that it was not solely her decision. Robert had his responsibilities to his people as his forbears always had, she could see that, and she had hers to him.

'Yes,' she replied slowly, 'I do understand and I am happy to accept your decision.'

'Good,' Robert said, 'I will let Mrs Bates know straight away. She and Bates will sleep a lot happier, I fancy.'

Charlotte duly arrived and Sarah received her in her sitting room. She found Charlotte to be a slightly more sophisticated edition of Lizzie. She will do very well, Sarah thought, I am sure we will get along.

Charlotte looked at the calm, wise face before her and wondered about her. It was certainly true that she was uncannily like an older version of the portrait at the head of the stairs. Her mother and father had always sternly discouraged idle gossip about his Lordship's guests but in the servants' hall, they seemed to think that Mrs Mannering was rather special. There appeared to be some link with the lovely young lady at the top of the main staircase, but it was not quite clear how. His Lordship was a direct descendant of the son she had died bearing and there were no other children. Oh well, Charlotte thought, I'll know soon. Mrs Mannering has the same lovely eyes and curly, smiling mouth. I was silly to think that being a beauty specialist was glamorous – it was jolly hard work being on your feet all day and sometimes the customers could be downright nasty.

With her newly-acquired wisdom, Charlotte sensed it was a lesson she had to learn and it certainly made her appreciate his Lordship's giving her a second chance. He's a real gentleman, she thought gratefully, to let me come back and not bear any malice because I wanted to leave Heronshurst. It will be really nice to wake up in the morning in my old room at the top of the house and be able to look right across the lovely gardens and lake to the fields beyond up to the skyline, and I did miss Mum and Dad, even if they are strict.

Charlotte had a feeling that her erstwhile flatmates would give their eye-teeth to be in her place, but the poor things hadn't had the same opportunities, she thought, a little complacently.

When Charlotte had gone, Sarah reviewed the situation – it was a revelation to her to realise that she, too, had obligations, not only to Robert but to Heronshurst and its occupants. It did not seem a new burden, strangely enough, rather something remembered from long ago and a duty to be resumed again.

During her first few days, when Robert was busy elsewhere

and did not need her, Sarah had wandered around the house and it seemed to her 'renewing her acquaintance'.

The two lifts that had been installed through the wells of the subsidiary staircases at the rear of the house were comparatively new, she thought. They had actually been built after the 1939–45 war, when Robert's father was alive. She also discovered a third lift that stopped in the centre of the galleried landing, cleverly disguised behind the door of what had been a dressing room.

The two rear lifts went from the basement to the top floor of the staff quarters and were installed primarily for them. Sarah learned later from Robert that his father had said, 'they (the staff) need them most, they have more to do and less time to do it.'

No wonder that Heronshurst kept its staff from generation to generation, Sarah mused. She noted that the house was built facing east, with all the main suites on the first floor occupying the width of the house, hers being on the southeast corner.

Other equally pleasant but slightly smaller suites ran down each side of the house and more opened off the passage behind the main staircase, which included the galleried landing.

On the ground floor, the ballroom occupied a large part of the south side with access both to the south terrace and the front drive. The dining room was at the end of the ballroom, with easy access from the kitchens via one lift, its windows facing south and the breakfast room led from it with both south and west facing windows.

Robert's study was at the end of the passage which ran past the ballroom, dining room and breakfast room, through which Sarah had first been shown the day she arrived and had both windows and French doors onto the west terrace. Next to it was the library running along a large part of the west terrace, the bookshelves set well back out of range of the westering sun.

Beyond the library was the green drawing room, a comfortable, pleasant room that Sarah and Robert often used in the evening. It was cosy in the winter and in the longer evenings, the sunset could be miraculous. There were other smaller rooms and on the north side, the larger, more imposing red drawing room, which was used for large gatherings when family and friends were entertained, occupying a passage on the opposite side of the house from the one which Sarah had traversed with such trepidation, but an even stronger sense of *déjà vu* on her arrival that first day.

As she reviewed the intervening time she smiled gently to herself and started at a light tap on her door. She glanced at her watch and realised with a start that she had been day-dreaming ever since Charlotte left, and called 'Come in.'

The door opened and Robert stood smiling at her. He said in a mock-aggrieved tone, 'Am I going to have tea by myself today?' It had become a ritual that he was reluctant to forgo.

'I'm so sorry,' Sarah said, smiling in return, 'I had lost track of the time until just this minute. Will you wait a moment while I wash my hands, please?'

As she went into her bathroom, Robert passed the time looking at the titles of her books. Tennyson, Keats, Milton, Wordsworth, Browning, Longfellow's *Hiawatha* – she obviously liked poetry – and the lighter Ogden Nash, Belloc, and Betjeman. Shakespeare, Dickens, Thackeray, Trollope, a beautifully bound and tooled set of Goldsmith, a complete set of Macaulay's *History of England*, dictionaries in English, French, German, Spanish and Italian and then suddenly, the unexpected – the four volumes of Louisa Alcott's *Little Women*. Without thinking, Robert lifted one down and on the flyleaf was the inscription, 'To Sarah, with all my love, Dad 1936.' He jumped guiltily as Sarah appeared.

'I'm so sorry,' he said, 'it was unpardonable of me to pry.'

Sarah smiled forgivingly and taking the book from his hand, said, 'Oh, *Little Women*, my father gave them to me at my request when I was fourteen. By the time I was sixteen, we were sorting out to move house and he suggested that I no longer needed them "now that you are grown up", but I insisted on keeping them. "Why?" he asked. "Because I want to read them to my daughter," I replied. He was very amused and commented, "You are looking a long way ahead, aren't you?"'

'And did you?' Robert asked.

Sarah understood what he meant and answered, 'Oh yes! And she read them for herself, many times, as I did.' She returned the book to the shelf and they went downstairs for tea.

Robert had heard Sarah mention only one daughter, who was married to an officer in the Royal Navy and had a son nearly four years old and a baby daughter of fifteen months. Over tea, he asked, 'Have you only the one daughter?' and could have bitten out his tongue the moment he saw the pain in the normally smiling eyes.

'Yes,' Sarah said, briefly. 'She should have had an elder sister and my husband did not want any more children.' It was over and done with, she thought, and she did not want to spoil the present by letting the shadow of the past darken it. What use was there in resurrecting the memory of the spiteful, jealous woman who had caused her to lose her first, longed-for baby, almost killing her, too, and of the man whose personality problems had wasted more than thirty years of her life?

Robert wanted more than anything, not to have spoken, but he had and now he wished that he could put his arms around Sarah, to comfort her. It really hurt him to see the effort she made to return to the present and normality. Serves me right, for being such a clumsy oaf, he thought.

Sarah's voice was steady, though quiet, as she asked him if he would like some more tea. He passed his cup in silence, to have apologised would only have compounded the blunder, but the gentle warmth and genuine concern in his eyes comforted her more than he could guess.

September was officially autumn, but the sun still held the warmth of late summer. It seemed a shame to waste it when winter would be on them all too soon, so, after tea, Robert suggested that they should take Merlin and walk all around the lake from right to left, picking up Neptune's path into the wood.

Robert still experienced the same feeling of wonder that he had the first time that they had taken that same walk and Sarah had said in such a matter-of-fact tone, 'The poor old boy looks rather more the worse for wear than he used to do.'

Merlin's excited barking attracted his attention. An inoffensive little squirrel had appeared and Merlin wanted to nuzzle it with his nose to see what it was made of as he always did with small creatures, but the squirrel had other ideas and started up a tree, corkscrewing round it as Merlin circled the tree, trying to catch sight of it. The squirrel reached the high branches safely and sat looking at Merlin.

Robert called to the dog, saying, 'Come here, you big bully,' and Merlin joined them, trying to say with his eyes that he had only wanted to make friends and had no intention of hurting the squirrel.

Sarah gave him a reassuring pat on the head. He really was very gentle with creatures smaller than himself, though she knew he would attack anything that threatened them seriously.

They continued their walk and arrived back at the house and went up to change for dinner, during which Robert told Sarah about the clay pigeon shoot that his bailiff, Grayson, had arranged for the following Saturday.

CHAPTER FIVE

Saturday arrived and still the lovely weather showed no sign of breaking.

'It should be a good day for the shoot,' Robert told Sarah. 'It is a real St Luke's little summer. Grayson arranges one every year about this time. He formed the club and every able-bodied man in the village belongs to it – tenants, farmers, my friends – and even one who is not so very fit, old Colonel Stewart who is crippled with arthritis from the waist down. "Old war wound," he says, "not the last one, the one before," referring to the wars. He is pushed to the firing point in a wheelchair by his ex-batman who is nearly as disabled as the colonel and drives him about in an ancient Land Rover. "Murder on the old bones," the Colonel says, "but practical and I can't afford a new one these days, with the cost of everything going sky high and the old dividends dropping."'

Robert's passable imitation of the Colonel's gruff voice made Sarah smile, even though she felt sorry for the old boy's predicament.

'He isn't as hard up as he pretends to be,' Robert maintained, 'and he would be very mortified if he thought anyone really believed him.'

He asked Sarah if she would join them at the shoot and she kept a discreet eye on the supply of food and drink that was provided from Heronshurst, to make sure that nothing ran out.

Several of Robert's staff were on hand to ferry more from the kitchens if necessary, between their turns at shooting. Mrs Bates and Mrs Briggs, the cook, were obviously well-used to catering for such an occasion and Sarah was impressed how efficiently the men hurried to and fro from the field beyond the walled kitchen gardens, where the shoot was held, to the kitchens. She noticed the head stable lad and his assistant, two of the under-gardeners, all ably assisted by tenants from the cottages.

The men all took turns at firing the clays and Sarah was admiring the skill of some of their shots, when Robert appeared.

'Come, Sarah, you must try, too,' he suggested. He handed her the gun, explaining the mechanism and how to sight it. 'Say when you are ready and I will release the clay.'

Sarah took a stance and said 'Pull'. The clay shot across the sky and she missed the first, then the second and a third. 'Oh, dear,' she said to Robert, 'moving targets are not very easy.'

'Don't worry,' he said comfortingly, 'just try to relax and follow the flight anticipating its trajectory.'

Sarah had a good eye and quick reflexes and she just managed to clip the edge of the fourth clay, then adjusting to the flight, she hit the next one right in the middle, disintegrating it and then hit the next five. She decided to rest on her laurels.

Robert said, 'Well done! I am proud of you. Have you ever shot before?'

'Not a moving target,' Sarah replied, 'only stationary ones and that was in my twenties,' adding demurely, 'But I did shoot for the County.'

Robert laughed delightedly, 'You are full of surprises, aren't you?' he remarked.

The shoot was over, everything had been cleared up and everyone returned to their homes. When Robert and Sarah walked indoors, Bates met them.

'There has been a telephone message from your office, my Lord. They requested you to call them when you came in. It was only ten minutes ago,' he added.

'Right, Bates, I will do that straight away, then we will have tea. Please excuse me for a moment Sarah. I cannot imagine what they would want that is important enough to telephone me on a Saturday.' He strolled along to his study.

Sarah went upstairs to freshen up and change into something less 'sporty' for tea.

Bates saw her come downstairs and go out onto the terrace and fetched the tea tray.

At that moment Robert arrived, too and remarked, 'Ah, I timed that well,' and after they had settled down and were alone, he said, 'It is a nuisance, Sarah, but I have to go to Geneva on Monday. That was my secretary – she knew there was no question of my not going, short of battle, murder and sudden death, so she booked me on a Swissair flight at noon on Monday.'

Sarah hoped her disappointment didn't show on her face. How possessive can I get? she thought, asking as casually as she could manage, 'Will you need to be away long?'

'Only two or three days at most, hopefully,' Robert replied. He considered explaining what was entailed but decided it was much too boring for Sarah. He hoped he had not imagined the flicker of disappointment in her eyes. Could it be wishful thinking? he wondered.

It was strange after years of being self-sufficient, that one person could so monopolise his thoughts that he would feel bereft without her. His first impulse had been to ask his secretary to make it two flights, but was deterred firstly by the speculation it might arouse – his secretary was very discreet, but she was a woman and Sarah must not be caused any embarrassment, and more importantly, by the feeling that it would be unfair to Sarah. It was also possible that another flight was not available on the same plane at such short notice, creating speculation for nothing.

Sarah was so happy at Heronshurst, filling the time that they were not together with a number of occupations. He knew, from what was said, that sometimes when he was too concerned with business to visit the tenants, she rode around accompanied by Merlin to fulfill his duty. The wives seemed to look forward to her coming – they certainly talked a lot more to her than they ever did to him. Dragging her off at a moment's notice on a business trip was not being fair, especially as she would have to amuse herself for most of the day. It was ridiculous to mind so much being separated – they did not spend all day every day together when he was home. But he knew the answer – at Heronshurst, she was somewhere in the vicinity and could be found easily and in the evenings, if they were pursuing their own interests, she was there.

Sarah, too, was thinking how empty the place would seem without Robert and her thoughts were running on much the same lines. For a fleeting moment she had the idea that he was going to ask her to go to Geneva with him, but it passed and he did not suggest it. She would have gone in an instant but there was no earthly reason why, from his point of view, he should have bothered to ask.

For something to say, Sarah asked, 'What is your secretary like?' and immediately could have bitten out her tongue. Oh, god! I sound like a jealous wife, she thought, but Robert didn't seem to find the question unusual.

'What is she like? Well, I suppose by some standards she is quite glamorous for a secretary. She has blonde hair cut in the style of that woman who invented mini-skirts in the sixties. What she probably considers her business suit has a jacket so long and a skirt so short that the hemlines practically meet!'

The almost disapproving tone of Robert's voice made Sarah laugh in spite of herself.

'And she is so deadly efficient,' he added, managing to make it sound like a defect rather than an asset.

'Don't you like efficient, glamorous women?' Sarah teased.

'She terrifies me at times,' Robert replied, adding, 'It rather depends on the woman. I am all for efficiency and glamour but it needs personal charisma to carry it off and that is all too rare. Perhaps I expect too much,' he concluded.

'I rather think you do,' Sarah agreed, laughing. Suddenly she lost any interest she may have had in the efficient, glamorous secretary.

Looking at Robert, Sarah found his phrase, 'personal charisma' echoing in her mind, wondering if he were aware that he had more than his fair share and deciding he probably wasn't, which was one of his greatest charms.

A distant memory from the past came to her of someone in the village where her mother was born, talking about her mother's family. They could all charm the birds off the trees and their greatest charm was that they were completely unaware of it.

Sarah realised how true that could be and considered the people she had known in her life who had charisma without necessarily being particularly physically attractive. Looking at Robert she understood when the two came together – looks and charisma – it was a very potent force.

The following day, being Sunday, was rather lazier than usual. Sarah and Robert went to the village church for morning service, as did a large proportion of the staff from Heronshurst. Lunch was a very quiet meal. Sarah remained silent because she thought that Robert was probably marshalling his thoughts for his forth-coming meeting in Geneva and did not want to distract him by chattering. Robert was quiet, not so much because he wanted to consider his meeting, but because he was reluctant to leave Sarah alone. Strange! In the past he had quite enjoyed popping off on such a trip.

They read the newspapers and Sarah disappeared to her room to write letters, while Robert prepared the necessary paperwork and checked his briefcase and passport. The tickets would be awaiting collection at the airport, all being well, if the efficient Clare had done her duty.

Robert sorted the few clothes he felt he might need for the next few days and laid them ready in his case, leaving it open until morning for the last minute things like toiletry. His valet would probably be offended but he should be used to it by now. Robert preferred to do the little things like that for himself and leave Aldridge to do the more serious valeting.

He glanced at his watch and wondered whether Sarah would remember tea without being reminded. For him, it had become a ritual that he was unwilling to forgo, so he was very happy on leaving his room, to catch a glimpse of Sarah disappearing round the corner on her way downstairs. Like him, she disdained the use of the lift. They both considered that while they were both active, they would like to stay that way and leave lifts until they really needed them. Robert hurried a little and caught up with her on the way out to the terrace, where tea arrived promptly.

Dinner was a very quiet meal that night with spasmodic bursts of conversation as each felt that they should make an effort.

'I will be at the Geneva "Wilton" if you need me, Sarah. I will leave you the telephone number before I go.' Robert did not really like the 'Wilton' but it was convenient as the conference was there and he had no need to travel to it and the facilities in that respect were first class.

Sarah's amused little smile made him curious. She caught his look and answered his unspoken question.

'The flunkey on the door in his brown top hat and tails always looks as if the job were really beneath him and he finds it a great effort to be even remotely civil to the guests.'

Robert laughed, 'Yes! You are right, he really does,' wondering how Sarah knew.

The following morning, Sarah and Merlin saw Robert off. While Frazer stowed his suitcase in the boot, Robert took Sarah's hand saying,

'Take good care of yourself while I'm away and call if you need anything.' He wanted desperately to say, 'Come to the airport to see me off,' but considered it would be tiresome for her, when she could follow her own pursuits away from the grime and fumes of the journey to the airport. He was unaware that she would have gone willingly – he needed only to ask.

Sarah said carefully, 'You take care, too. We will see you in a few days.'

Robert sat in the car, checked that his briefcase was there and with a final wave as the car moved down the drive, he was on his way.

Sarah looked at Merlin. 'A long walk is what we need,' she told him and he was only too willing to agree wholeheartedly to the word 'walk'.

They seem to have walked for hours and when they returned, even Merlin was glad of a rest. He ran so much further, following interesting scents and then returning to make sure that Sarah was all right that he probably covered six times the distance that she walked.

Even so, it was still only eleven o'clock and Robert had gone just after eight-thirty. It was going to be a long two or three days, Sarah decided.

She went up to her room, where Charlotte was still performing her duties.

'I'm just finishing, madam. Is there anything more I can do for you?'

'No, thank you, Charlotte. Everything looks very nice.'

'Thank you, madam,' and Charlotte went downstairs to Mrs Bates. Mum always liked to see that she did not waste time mooning about as she called it. She would soon find some little thing for Charlotte to do. That was the drawback with family, she thought, but it was lovely to be back at Heronshurst and she did not really mind.

To pass the time – how awful to feel one is killing time when it is so precious – and because she could not settle to anything, Sarah had a quick shower to freshen up from her walk, donned a simple dress and sat at her bureau thinking she should be doing some writing, but nothing came and after desultorily tidying up some papers that had got disarranged, trying to concentrate on a chapter from the book she was reading, she found it was lunchtime.

After lunch, she went to find Mrs Bates to see if she needed anything and they discussed meals for the time that Robert would be away, since it would be only Sarah there to eat them, and then considered finding something for the jumble sale being organised by the local boy scout troop in aid of funds.

By this time, it was still only three o'clock and Sarah went to the stables, where Foster soon saddled Apollo for her and she went for a long, hard gallop with Merlin, who had got his 'second wind' by then, racing happily behind her.

Dinner was a very lonely meal that night, as was the rest of the evening. Going to bed, Sarah told herself very firmly that she must make better use of her time for the next two or three days, at least time would not drag so much. There were several young and middle-aged farmers' wives who would be glad of a chat, if her usual visits were anything to go by. It was going to seem a long while.

CHAPTER SIX

The telephone rang in Sarah's room the following morning just as she had finished dressing after her shower. She glanced at her watch as she was putting it on and found, as she had thought, that it was only just after seven. It was rather early for a social call and for a moment she wondered if anything was wrong, but then relaxed. If anything had gone wrong that should concern her, she would have known, as she always did.

Picking up the telephone, she heard Bates say, 'It is his Lordship calling from Geneva, madam.'

She was not worried, but she did wonder why Robert was calling so early in the morning.

His voice said, 'Sarah?'

Was she imagining that his voice sounded a little strained or was it the effect of the telephone line?

'How are things, Robert? Is there a problem?'

Robert's voice sounded more normal as he answered, 'Well, there is and there isn't. It all depends on you.'

'That sounds very intriguing. What is it?'

'In the first place,' Robert told her, 'we start working about eight o'clock, hence the early call, for which I humbly apologise – it is lucky you are still on BST or it would have been even earlier, but as you are normally an early riser, I hope you will forgive me?'

'That does not matter at all, Robert. It is nice to hear you,' Sarah told him.

'The other thing is,' Robert went on, 'the day starts with that horrible invention, a working breakfast. You know our trans-atlantic cousins, though how anyone is expected to operate satisfactorily either eating or speaking when trying to do both together, I'll never know. It's a wonder that the paperwork isn't plastered together with butter and marmalade, washed over with the occasional cup of coffee that gets spilled.'

Sarah's soft laugh drifted over the telephone.

'We are expected to work right through lunch, when coffee and sandwiches are sent in and finish about three o'clock in the afternoon. But that is not really the problem. How are you getting on, is everything functioning satisfactorily at home?'

'Yes, Robert, everything is fine,' – except that I miss you, Sarah added to herself.

Robert finished in a rush, 'Sarah, can you possibly bear the prospect of joining me here, please? I am afraid you will be left to your own devices until three o'clock in the afternoon, but after that we have the rest of the day to ourselves, to play at being tourists and the evenings will not seem so interminable if you are here to have dinner with me. Do please say you will come.'

Sarah's heart was singing, she could have danced around the room for joy but she controlled her voice carefully as she replied, 'Of course, Robert, if you would like me to.'

'Bless you!' he said happily, 'I can telex to London for your flight at noon on Swissair and you can pick up your ticket when you check in. After I have finished speaking to you I will give Frazer instructions to drive you to the airport. I am afraid I will not be able to meet you quite by then but I will order a taxi to collect you at Geneva and drive you straight to the Wilton. I have checked that they can accommodate you. I will see you as soon as I can after three o'clock – in time for afternoon tea,' he added. 'You don't know how much better I feel.'

'Very well, Robert, until three o'clock then.' You are not the only one who feels better, Sarah thought, if one could die of sheer happiness, I would probably expire right this minute.

She ran downstairs for a hurried breakfast, while Charlotte quickly packed the list of things that Sarah had hastily scribbled. Luckily her passport was valid for another six years, so that was no problem.

By the time she was ready, it was still only eight o'clock and Frazer and the Rolls were already awaiting her at the front door.

Bates saw her out and Merlin stood beside him, looking utterly forlorn.

'We will both be back soon, I promise,' Sarah told the dog, dropping a kiss on his forehead.

Frazer stowed her suitcase and put her in the car. As it purred along the drive, the song that Joyce Grenfell used to sing in the

43

war, kept running through her head, 'I'm going to see you today, all's well with my world.'

They arrived at Heathrow in good time to check in for her flight. The ticket was ready and waiting for her and after sitting in the departure lounge for a while, happily relaxed and watching all the people coming and going, her flight was called and she went up the steps of the aircraft as if she had wings on her feet. Sarah felt as if she could have flown to Geneva and Robert without the need for an aeroplane.

They arrived on time at Geneva and having picked up her luggage and gone through the formalities, she found the taxi that Robert had ordered for her and it was only just after two o'clock when she arrived at the hotel.

The receptionist had a reservation for her and she signed in, thinking that there was just time to freshen up before meeting Robert.

'Lord Falconbridge requested that you should await him in your suite, madam. He hoped not to be later than three o'clock,' the receptionist said in faultless English.

'Thank you, I will do that,' Sarah replied, smiling and hoping her French was as good.

The receptionist returned her smile, privately thinking that Mrs Mannering was a very lucky woman. Sarah would have been the first one to agree with her, but not for quite the same reason.

She expected her suite to be the usual elegant, impersonal affair one was generally given in such places until she went in and the scent of roses met her. On a low table in her sitting room was a bowl of exquisite pink blooms, beautifully arranged, the small card beside them read, 'Welcome, Sarah and thank you. Robert.' She held the card against her lips for a moment and then hurried to change out of her travelling clothes and freshen up.

She was scarcely finished, when a light tap on the door heralded Robert's arrival.

'Thank you for coming, especially as it must have been rather a rush for you,' he said, taking her hand and holding it in both of his.

'I was happy to do so and thank you for the beautiful roses,' Sarah said simply. 'Would you like tea sent up or would you rather go down for it?'

'Oh, we'll have it sent up,' Robert answered. 'You must be tired after your journey – although I must say, you don't look it. I have not had time to explore yet.'

'Very well, but tomorrow we will walk beside the lake to a

little place called "Lac du Perle" and have tea on the lawns outside while we watch the world go by and the swans on the lake.'

'That sounds nice,' Robert agreed, wondering for the hundredth time how Sarah did it.

He telephoned room service, then relaxed in one of the armchairs, stretching out his legs with a luxurious sigh. 'This is pleasant,' he said, smiling contentedly. 'I'm actually looking forward to the next day or so now, from three o'clock onwards.'

After tea, they strolled along the Quai du Mont Blanc, across the Pont du Mont Blanc to the Jardin des Anglais with its well-known flower clock, returning along the Quai de la Poste, over the Pont de la Coulouvreniere and back along the Quai des Bergues to the hotel in time to bathe and change for dinner.

In the morning, after Sarah had breakfasted alone, she wandered through the arcade belonging to the hotel, with its wonderful, elegant shops. She loved looking at beautiful things, it gave her a lot of pleasure, but she did not covet them. Strolling past a large glass case full of expensive jewellery, her eye was caught by a brooch in the centre of the display. It was a unicorn wrought in gold with a main and tail so exquisitely chased that they seemed to flow with movement. The eyes were set with large diamonds and the tail and hoofs with smaller ones. It was a lovely work of art and she adored it, having always been fascinated by their mystique and legend. She had a model of one on her desk that her daughter had given her for, what she called, an 'unbirthday present'.

Moving on, she wandered out on to the street and along the lake into Quai Wilson, named after the American President who proposed the Fourteen Points for Peace, after the Great War in 1918, and secured the basis for the League of Nations.

Going into the gardens of the Lac du Perle, Sarah sat and watched the sunlight dancing on the water, the swans lazily swimming and the Jet d'Eau fountaining across the other side of the lake, the Cathedral standing up high in the old city beyond and Mont Blanc in the far distance.

There was no point in going back to the hotel for lunch, so she had a light snack in the restaurant, before walking on to the Botanical Gardens. As she was returning, a vivid flash split the sky, thunder crashed, the heavens opened and down came torrential rain. Sarah was taken completely by surprise – she just hadn't noticed any build-up of cloud. She ran across the road and took shelter in a little café. The rain was much too heavy to last

45

very long and when it stopped she walked back to the hotel, noticing a rainbow arcing over Mont Blanc. Being delayed by the storm had made her later than she meant to be and she found a very worried Robert waiting for her at the hotel.

'They said you had gone out, but I did not know where you were,' he said, very relieved to see her safe and sound.

'I'm sorry, Robert. If it had not been for the rain, I would have been back much sooner,' Sarah apologised.

'You are safe, that is all that matters,' Robert smiled.

Over dinner that night, Robert suggested that they should stay on an extra day and spend it together.

'I feel I deserve it,' he said, 'after the grind of the last few days. There is no real need for us to rush back immediately. Just one more day with my nose to the grindstone and then we can be free. We will hire a car, where would you like to go?'

'Could we drive around the north edge of the lake to Vevey, on to Montreux and visit the Château Chillon?' Sarah suggested.

'By all means, that sounds a wonderful idea, we will do just that,' Robert agreed.

The following morning the sky was still overcast and Sarah decided to go to the museum in the older part of the city. She walked along the hotel side of the lake, crossing over the Pont de l'Ile, across Place Bel Air, approaching the museum by the Rue de la Corraterie. When she came out, the sun was shining so she walked to a little café called 'Le Cabin de l'Oncle Tom' for lunch and back to the hotel along the Boulevard Georges Favon, across the Pont de la Coulouvreniere into the Quai des Bergues.

Later at afternoon tea, Robert asked, 'Shall we try and find somewhere else for dinner tonight? Somewhere a little cosier than this ... emporium.'

Sarah wondered how the hierarchy of the Wilton would react to their hotel being classed as a store or market, but she knew exactly what Robert meant. She thought for a moment, wondering if the place she was considering would really be suitable for Robert, but he did say 'somewhere cosier' and that would certainly apply to the little place she had in mind. 'There is a little place in the Boulevard Georges Favon,' she said, a trifle doubtfully, 'that would definitely come under the heading of "cosy". It is not chromium-plated or streamlined, but the food is excellent and the service first class. We can walk to it easily from here and it is completely safe at night.'

'If you approve of it, I am sure I shall,' Robert told her, and that evening Sarah found herself retracing her steps of the afternoon.

46

The restaurant was well patronised, but there was a table for two, nicely situated so as to be reasonably private. While they were waiting for the food they had ordered, the owner came over to greet Sarah and they had an animated conversation in French. Robert was introduced and was amused by the expression of disappointment on the face of the owner when he realised that Robert was not Sarah's husband, as he had assumed.

After he left their table, Sarah said, 'He always claims he cannot speak English, but I find that hard to believe as all his waiters do.' She laughed, 'Perhaps he can eavesdrop better!'

Robert asked, 'Sarah, do you know every town in Europe and does everybody know you?'

She looked astounded, 'No, of course not. Why do you ask?'

'Well, you obviously know Geneva like the back of your hand and he greeted you like an old friend.'

Sarah burst out laughing. 'I was here two years ago with my sister. She telephoned me from Africa and asked me to arrange a holiday in Switzerland near enough to visit the Château Chillon. I booked bed and breakfast in a little hotel not far from here, so we would be free to wander all day, eating where and when we felt like it – which, in the case of my sister, works out at no more than two hours at the most! Nevertheless, she is as slim as a reed,' Sarah added affectionately.

'We usually dined here in the evening as they always made such a fuss of us from the first time we came here and we enjoyed it – apart from the food being extremely good for such a small place. We actually passed the little hotel where we stayed on the way here tonight. When I knew we were coming, I sent to the Tourist Information Centre here in Geneva and they sent me a very clear detailed street map and masses of information, which I studied for about six weeks prior to coming, so that we would know our way around. My sister was very impressed – she thought it was magic when I could find my way anywhere!'

'So it was as simple as that?' Robert remarked, laughing.

'Yes, as simple as that. Why – shouldn't it have been?'

Robert realised that he should be able to distinguish the ordinary from the extraordinary and when a door opened into the past and Sarah went through, it closed again when she returned and to her was probably no more than the blinking of an eye.

Just at that moment, an old man arrived at their table with a basket of long-stemmed roses. He laid one down on the table and

Robert gave him a note, waving away any change. Thanking him profusely, the old man shuffled off.

'That was very generous,' Sarah said softly, 'he probably won't need to sell any more tonight.'

Robert looked thoughtful. 'There but for the grace of God...' he left the sentence unfinished and Sarah thought, as she had many times, what a kind, perceptive and considerate person he was. He did not take anything for granted – least of all, his privilege.

When they had finished dinner, they walked back the way they had come. The lights were reflected in the lake and Robert wanted desperately to take Sarah's hand in his and be like the lovers strolling by.

He had ordered the hire car for eight o'clock in order to have a nice long day, so after a brief chat in Sarah's sitting room, they said 'Goodnight' and retired fairly early. On his way back to his room, Robert thought, I *know* you are going to be my wife, Sarah, it *must* work out that way, but I wish I did not have to wait so long.

CHAPTER SEVEN

The following morning dawned clear and bright. Robert and Sarah were able to have breakfast together for the first time since she arrived. Promptly at eight o'clock, Robert received a message to say that the hire car was ready and waiting. He had decided to drive himself as he did not want a third party intruding on his precious day with Sarah.

With her help reading the road signs, they set out along the road running parallel with the north edge of Lake Geneva, travelling through Coppet, Nyon, Rolle and Morges, stopping in Lausanne Square for coffee. Afterwards they continued on to Vevey and Montreux, arriving in time for an early lunch at the Suisse et Majestique.

It started to rain as they left the hotel, but cleared up again as they came over the highway at the foot of the Dents du Midi.

Sarah said suddenly, 'There it is!' and below them was the Château Chillon, appearing to rise out of the lake. They parked the car in a little road beside the château and walked through a gate and along a path running parallel to it. Before crossing the small wooden bridge that had replaced the original drawbridge, they paused to appreciate the conspicuous curtain wall, flanked by three semi-circular towers, aimed at doubling the defensive system on the landward side which posed the greater danger and so into Chillon with its three successive courts stepped one above the other, the gateway and guardhouse ward, the constable ward and finally, that of the count and duke.

They learned of its long history. How Bonivard and Byron were incarcerated in the dungeon. Chillon occupies the narrow strip of land affording the only passage between the lake and the sheer mountainside, which as Sarah remarked to Robert, 'That explains the illusion of its rising out of the lake, when viewed from above.'

For centuries it had been a strategic fortress guarding the international approach road to the Great St Bernard or Simplon passes.

They viewed the Great Halls of the Constable, the Bernese kitchen and chamber, the Lord's chamber, fourteenth century living quarters and a large hall, once heated but now open to the sky.

The chapel dedicated to George boasted a magnificent painted ceiling and led to the large upper courtyard, still bearing charcoal graffiti from the fourteenth century.

'We think that sort of vandalism is a curse of the modern age – nothing is new!' Robert whispered to Sarah.

At the northern end of the Great Hall of the Court, originally known as the Hall of Justice and turned into a torture chamber in 1652, were the clergy's lodgings and access to the keep was by way of the Treasury, used as a prison during the Bernese period. Even today, Chillon remains the closest to what a baronial castle was in the middle ages.

As they returned to the car, Robert remarked, 'It makes Heronshurst look positively modern, doesn't it?'

Sarah felt dwarfed by both its size and age, as she always did after seeing such places.

They drove back into Montreux for tea and then walked along the promenade beside the lake, with its myriad swans until they reached the view of the château that Sarah wanted to see.

'We had an oil painting of it in the hall when I was tiny,' she explained. 'My father said my mother brought it back from here and he had it framed for her. I remember gazing up at it and thinking how mysterious and romantic it was. I used to half-close my eyes and try and imagine I was in the picture and always hoped to see it one day. Then suddenly the picture wasn't there any more and for a while, I felt quite bereft. But one soon forgets with so much happening when one is young. I didn't know then – no one thought it important enough to tell me – my sister had taken it as a memento of home when she went to Africa.'

'And here it is in reality,' Robert said, adding with a great deal of satisfaction, 'and we are seeing it together.'

Sarah smiled at him, thinking that never in her wildest dreams did she envisage coming here with such a special person.

It was about six o'clock when they arrived back in Geneva and they parted company to go to their respective suites to get ready for dinner. Later they strolled along the lakeside, enjoying just being together, both aware that it was their last evening in Geneva.

'It is very pleasant to be able to do this without feeling apprehensive as one might in some of the bigger cities in the world,' Sarah remarked. 'I have seen ladies who must be at least seventy years old, walking alone and quite unafraid quite late at night, which they couldn't do in a lot of places.'

She thought suddenly of Merlin and remarked, 'I wonder how he is getting on without us?'

Robert was getting quite accomplished at following Sarah's quick changes of thought and said, 'It was bad enough, one of us deserting him, but when you came too, he probably feels he doesn't want to speak to either of us again,' and they both laughed at the ludicrous idea of Merlin's sulking.

'That is the wonderful thing about most animals, they never seem to bear grudges as many humans can,' Sarah commented.

Their plane was due to take off at ten-thirty the following morning and, after an early breakfast, Robert excused himself and disappeared. Sarah thought he probably had some last minute business calls to make and was not unduly concerned but he returned much quicker than she expected and they had their luggage collected and loaded into the waiting taxi, while they checked out.

As they left the hotel, Robert looked across the lake at the Jet d'Eau, the old city and Mont Blanc in the far distance and vowed to himself that they would come again some day – hopefully in the not too distant future – but stay in one of those romantic little lakeside hotels that existed, and not need to attend any business conferences.

Having arrived at the airport and gone through the usual formalities, they were soon airborne, though Sarah insisted that they were five minutes early taking off.

The air hostess announced, 'The time by the pilot's watch is ten-thirty.'

Sarah commented, 'Oh no, it isn't, it is only ten twenty-five.'

Robert laughed and said, 'Your watch must be wrong. The pilot needs to be exactly on time coming in to a busy airport like Heathrow.'

'No, it isn't,' Sarah insisted, 'this is my travelling watch – it never gains or loses a second.'

51

Robert smiled indulgently and no more was said about it.

When they were settled down, Robert thought what a pity it was that there was so much room between them. He understood that it was a lot more cosy in the tourist section. He would like to have held Sarah's hand – perhaps it was as well that he couldn't. He decided that now was as good a time as any, before the trip was actually over, to give Sarah the little memento he had bought her before leaving. Frazer would be meeting them and driving them home and, though he was the soul of discretion, Robert did not want to feel that he was being watched, neither did he want to wait until they got home.

He reached into his pocket and pulled out a small jeweller's box and handed it to Sarah, saying, 'This is to say "thank you" for coming at such short notice and hopefully, to bring back happy memories.'

Sarah looked surprised as she took the box and opened it. Her expression changed to sheer wonder and delight, 'Oh, Robert, it's perfect.'

He was pleased, 'You really like it?'

She gently touched the flowing mane of the unicorn brooch that she had admired when she was alone and Robert was busy.

'How could you know that I would love it so much?'

'Well, they are mystical, magical creatures and it seemed appropriate for the occasion and I noticed you had one on your desk,' he told her.

The shining of her eyes owed a little to unshed tears but they were very happy tears and her expression said more than words would possibly convey.

'Here, let me fasten it for you,' Robert said, leaning across the space between them and deftly pinning it to her jacket lapel and securing the safety catch.

If he had wondered whether it was the right thing to buy, he could not be more happy about it as he noticed that, from time to time Sarah touched it gently all the way back to Heathrow.

As they were about to descend, the Swiss pilot's voice announced, 'They are not ready for us yet, we have to stop up here for a while.'

'He makes it sound as if he is waiting at an aerial traffic light,' Sarah remarked, making Robert laugh. 'I said his watch was fast,' she added as they cruised round, seeing Windsor Castle for the fifth time.

'You were right. Are you always right?' Robert asked teasingly.

'Yes!' Sarah replied firmly. 'Sickening, isn't it?' She grinned at him, adding, 'You will learn that I only bet on certainties!'

When they did finally land, it was such a featherlight touchdown that Sarah, who was sitting by the window, was surprised that they were actually on the runway and already slowing down.

'Pity his timekeeping is not as good as his flying – but I suppose it's better that way round. It would not be much good being on time if he crash-landed!' Robert remarked and they both laughed.

They were not very long getting through and Frazer was waiting for them as usual and soon they were speeding free of the airport.

'We ought to stop somewhere for lunch,' Robert remarked, wondering where it was best to turn off the motorway.

'I know just the place,' Sarah said, 'we can take the first exit that leads to the M40 and then on to the A40 and I will direct Frazer from there, if he doesn't already know it.'

'It sounds intriguing,' Robert remarked, giving Frazer the necessary instructions.

Some time later, when they were on the A40, Sarah said, 'At the next roundabout, go three-quarters round it and take the minor road, then almost immediately, first left down a small lane.'

Frazer skilfully negotiated the turns and slowed down in the small lane.

At a T-junction, Sarah said, 'Right here and then pull into the car park of the inn on the left-hand side.'

The inn in question, was a slate-roofed, Cotswold stone building that looked as if it were left over from a bygone age.

'Don't worry, Robert, it is very civilised.'

They had a surprisingly good meal in a small timbered room, although as Sarah mentioned later, they could have gone into a large dining room which had been added very unobtrusively at the back of the building.

'But that,' Sarah remarked, somewhat disparagingly, 'will be full of high-powered executives of all nationalities on expense-account lunches.'

Robert laughed and said he knew the feeling.

Frazer had insisted on going into the bar for a ploughman's lunch. His missus, he said, would have a steak and kidney pie waiting for him at home and he wasn't going to ruin his appetite.

'I suppose if I ask you how you knew this place existed in the back of beyond, you will say "it is quite simple",' Robert remarked to Sarah.

She laughed. 'It couldn't be more simple,' she told him. Then more seriously, 'My father used to bring my mother here for afternoon tea in 1910, when they were courting. They usually had scones with strawberry jam and cream and rich fruit cake, all home-made, and a pot of tea for one shilling. Incredible, isn't it, when one compares today's prices? He would drive her over in her father's horse and carriage and one day, on the way home, the horse got impatient for his feed and broke into a fast trot, took a corner a little too sharply and clipped a wall with the wheel hub. It did not do any real damage apart from scraping the paint slightly and my grandfather told him it wasn't because he couldn't drive the horse, but because he couldn't talk to him.'

'A man after my own heart!' Robert laughed. 'I always believe in talking to horses rather than digging one's heels in them or using a crop and I have noticed you do, too.'

'Yes,' Sarah agreed. 'Horses are a lot more understanding than many people give them credit for. "Horse sense" is not just a myth.'

'Your parents must have been very young then,' Robert remarked.

'My father was eighteen and my mother twenty-one,' Sarah replied. 'He was born in the Royal Borough, his father was in the "Blues" and my mother was born in a tiny village near here that had only six houses, two pubs, a church, a windmill – and a village pump, even when I knew it as a small child. It has since developed quite a collection of bungalows for commuters to Oxford – they have a strangely Continental look with their pastel colours.'

'How did they meet – so far apart?' Robert asked. He found dwelling on the odd coincidences that brought people together, sometimes from worlds apart, very fascinating.

'My father had just returned from a trip round the world and was staying in a hotel in Langham Place, temporarily. He happened to notice that a beautiful girl passed by at the same time each day across the road from his window and wanted desperately to meet her. It was not so easy in those days and they had no mutual acquaintances. As a last resort, he waited around the corner of a side street until she went by – and "accidentally" bumped into her! She was obviously as impressed with the handsome young man as he was with her and after one or two

54

decorous meetings, she invited him to meet her family. Hence the fact that he drove her here in her father's horse and carriage.

'I got into the habit of driving here when things got difficult. It was very therapeutic and made me feel ready to face the fray again. It was as though there was something – or someone – here to comfort and console me.' She could not tell even Robert at that moment, how her mother had come to her in that sunny village street and the wonderful feeling of tranquillity and peace that she brought with her, so that just thinking about it could bring back that feeling of calm for months afterwards.

Having finished their lunch, they returned to the car to find Frazer already at the wheel and soon they were on their way back to Heronshurst and a rapturous welcome from Merlin and a rather more sedate one from Bates.

By the time Sarah had freshened up, shared the usual tea ritual with Robert and returned upstairs, Charlotte had unpacked and sorted out all the things that needed attention.

Sarah handed her a small packet, beautifully wrapped with the name of a famous couture house on the paper.

Charlotte opened it immediately to disclose a silk square with the crests of the Swiss cantons, interspersed with all the small mountain flowers. 'Oh, madam, it's lovely,' Charlotte exclaimed enthusiastically. 'It will look so smart with my best black blouse.'

'I'm glad you like it,' Sarah said. 'You take such good care of me, it is a small token of my appreciation.'

Charlotte blushed, looking after Mrs Mannering was a whole lot nicer than hairdressing, she thought.

At dinner that night, Robert introduced the subject of the Hunt Ball. 'Grayson takes care of the main guest list, they are people who expect to be invited each year but not particularly associated with Heronshurst. A small number will probably drink too much and generally behave rather like juvenile delinquents, but that will be par for the course and an annual hazard. Needless to say, Bates strongly disapproves,' Robert said, somewhat ruefully. 'He will make sure the more fragile irreplaceable items are tucked away safely. I make my own list of friends. Are there any names you would like to add to it?'

Sarah gave some thought to the question, then said, 'It is very kind of you, Robert, but I got separated from any of the people I might have liked to come.'

Robert did not comment, privately hoping that one day, Sarah would not even remember her life between leaving her childhood home and coming to Heronshurst. He hated to see the dimming of her normally happy expression.

The following morning Sarah was brushing her hair after dressing and considering the problem of having it cut. She did not want to return to the salon where she had had it styled for years and wondered whether she could go to the village hairdresser. It would certainly save a lot of time and bother and she was not particularly vain about her hair.

She became aware that Charlotte had passed behind her and reached out her hand as if to touch Sarah's hair, then drew it back again.

Their eyes met in the mirror and Sarah mentioned her predicament, asking, 'Do you think the village hairdresser would cut my hair for me?'

'Oh, madam,' Charlotte breathed, eagerly, 'Would you let me try? I was just thinking how I would love to be allowed to style your hair.'

'That is an idea,' Sarah replied, 'I had forgotten for a moment that you are a trained hairdresser. How about now?'

Charlotte looked surprised for a moment but quickly recovered and said, 'I'll just run and get my equipment, it is in my room.'

She soon returned and set her tools out in the bathroom, placing a chair for Sarah in front of the wash-basin, where she had fixed a spray on the taps.

Sarah sat down while Charlotte shampooed her hair and then trustingly let her go to work cutting it.

Charlotte worked quickly, but with complete concentration, deftly combing, cutting and shaping Sarah's hair. She requested her to move into the bedroom where she plugged in the hairdryer and blew it dry, flicked it with a brush, took off the cape and looked critically in the mirror at Sarah's hair for a few seconds and said, 'There, madam, will that do?'

Sarah studied her reflection. 'Really, Charlotte, you have done it well. Yes, that will do very nicely.'

Charlotte was gratified. It was agreeable to be able to keep up her skill as a hairdresser, especially working on madam's lovely hair. It was such an easy texture and a pleasure to handle.

After a quick glance to make sure she was free of loose hair, Sarah ran downstairs to join Robert for breakfast. He had already arrived and was looking at his mail, while he waited for her. She quickly helped herself to breakfast and sat down, remaining silent after her initial morning greeting to enable Robert to concentrate on his post. She felt his eyes on her and looked up.

'Is it my imagination, Sarah, or have you had your hair cut since I saw you last night?'

She laughed and replied, 'No, it is not your imagination, Charlotte has just done it for me.'

Robert looked taken aback. 'And you let her?' he asked, in amazement.

'Yes, of course. Why not? She is a trained hairdresser, remember, and it is only hair – if she had done it badly, it would soon have grown again, but she hasn't. I am very happy with it.'

'It is really first class,' Robert agreed. 'Your hair always looks impeccable and it has never looked better. I was just surprised at your taking the chance.'

'Thank you. As I said, she is a trained hairdresser and she liked to be able to "keep her hand in" as it were.'

It isn't the first time I've been made aware of her complete lack of vanity, Robert thought.

CHAPTER EIGHT

Robert and Sarah spent most of the following morning sorting out and writing invitations to his personal friends for the Hunt Ball and Sarah helped address the envelopes and then took Merlin into the village to mail them at the local post office, while Robert concentrated on some work that he needed to do.

It was going to be Harvest Festival the next day, Sunday, and the bakery had all the traditionally shaped loaves that she had loved as a child, including her favourite, a huge sheaf of corn, on display in the window.

Sarah loved the little village of Heronsbury and was glad it had escaped much of the civic vandalism that had overtaken a lot of small villages since the war, with the sudden advent of cars and a desire to live in the country while working in a town. True, there needed to be new houses, but Robert had used his influence to ensure that they blended with their surroundings and the balance of the village was preserved and also that there was enough reasonably priced accommodation to encourage the young people to stay in the vicinity when they wanted to marry and set up their own homes. After she and Merlin left the village, they went home the long way round through the woods.

Robert had finished his work much sooner than he had anticipated and went to find Sarah. Bates told him that she had not yet returned and Robert guessed that, since she had Merlin with her, they would come back via the woods and he decided to go and meet them.

He followed the path that led eventually to the village and just as he reached the edge of a clearing, he caught sight of them both sitting very still, their eyes looking in the same direction. Robert stopped, wondering what was absorbing their attention.

At that moment, Merlin sensed his presence and glanced

briefly at him, returning to his original contemplation of something that was out of Robert's view.

Sarah was sitting at the base of a tree, leaning against the trunk with Merlin close beside her. One of her hands was extended, holding out something he could not quite discern. Her voice came to him, saying softly, 'Come here, we won't hurt you.'

A few seconds passed, then Robert was amazed to see a squirrel move slowly into his line of vision, warily approaching Sarah and Merlin. It walked a few paces, stopped, its eyes on Sarah's outstretched hand, then moved closer. Finally it extended its neck and took what Robert could now see were beech nuts on the palm of her hand and retreated to the other side of the clearing.

Merlin did not move a muscle, unlike the previous time when he had tried to make the squirrel's acquaintance, when the three of them were in the woods.

Robert wondered how Sarah had persuaded Merlin to sit so still and the squirrel to eat from her hand. He wished that he had brought a camera with him.

Sarah looked up and saw him, getting up with a warm smile of greeting and they returned to the house for lunch. She will never cease to amaze me, Robert thought.

The Harvest Festival display in the church the following morning, filled the air with the mingled scent of apples, bread and fresh vegetables, piled up around the pulpit which Sarah found very evocative of her childhood.

The produce would later be distributed among the senior citizens and the more deprived families in the village and on the following Saturday, there was to be a Harvest Supper for all in the village hall.

During that afternoon, Robert was amusing himself with the crossword in the Sunday newspaper. He usually finished them fairly easily but this time he got stuck on one clue that somehow escaped him. On the face of it, it was no more difficult than any of the others. He read the clue out to Sarah. '"In favour of a reversed segment to a point, can be at another point, to postpone."'

Sarah looked up from her newspaper. 'Say that again, please, slowly,' she requested.

Robert obliged and Sarah closed her eyes for a few moments, then opened them and said, 'Procrastinate.'

'I beg your pardon?' asked Robert.

'The word is "procrastinate", "pro" – in favour of, "arc" – a segment reversed to "cra", to a point – s for south, "tin" – another name for "can", "at" another point, e for east. Procrastinate – to postpone.'

Robert burst out laughing. 'You are right, of course. Why couldn't I think of that?'

'I expect you were trying too hard and hit a blank spot,' Sarah said, smiling. 'I came fresh to the problem. Another time you would get it at once. Perhaps the same person helped me who helps me play chess,' she added, grinning mischievously, quoting his words the first time they played chess.

'That wouldn't surprise me at all, there are many things you know that astound me,' Robert replied, grinning back at her.

'Oh,' Sarah said airily, 'I'm a woman. If men understood women, they would never believe it!'

'As our transatlantic cousins say, "You can say that again!"' Robert exclaimed fervently. But privately, he thought he understood Sarah reasonably well, except when she seemed to leave him to go off on another plane for a few moments. She was so straightforward, with no devious little tricks, as so many women had that he had known in the past.

During dinner that night, Robert announced suddenly, 'I think it is high time you met some of my friends – the nicer ones, that is of course,' he added, smiling. 'I suggest we have a small informal dinner party. I can think of several that I would like particularly to meet you. They will be at the Hunt Ball and if you have met them previously on a less formal social occasion, they will not be strangers to you. There is old George – that is a figure of speech – he is approximately my age.'

Sarah smiled and waited for Robert to continue.

'George Faversham, that is. We were in the RAF together from the beginning of our service life during the war. We can ask Adrienne Hamilton as his partner, they are quite old friends. Poor old George lost his heart to a young WAAF when he was only nineteen. He knew nothing about her and it was doomed from the start. She was very impressionable and quite frankly, out to improve her lot. She left George for an allegedly wealthy Texan US army officer who had remained in England after the war ended. They went back to the States eventually and needless to say, George is now divorced from her. I think it was a case of "once bitten, twice shy" and he has never remarried. He is a nice chap – pity it had to happen to him, there must be many nice women around who would have seen him as an ideal husband.'

Sarah considered Robert's last remark and thought the same thing applied to Robert, himself. The trouble with 'nice women' she thought ruefully, was that they believed men liked to 'make the running'. Sarah herself thought that this was probably true of the only men that were worth having.

Robert continued, 'Adrienne was a victim of the war, too. Philip, the man with whom she had grown up and later married just before his ship sailed, was torpedoed out East. They were from two of our local families and the three of us had known each other almost from our cradles. Adrienne's lasting regret is that they did not have a child. She joined the WRNS and after the war was over, she set herself up in business, doing interior design. She had received honours in art doing her matriculation, but as you know at that time, things were in a state of flux and she did not go on to university, wanting to spend as much time as possible with Philip in those troubled times. After she lost him, she wanted to do something vital for the war effort and she was recommended by her chief officer in the WRNS to go on a course to "brush up" her French and German and took a commission, later interpreting for the Free French and interrogating prisoners.' Robert paused, wondering if he were boring Sarah with his long dissertation on people whom she had not yet met.

It was obvious that Sarah was engrossed in what he had been telling her as she asked, 'What happened then? Things were difficult after the war, weren't they?'

'Yes,' Robert agreed, 'but people were tired of "making do" and the general shabbiness of everything and Adrienne's business flourished after a slow start in the aftermath of hostilities. She is very good at her job and now, I believe, has six or seven branches, each run by a very efficient manageress, whom she trained over the years, having recruited them from Art School.'

'Did she never feel she wanted to get married again?' Sarah asked.

'I would think that she has had several other offers of marriage but she is content the way things are,' Robert answered. 'I believe you will like her and enjoy her company, I imagine she is your sort of person.'

Sarah mulled over Robert's words and thought it would be nice if he were right. His judgement of people was usually infallible. She found herself looking forward to meeting Adrienne and the possibility of having a woman friend again after all this time. She had necessarily lost touch with all those she knew in her youth.

Robert said, 'We will include my younger brother, Richard, and his wife, Helene, who is French. Richard does not get about a lot, he was captured by the SS when liaising with the French underground movement and suffered badly at their hands.' Robert refrained from mentioning that he was largely responsible for freeing Richard.

'As I mentioned briefly to you, he is heir to Heronshurst and after him, his son, young Richard, born in 1948, who married after getting his law degree and joining a prestigious law firm in the City. His wife, Sophie, was up at university with him, reading medicine. I don't think we will include the young people this time, charming though they are. They would feel a bit isolated among the older generation. There are two men with whom I was at prep. school originally, and later, public school, with whom I have remained friends. Harry Goodchild is married to a nice quiet little woman who is a lot more intelligent than most people give her credit for being, I suspect. There is a rumour that Harry is having a mid-life crisis and trying to recapture his lost youth with a fashion model, but I hope it is only conjecture. Marion, his wife, deserves better than to be humiliated by idle gossip. Stephen and Elizabeth Stanway are a devoted couple with four delightful children, two boys and two girls, the youngest of whom is still up at university. That will make ten of us. I think that will make a pleasant dinner party, don't you?' he appealed to Sarah.

'It sounds fine,' Sarah answered, mentally reviewing her wardrobe and wondering if she needed to buy a new dress. Thanks to Robert's generosity, it would not be a problem. Her mind ranged over other occasions when it would have been and she rapidly shut her mind to them and tried to keep to her vow to take one day at a time.

'Mrs Bates knows all of them and their likes and dislikes regarding food – she and Mrs Briggs will contrive a very enjoyable meal between them. We will send off the invitations in the morning after we have decided on the day, if that is all right with you?' he finished, rather anxiously.

'Robert, I appreciate your consideration in asking my opinion, but it is your home and they are your friends, after all. I am more than happy to comply with your plans. As you said, they will not seem so much like strangers at the Hunt Ball. Since the dinner is informal, I presume it is not long dresses for the ladies?'

'Oh no,' Robert answered, 'just one of those becoming little dresses you wear when we dine alone.'

The following morning, having decided on the date for the informal dinner party, they wrote the invitations together.

'Do you always do this yourself,' Sarah asked Richard, wondering why he did not have a secretary at Heronshurst as well as in his office.

'Not usually. As you know, Grayson takes care of the big events and invariably I dump a list on Clare and she has to find time to do it as well as her office work. She is very magnanimous about it and as I said, horrifyingly efficient. One secretary is quite enough,' he finished, grinning at her and his expression told her that he had had problems in that area in the past which, feeling the way she did about him herself, didn't surprise her in the least. Her one horror in the otherwise idyllic set-up was that he would discover how she felt and be embarrassed. If that ever happened she would feel compelled to leave – it would be too humiliating. She hoped her thoughts were not reflected on her face.

The night of the dinner party arrived and Sarah dressed with a certain amount of trepidation. For Robert's sake, she did not want to give any grounds for criticism either in the way she looked or behaved.

Charlotte dressed her hair with her usual care and attention so that Sarah felt, at least in that sphere, there was no cause to worry. She took several dresses from her wardrobe, wondering whether perhaps she should have bought a new one. But she always felt happier, when faced with a special occasion in unknown company, to wear something that was familiar and in which she felt comfortable.

I must be odd, she thought. The first thing that most women did when faced with an unknown situation, was to go out and buy a new dress to give their morale a lift.

Charlotte broke into her thoughts. 'The amethyst velvet looks lovely on you, madam,' she said unexpectedly, sensing Sarah's dilemma. It was unusual for her to comment without being asked and Sarah was touched by the concern that made her speak out now.

'Thank you, Charlotte, I believe you have made up my mind for me. I will wear my unicorn brooch on the shoulder and my amethyst drop earrings with matching ring and bracelet.'

Having made the decision, she was soon dressed and ready for the fray, as she privately considered it, going downstairs to be available to help Robert greet the guests.

The unspoken approval in his eyes did a lot more for her morale than her mirror had done, although she had been reasonably satisfied with her reflection.

The first guest to arrive was 'old George' and she could see what Robert meant when he said he was 'a thoroughly nice chap'. He took Sarah's hand in both of his saying, 'So you are Sarah – Robert is lucky,' without actually specifying why.

Adrienne arrived almost on his heels and Sarah, remembering what Robert had told her, wondered why she and Robert had never got together. She was utterly charming, witty and still very attractive at fifty-one, as Sarah had calculated from what Robert had said.

Robert's brother, Richard, younger than Robert by three years, looked much older. His ordeal as a captive of the SS had obviously left its mark. He limped, but disdained a walking stick and, in spite of everything, it was easy to see that they were brothers.

His wife, Helene, was a chic, very slender Parisienne who chattered volubly in her attractive accented English.

Robert had not actually said that they had met during Richard's liaison with the Resistance but it was implicit in what he had told her.

Harry Goodchild was a bluff, hearty character with the remains of good looks rather gone to seed. Marion, his wife, was quiet as Robert had said. Sarah mentally agreed with him that she was probably very intelligent when one got to know her.

Last to arrive were Stephen and Elizabeth Stanway who, having been devoted to each other for years and brought up four children together, looked as if each would appear incomplete without the other.

The dinner was a great success. Mrs Briggs had really excelled herself and the guests talked easily as people who have known and liked each other for several years. They went out of their way to include Sarah in their conversation and she was appreciative of their consideration, quite happy to listen and speaking only when it was appropriate, watching carefully to ensure that their guests wanted for nothing.

During the course of the evening, under cover of the general chatter, Adrienne had murmured to Sarah, 'We must get together sometime, I'll ring you.'

Sarah had smiled and replied, 'I would like that. I will look forward to hearing from you.'

When the evening ended and Robert and Sarah were showing out their guests, 'old George' had kissed her cheek saying loudly, 'If you are not careful, Robert, I'll be robbing you of this woman.'

Sarah felt slightly embarrassed but Robert merely laughed saying, 'No chance, old boy, I am head of the family and I would not give my consent,' and the tricky moment passed.

'You must not mind old George,' Robert said to her later, 'He did not mean to cause you any embarrassment. I thought the evening went very well, didn't you? You look superb, I was very proud of you and you made a great impression on everyone.'

'Thank you, Robert. They are very pleasant people and I enjoyed their company. Adrienne said she will telephone me to meet again.'

'Did she now?' Robert sounded surprised. 'She does not usually bother much about women friends. She is so busy herself that she does not have a lot of time for them, but I should not be surprised really, I thought you two would get on well. I have known her since we were children, as you are aware,' adding to himself, and you, my darling, for all of time.

CHAPTER NINE

The day of the Hunt Ball had arrived and Sarah had had to face the fact that, like it or not, she had to go and buy a new dress. Robert had made it easy by suggesting that she should travel with him when he went to Town and spent the morning looking for a suitable dress.

'We can have lunch together, if you can tear yourself away,' he said, smiling, 'then if you still haven't found anything you like, I will come and help. I should be finished with business by then.'

She accepted both offers gratefully and they established the time and place for lunch before parting company for the morning and that was how she found herself surrounded by what seemed like hundreds of dresses. This is what is known as 'being spoiled for choice' she thought, and having tried on several, some of them twice, she was amazed to find it was time to go to meet Robert for lunch.

She had whittled the number down to a short list of six, thinking that, as Robert had offered to help, she would leave the final decision to him. After all, it was his social event and she wanted to look right for the occasion. She was glad she had met his closest friends and was happy to be seeing them again.

There was one dress of the six that she privately thought was right for her and the most flattering but, on a whim she could not explain even to herself, she decided to leave it till last to try on when she and Robert returned after lunch.

He sat on one of the little gold chairs looking, for once, slightly out of place, while two of the sales girls preened and ogled to attract his attention. Sarah was amused and not a little gratified, to find that he concentrated solely on her and the current dress she was wearing, giving each one serious consideration as if the whole affair were of the utmost importance.

As she paraded in each one, he admired its best points and waited patiently until she appeared in her favourite one.

'Oh yes! Sarah, that is the one – no question about it. It looks as though it were designed exclusively for you.'

Sarah was delighted that he had confirmed her own opinion and turned this way and that, walking to and fro to give Robert a good view. The dress was made of a smooth silver fabric, the colour practically indistinguishable from her hair. The bodice fitted closely, at the same time moving fluidly with her body. The neck was high and curved simply against her throat. The sleeves were long and full, caught at the wrist in a tight cuff, but slashed underneath so that the fabric floated and settled like a cape. The skirt fitted closely over her hips, widening towards the hem, which was ankle length at the front, with a hint of a train at the back and there was a wide matching sash at the waist. Her shoes harmonised in silver and were very plain and well-fitted with a low comfortable heel.

The whole effect was dramatic, without being overdone. Robert was enchanted. 'I can't wait to see the impression that creates at the Hunt Ball,' he commented, as Sarah waited while the dress was being carefully packed.

'I can't thank you enough,' Sarah told him, 'for making it such a pleasant occasion. You have been very patient and forebearing.'

Robert laughed, 'I thoroughly enjoyed it,' he said, 'we must do it more often – you certainly set off a dress well.'

Some days later, Robert handed Sarah a small package, saying very carefully, 'I saw these in Town when I was last up and couldn't possibly resist them, I hope you approve.'

Mystified, she unwrapped the package to reveal a jeweller's box with the name of a very exclusive house. Opening the box, the sight of the contents took her breath away. 'Oh, Robert! Thank you, how beautiful they are!'

'They seemed to me to have been designed especially to go with your new dress,' Robert said. 'It is so lovely in itself that it does not need a lot of adornment and even I, as a man, realise that you can't really wear gold with it.'

Sarah gazed at him in awe, he really was so perceptive – and generous. The look in her eyes more than compensated him for any effort he may have made.

She looked again at the contents of the box, marvelling at the sheer beauty of the perfect pearl drop which shimmered as her hand moved, now palest opalescent pink, now almost silver, set in tiny platinum shells and suspended on a slender platinum chain. The earrings matched perfectly. Although Sarah was not mercenary, she could not help thinking how expensive they must have been. Robert was so generous – if he thought something would please her, he never seemed to consider the cost, and somehow it was given so naturally, creating the impression that it was she who was doing him the favour by accepting. There was never any embarrassment in receiving the gift – or a feeling that she should refuse, thereby appearing discourteous.

Robert thought how gracefully and gratefully she accepts, it is a pleasure to choose presents for her. None of that ridiculous, hypocritical, 'Oh, you shouldn't have bought it' nonsense that spoils the joy of giving.

Now it was time to dress. One part of Sarah was a little apprehensive, but she had to admit it was going to be a delight to wear that lovely dress and the wonderful pearls. Any woman would be ecstatic.

Charlotte had been enchanted by both the dress and the pearls and could not wait to see Sarah in them. She had carefully arranged her hair and was standing by to give it a final touch when Sarah had finished dressing and was ready to go down.

Sarah had relaxed in a warm bath and would soon be dressed and prepared to meet the guests. Robert had asked her to stand with him at the head of the stairs to receive them, when they would pass along the galleried landing to cloakrooms that had been made available to them, returning to the ground floor by the stairs at the other end of the landing.

It was no accident that Robert had chosen the side nearest to the portrait of Estelle. Sarah was very happy about it as she felt somehow that Estelle was behind her both literally and metaphorically and it comforted her.

She gave herself one last critical look in the long mirror in her room and opened the door to find that Robert was about to knock.

'You look absolutely wonderful,' he said simply.

Sarah smiled. 'Thank you. So do you.'

It was difficult to make up her mind whether he looked most handsome in tails or tweeds and she decided it was both!

Robert held out his arm and as she put her hand into it, she thought that, apart from shaking hands, it was their first physical contact and a little shiver ran down her spine. Just walking along holding his arm seemed somehow intimate.

Robert smiled down at her, thinking, I am really looking forward to this evening. There is a lot to be said for ballroom dancing, I can hold her in my arms with complete propriety.

As they reached the top of the staircase, the first guests were arriving and being directed up to them. Most were well known to Robert, so there was no need to announce them, but he quietly introduced those to Sarah whom she had not met.

Finally, everyone had arrived and Robert and Sarah went downstairs to mingle with them in the ballroom. The orchestra struck up with a slow foxtrot and turning to Sarah, Robert said, 'May I have the pleasure of this dance with you, please?' and they glided across the floor.

He was a superb dancer, which slightly surprised Sarah, but then anything he chose to do he did supremely well. It was very easy to follow his steps and presently they were joined by many other couples.

This must be heaven, Sarah thought, if it is a dream, please don't let me wake up, and she gave herself up to the sheer bliss of floating around in Robert's arms in her lovely dress, with the beautiful pearls he had given her.

She murmured something quietly to him but could not be sure whether she said, 'You are a dear to think of these lovely pearls,' or 'You are so dear to think of these lovely pearls.' There was a wealth of difference in the meaning, he thought and hoped it was the latter, but he only said, rather complacently, 'I was right about them, wasn't I?'

'Yes,' Sarah answered, 'Are you always right?'

He took his cue from her and replied, 'Yes, sickening, isn't it?' and they laughed together in a way that made several people nearby look closely at them.

After several dances, Sarah was circling the room, exchanging a word here and there with guests, ensuring that they were happy and comfortable, while Robert was chatting to George Faversham.

Suddenly Robert's attention was drawn by a slight disturbance at one of the doors and looking round, he saw a woman who had obviously had too much to drink, walking unsteadily across the room. He was furious when he recognised her and thought, how dare Harry bring that horrible woman here? She was heading straight for Sarah and knowing the woman's reputation, Robert started to head her off but George caught his arm, murmuring in his ear, 'Steady, old boy, Sarah is more than capable of coping with that odious woman.'

Robert tried to break free of George's restraining hand but he only tightened his grip and Robert had to stand and watch helplessly as the woman who called herself Magda Dupre reached Sarah.

'Oh,' she said, 'I have been dying to meet you. You are a lot older than I thought you would be.'

A sudden hush fell on the assembled throng as her strident voice rose above the level of normal conversation.

'That woman has a voice like a foghorn, but less musical,' Robert fumed, seething inside.

In the sudden hush that followed her remark, Sarah's quiet voice carried easily, 'Oh, really? Yes, I am old enough to have met people like you many times in my life. Now will you excuse me please, I have to attend to our invited guests.' There was a tiny emphasis on 'invited' and for the first time, Robert saw a wide smile on Sarah's face that did not reach her eyes.

As Sarah turned away with great dignity and her head held high, a little ripple of approval ran round the room and general conversation started up again.

Someone near Robert clapped softly and turning his head, he saw it was Adrienne. She gave him the merest suggestion of a wink and turned to follow Sarah.

George loosened his grip on Robert's arm.

'Thanks George,' Robert said briefly, moving off to try and reach Sarah.

'Any time, old boy, I told you that Sarah was more than a match for that revolting woman.'

By the time that Robert had managed to get to the other end of the room where Sarah was heading, he had lost sight of her, several people having waylayed him en route to express sympathy and admire Sarah's dignified handling of the situation.

Adrienne was nowhere to be seen either and Robert assumed, rightly, that wherever they were, they were together.

I hope Sarah is not upset, Robert thought, she hates people being gratuitously rude. I trust Adrienne can comfort her and he wished he were in the position to do so himself.

Adrienne had caught up with Sarah and, slipping a hand through her arm, she gently but firmly guided her into the passage.

Realising that Adrienne wanted to speak privately, Sarah

walked to the end of the passage saying, 'Robert's study is most likely to be empty at the moment. He won't mind our using it.' Shutting the door behind them, she turned to hear what Adrienne had on her mind.

Sarah was momentarily reminded of the first time she had entered that room, what was it? Six weeks ago?

Adrienne was speaking, 'It's the first time I have seen Robert look so angry and we practically grew up together, being much of an age and living in the same locality. He looked like a tiger prepared to defend its young. Luckily George held on to him and so prevented a scene. I expect George thought as I did, that you were more than capable of dealing with that poisonous woman. Why Harry brought her here of all places, I'll never know. I am sorry it happened.'

Sarah smiled serenely, 'I really have had a lot of practice dealing with her brand of spitefulness. It does not worry me now.'

Adrienne giggled, 'If George hadn't held on to Robert, he would have charged into battle like a knight defending his lady,' she said, completely mixing her metaphors.

Sarah smiled, 'He was a tiger defending its young, just now,' she reminded Adrienne.

'Oh, you know what I mean.'

They both laughed and Sarah said, 'We should return to the guests, everyone will be wondering where we are.'

There was still a trace of the smiles on their faces as they returned to the ballroom. Robert felt distinctly relieved to see them both.

As soon as possible without making any undue fuss, he made his way to Sarah.

'I'm so sorry that you should have been subjected to such rudeness in my house,' he said very quietly.

Sarah's expression was quite serene as she looked up at him. 'Please don't give it another thought, Robert, it was her problem, not mine.'

Realising that George was right, Sarah *was* more than capable of dealing with people like Magda, he became aware that if George had not restrained him, he would have given way to his primitive instincts and probably caused Sarah more embarrassment than Magda had done. It was a sobering thought now he had calmed down. He couldn't remember a time when he had felt so incensed about anything – certainly not to the point when he felt positively violent.

On reflection, it was almost insulting to an intelligent, well-balanced person like Sarah, to think that she was unable to contend with such people without his rushing to defend her. He remembered her phrase 'people like you' and smiled to himself. It was masterly – no way could Magda deny that she was like herself and by no means could the words be construed as offensive, unless Magda herself admitted that her behaviour was far from perfect. It was obvious that everyone felt that Magda had only received her just reward for her rudeness and if she was affronted, it was only by her estimation of herself.

Robert surveyed the room. There was no sign of Harry or the infamous Magda and he hoped that they had made their departure. He couldn't know that Magda had demanded to be taken somewhere 'away from all these boring people' and Harry had been only too glad of the excuse to make himself scarce.

I will have to have a word with Harry, Robert decided. It is one thing to consider other people's morals are none of one's business, but quite another when they encroach on one's own life and friends.

CHAPTER TEN

By morning Robert had regained his perspective of the 'Magda' incident and realised that it was a mere ripple and had not spoiled the event.

Discussing the Ball with Sarah at breakfast, he said, 'I really enjoyed last evening – I don't usually. Thank you for your part in making it such a success.'

Sarah looked up in surprise. 'I didn't do anything special, but thank you for the compliment.'

'You made a great impact as I knew you would. Your dress looked wonderful on you.'

'Adrienne looked attractive, didn't she?' Sarah said thoughtfully. 'She is such a nice person, I like her enormously. I wonder why she and George don't pair up?'

Robert laughed. 'Are you match-making?' he asked, then more seriously, 'In answer to your first question, yes, Adrienne did look nice, she always dresses well,' he said in the sort of tone a man uses about a favourite sister, 'but as to her and George's getting together on a permanent basis, they would drive each other mad inside a month. Adrienne is too self-contained and knows exactly where she is going and George is a bit haphazard and casual, much as I like him. Besides, the spark isn't there,' he added, enigmatically. 'By the way, wasn't Adrienne supposed to be staying overnight?'

'Yes,' Sarah replied, 'but I suggested she had breakfast in bed. She works so hard, it won't hurt her to have a lazy morning.'

Robert smiled. 'You had a pretty late night – or should I say early morning? by the time everyone had gone. Aren't you tired, too? Although, looking at you, I must say you seem as fresh as the proverbial daisy.'

'No, I'm not tired. Merlin and I went for a breather before breakfast and the occasional late night does not affect me unduly,' Sarah replied.

As Robert had to leave that morning to go up to London for a few days and remembering that she had come to Heronshurst originally to apply for the job of cataloguing Robert's special collection of books, Sarah decided it would be a good idea if she made an effort to do it while he was away. He had made no further move to get it done. He had said at the beginning that he did not think that it was really a job for her but that was as a full-time post and she was sure that if he was presented with a fait accompli, he would be pleased. Robert had done so much for her and given her so much, it was the least she could do for him in return while he was away and she could easily fit it in with her other duties if she did not need to be on hand for anything else with which he might need help.

As soon as Robert had driven off, Sarah settled down and worked steadily, beginning by listing, collating and indexing and creating cross-references to subjects, titles and authors. She realised it was going to take up a lot more time than she thought but if she hadn't finished by the time Robert returned, she could fill in the moments when she wasn't needed elsewhere. The biggest problem was not to get side-tracked by all the fascinating books on which she was working. It should be finished well before Christmas.

Halloween was only a week away and the children on the estate and in the village would be looking forward to the big party that was arranged for them, with apple-bobbing and chestnut roasting, then right on the heels of Halloween, Guy Fawkes night.

To try and eliminate the possibility of accidents, the Guy Fawkes celebrations were organised by a band of willing helpers in the village, mostly the young married men with children of their own. The huge bonfire was built well away from anything that might create a hazard and children were prevented from straying too near it.

Hot baked potatoes and toffee apples were on hand at a safe distance and provided enough incentive, with the well-organised firework display, to keep the children from unsupervised discharging of fireworks. It had the added advantage of being free, being funded by the estate. There were always plenty of adults around to keep a watchful eye on the children and ensure that they did not wander too far away.

One morning after Robert returned, he asked at breakfast, 'What shall we do for Christmas?'

For a moment, Sarah was nonplussed and countered by asking, 'What do you normally do other years?'

'The staff have their own celebrations that hardly vary from year to year, but for the last few years I have not planned anything very much. There are always people who invite one and I need not be alone, but I thought as you were here we might plan something special for ourselves.'

Sarah still felt somewhat at a loss. Although during the weeks she had been at Heronshurst, it had come to feel as though she had never been anywhere else, she had to remind herself that, like it or not, she was a newcomer.

She tried hard to think of something constructive to say. 'What about Adrienne and George,' she asked, 'are they alone at Christmas?'

'I think they get invited if it seems they are likely to be alone,' Robert replied. 'Were you thinking of a house-party?'

Sarah hesitated, feeling rather awkward, 'How would that fit in with what you have in mind?'

Robert said, 'I think it is a wonderful idea. We will have only the people we really like and with whom we feel at home – and not too many,' he added, 'more like a family party. How about the people we had to our first dinner party, plus young Richard and Sophie, if they want to come, and your family so that we have some children. We should have children at Christmas.'

'That is very kind of you,' Sarah said. 'My daughter's husband, Tom, will unfortunately not be home for Christmas this year. As you know, he is a naval officer and has managed to get home for the last three years but this year is out of the question as far as he is concerned.'

'All the more reason for having Laurel and the children, then,' Robert replied, 'providing, of course, that they would like to come.'

'I am sure they will,' Sarah assured him, beginning to look forward to Christmas.

'That is the preliminary plan, then,' Robert said. 'Now we must get the invitations out quickly and hope everyone has not made prior arrangements already. I am beginning to look forward to it for once,' Robert remarked, unconsciously echoing Sarah's own thought.

'Thinking about Christmas,' he continued, 'there is an annual party for the estate and village children, which is held after Christmas. It takes place in the village hall, being the most convenient building to erect the number of trestle tables needed to accommodate them all. It used to be a pre-Christmas event, but the youngsters got over-excited too soon and having already had one present, got even more impatient for *the* day, which added to their mothers' stress prior to their family celebrations. Then one year, my mother suggested it should be held on the Saturday after Christmas, providing it did not clash with either New Year's Eve or Day. The years that that happens, it is held a week later. My mother felt that it would be more convenient for the young mothers not to have to cope with any extra pre-Christmas excitement and it had the added advantage of providing a lift in the period between the end of the festivities and the children going back to school, when they might be feeling flat and bored after the fun of the festivities had died down.'

'That was good idea,' Sarah said, 'the mothers must have found that much more helpful. Who is responsible for choosing and wrapping all the presents? That must be an enormous task in itself.'

Robert grinned. 'Would you believe Grayson?' adding hastily, 'Not that he wraps them, but he certainly undertakes the bulk of choosing and ordering the right presents in the right ratio of boys to girls.'

'Your bailiff!' Sarah exclaimed.

'If you think about it, who has most of the facts at his fingertips? He is the person who sees most of the families associated with the estate who represent a large portion of the village. He sees their children born, grow up, knows the proportion of boys to girls, while visiting their homes on estate business at least twice a year. It is easy to ascertain within a little, what interests the children have. Most little girls like dolls, but it is just possible that one might prefer a train set. He will know and he keeps a large ledger with all such facts tabulated, then he telephones to the buyer of a large London toy shop, discusses it at length, then confirms the order in writing with a detailed list and the shop gift-wrap and label each one accordingly. They then deliver the toys in bulk to Grayson's house, where they stay safely until the day of the party. The small minority of children with whom he is

76

not acquainted are listed, with their preferences, by the head-mistress of the local school, who just happens to be Mrs Grayson.'

Sarah laughed heartily. 'You really do have everything but-toned up here, don't you?' she commented.

'We try,' Robert said modestly, 'we try.'

She did not need to ask, even if she had been rude enough to do so, who footed the bill for such an undertaking.

'Between the two of us,' Robert confided, 'I think he thoroughly enjoys the rather complicated exercise. His own children are grown up now, he has three, but when they were small, my mother discovered somehow that he had not included them on his list and when she reminded him, thinking that perhaps he had forgotten, he said he "didn't think it was seemly". She soon put him right on that score!'

He sat deep in thought for a few moments, then announced, 'We must get some special invitation cards printed for our Christmas party.'

The 'our' gave Sarah a warm glow inside.

'To save what will probably amount to several days' delay, getting them printed at this time of the year, we will go to that man in the village who does a variety of printing jobs. He is really very good and I think he will enjoy designing something really special for us. It will make a welcome change from the humdrum printing as he is very artistic but does not have a lot of oppor-tunity to indulge his talents.'

'Do you know everyone in the village?' Sarah asked.

'More or less,' Robert answered, 'we have grown up together, as our families have done for centuries,' he added simply.

As it transpired, the printing man, Adam Carter, produced a really elegant, attractive card in gold and white.

'It looks very impressive and *very* important,' Sarah remarked when they were delivered.

'So it should,' Robert replied, 'we will be there!' and they laughed as they sat down to address them and send them off post haste before the recipients had made other arrangements for Christmas.

They were not to know that Adrienne had already accepted an invitation to go to Europe, rather against her better judgement, but hastily cancelled when the invitation arrived from Herons-hurst. It had been much too long since she had spent Christmas there and nothing on earth would have prevented her from accept-ing. Since Robert's parents died, he had seemed to be living in a solitary world. He had not exactly become a recluse – his friends saw as much of him as they always had and he was just as sociable as ever, it wasn't anything she could put her finger on but she had grown up with him and although it sounded fanciful, he had the air of waiting for something – or someone. Things seemed to have changed since Sarah arrived and he had 'come alive' as she put it to herself. Adrienne wasn't very sure yet how this had come about but she blessed the occurrence. She liked Sarah enormously and felt a rapport with her that she had never experienced with any other woman of her acquaintance. She had always regretted not having a sister, but if she had been lucky enough, she would have liked her to be like Sarah.

Having been brought up in the environs of Heronshurst, Adrienne had a finger on the pulse of local opinion and she knew that Robert's tenants seemed to have taken to Sarah as well. It was strange that no one questioned her arrival or even wondered from where she came – they just accepted her – but there seemed to be a tacit agreement among them that somehow she belonged to the Falconbridge family and it was equally strange that in a small village which normally abounded with gossip, no one was prepared to discuss Sarah, other than to appreciate all she did for them.

While Robert and Sarah were busily writing the invitations, he said, 'We will enclose a personal note to Richard and Helene, young Richard and Sophie and Lauren and Tom. We will write a few lines each, I will start and you can finish – I always get stuck for a good ending. That is, if you don't mind,' he added apologetically.

Reading through what he had written to avoid repeating anything, Sarah thought that he might not be able to finish, which she privately doubted very much, but he certainly made a charming beginning.

To Lauren and Tom he wrote 'We would be so happy if you could add to our family party at Christmas. I understand you may be away, Tom, in which case, perhaps you could all manage a day or so when you are next on leave, but if circumstances change, as they have a habit of doing in the Services, we will be delighted to see you with Lauren, Patrick and Alexandra.'

The invitations were duly despatched and replies with acceptance received within ten days except for the Stanways, who were having a family house party of their own with their four children and their friends.

'All being well,' Robert remarked with great satisfaction, 'we will have a thoroughly enjoyable Christmas. It will be nice to have some children as well,' referring to Sarah's family.

She was looking forward to it immensely, having wondered about seeing them during Christmas and whether she should be on hand at Heronshurst all the time during the festivities. Now Robert had arranged everything to perfection. The prospect of the children being there in a strange house did not worry her at all. They were lively and full of fun but had been brought up to have a healthy respect for other people's property and, although they answered well when spoken to, they did not try to monopolise the conversation.

The next few weeks flew by and Christmas was only a week away. Sarah had bought all her presents and they were wrapped elegantly and just awaiting the final trimmings, which she was preparing to do now, checking them off against her list as she finished each one.

A tall Christmas tree had already been installed in the red drawing room, ready to be decorated and have the presents arranged around the base, to be opened after breakfast on Christmas morning.

Sarah knew that Lauren always planned a small stocking of interesting little things to keep the children occupied in the early hours before the adults were awake. What child could sleep as late on Christmas morning as they did the rest of the year? Sarah's father had done the same for her and her brother and sisters and she had perpetuated the idea for Lauren.

It was only since she had been adult that Sarah really became aware of all the thoughtful and caring things her father had done for them when they were young, that she supposed were usually a mother's province. It must have been a big responsibility for him to raise four children with only a housekeeper and domestic help, especially as three of them were girls.

She felt eternally grateful to him that he had refused to let any of his family adopt them individually as they had wanted to do. His elder sister had wanted to take Sarah to help fill the gap left in her family at the sad loss of her little daughter from poliomyelitis and although Sarah would have had two adopted brothers and a sister, it wouldn't have been the same as being the baby in her own family and having them so fiercely protective of her. Her father had told her that her mother's last words to him were,

'Please don't let the children be separated,' and he had promised and kept his word faithfully, not marrying again until twenty-eight years later, long after they had all grown up.

In spite of the tragedy of losing their mother so young, all of them being under ten years of age, they had had a very happy childhood together and the older ones had always taken very good care of her.

Now they were scattered half the world away but the bond was still close. What a pity they had not been nearer when she needed them so badly, but one could not burden them with one's own worries when they were too far away to help and, in the last analysis, one had to rely on oneself.

She was miraculously happy now, even though she missed them, particularly at this time of the year, but nothing could spoil the happy memories of when they had such fun together.

Sarah had realised since that it must have been easier for her, as the youngest she had had them to watch over her, but the others were old enough to remember their mother vividly but too young to be able to cope easily with the trauma of losing her.

She had to admit that their housekeeper was as efficient in her way as Mrs Bates, although she had had to do a lot more of the practical side of running a home. Her Christmas tea parties were a sight to behold. She always forbade the children to go into the morning room which was commandeered for the occasion, before everything was completely ready, but it was well worth the wait, when the whole scene burst miraculously before their young eyes.

Sarah loved that first glimpse of the elegantly arranged table with her favourite thing – the beautiful cracker by each plate, shining and sparkling in its pristine state, the decorations on the outside promising more within.

Thinking about it now, she remembered one particular year, when the crackers had a fairy doll on the outside, each one dressed in a different pastel-coloured dress like sweet peas. Because she was the youngest and a girl she had been allowed to keep every one. How she had loved them! Were children these days made as happy by such simple things? she wondered. Perhaps they were, she had heard Lauren talk about equally simple things that remained in her memory and Daniel had once told his mother not to bother to bring any toys when he came to visit Sarah, because 'Grandma has thousands'. 'Do you really have so many?' Lauren had asked and had been vastly amused when Sarah answered, 'He usually plays for hours with my box of clothes pegs, clipping and unclipping them into various shapes.'

A glance at her watch told Sarah that it was time to join Robert for their daily ritual of afternoon tea, no longer on the terrace at this time of the year, but in the small green drawing room. A very precious time nevertheless.

CHAPTER ELEVEN

The big day had arrived. Somehow, Sarah had never lost her childish delight in Christmas although circumstances over the past few years had done much to diminish it. But today was going to be very special.

The guests had all arrived safely and settled in. Robert had insisted on sending Frazer to fetch Lauren and the children, although she was quite capable of driving the eighty or so miles herself, since Tom had not been able to get leave.

'It will be less of a responsibility for her with two young children for whom to care, especially if the weather worsens, as it can this time of the year and you will not have to concern yourself about your ewe lamb,' he finished, smiling at Sarah.

Even after four months Robert could still surprise and touch Sarah with the extent of his consideration and thoughtfulness.

The children were rapturous in their greeting of Sarah, but had been rather quiet before bedtime, bearing in mind that it was Christmas Eve.

Both Lizzie/Elizabeth and Charlotte had lost their hearts to them and when they were not otherwise occupied with their duties, seemed to enjoy spending time amusing them, leaving Lauren unusually free, which felt strange to her.

Mrs Bates had offered Lauren the choice of two of the guest rooms or the nursery suite and she had chosen the latter. 'There will be much less chance of the other guests being disturbed by excitable children on Christmas morning,' she told her mother later.

The children had had breakfast there and were under Lizzie/ Elizabeth's watchful eye, with their stocking presents, while the adults had breakfast and now everyone was gathered round the huge tree to receive their presents.

It looked magnificent, nearly everyone in the household had contributed to the decoration and Bates had fitted up the lights. He considered it was his privilege to play Father Christmas and had arranged the gifts in such a way that he could distribute them evenly.

Sarah had given a great deal of thought to her present for Robert.

Although she seldom consciously considered his wealth, she was aware that there was very little she could give him that he could not afford to buy bigger and better for himself. She watched carefully now as Bates handed him the rectangular package that she had wrapped for him with such care and attention and was glad that Bates had chosen to give him that one first and allay her anxiety.

Robert read the gift card attached and glanced across at Sarah, giving her that little smile that started in his eyes and which she had come to think of as special. He unwrapped the gift with care and looked at it with an expression of surprise and wonder. Just for a moment, he wished they were alone so that he could thank her properly.

He gazed at the beautiful, delicate water-colour of the beech wood in the background and old Neptune sitting by the stream. A shaft of sunlight through the trees struck the water so that it appeared to move. In the foreground, a heron was poised at the moment of landing in the stream, wings half open and its feet down to land.

At first, Robert wondered where on earth Sarah had found such a delightful and personal present. It was obviously their wood with old Neptune and there were still herons about if one was lucky enough to catch sight of them, though not as many as there had been when the house was first named. Then he noticed the title in small letters at the bottom, 'Heronshurst' and in the right-hand corner, the tiny initials S.E.M.

Sarah never ceased to surprise him. It was the first time he knew she painted and certainly not as well as that.

Robert was oblivious of the hubbub of talk around him as people received their presents and voiced their thanks for them. He continued to gaze at the picture, noting how the heron's feet were just breaking the surface of the water and he felt that if he touched it, his fingers would be wet.

Finally, he looked up and caught Sarah's anxious regard. Did he like it? she wondered.

Robert's expression said it all, and she relaxed with relief, not so concerned about the engraved gold pen and pencil set which was her other present to him. Bates handed her a small packet wrapped in silver with a pattern of snowflakes on it. The attached card read, 'I could not find a piece of gift-wrapping paper big enough to wrap it for you. Many happy Christmases at Heronshurst, Robert.'

Sarah unwrapped the packet and opened a small box to find the keys of a BMW car.

Sarah was completely overwhelmed and looking up, saw that Robert was talking to the children, who were thanking him for their presents. It gave her a moment to collect her thoughts. She would have liked to thank Robert when they were not surrounded by so many people.

At that moment, Robert looked up and Sarah silently mouthed her thanks to him. He smiled, understanding her thought and hoping to be able to talk to her alone, to thank her properly for the wonderful picture and the elegant pen and pencil set.

Sarah's present to Lauren had posed no problems but had appeared almost magically just as she was wondering what to give her. She watched now as Lauren was unwrapping the gift to reveal a delicate porcelain figurine of a young girl reading a letter. The graceful folds of her turquoise gown fell around her feet, the porcelain lace at her throat, cuffs and the hem of her dress was so fine it appeared to be soft to the touch.

Sarah hoped that Lauren would think to read the inscription on the base and almost as though she caught Sarah's thought, Lauren turned over the figurine to read 'A Letter for Lauren' and the number of the limited edition, which was repeated on the certificate accompanying it.

Their eyes met and though Lauren was smiling, her eyes shone with unshed tears. Letters were of especial significance when one's husband was away in the Services, even in peace time and telephone calls, when available, were never so precious. Lauren blew her a kiss and Sarah was glad that the gift was a success.

Robert's present from Lauren was a cashmere sweater in a soft oatmeal shade. Sarah had discovered the correct size from Aldridge. Robert was delighted and walked over to kiss Lauren's cheek by way of thanks while Lauren was able to thank him for the beautiful diamond-studded gold pendant in her zodiac sign that he had given her.

Adrienne's voice in Sarah's ear murmured, 'Some people have all the luck!' and her melodramatic tone made Sarah laugh.

Finally all the presents were distributed and the hum of reciprocal thanks died down. Patrick proceeded to gather up the discarded wrapping paper, carefully detaching the gift tags and returning them to the right recipients, while Alexandra toddled behind him, trying to help.

Noticing what he was doing, Bates fetched a large bag and joined him, while Robert looked on, smiling as it took him back to Christmases long ago, when his mother had encouraged him and Richard to do the same thing, as she did not consider it was fair to leave it all to the staff at such a busy time. Soon everything was tidy again and most of the guests accompanied Robert and Sarah to the little village church for the morning service, coming back to the coffee which Bates had prepared for the adults, with orange juice for the children.

After the usual enormous Christmas lunch that most people indulge in, Sarah, Robert, Lauren, Adrienne and the children went for a walk. It was cool and fresh, but sunny, with a suggestion of a nip in the air that could presage frost later that night.

The children had lost their hearts to Merlin and for once he deserted Sarah to keep his eye on them and make sure they did not wander far without him. She felt that she and Lauren could relax, knowing that they had a more than efficient nursemaid and protector.

At one point where they had to go in single file as the path narrowed, Robert was able to get a quiet word with Sarah.

'The picture is lovely,' he told her, 'I had no idea that you could paint like that.'

Sarah smiled, 'The subject never came up,' she said.

'I am fascinated to know how you managed to paint it without my knowing and how you were able to pick on such a special subject.'

'In answer to your first query – in my room when you were busy elsewhere and the subject presented itself quite unexpectedly when Merlin and I were waiting for "our" squirrel. There was a loud flutter of wings and the heron landed in the stream. It was the first time I had seen one here, I was thrilled. It was so spectacular with the sunlight through the trees, glancing on the water and lighting up the heron's plumage, with old Neptune in the background. I wanted to tell you about it and that seemed the best way to describe it to you. Words would have been somewhat inadequate. I wanted you to see it the way I did and that seemed the only way of doing it,' Sarah said, simply.

'It was a wonderful present, which I shall treasure always and hang in my study where I can gaze at it often when I need a mental lift from humdrum work,' Robert told her.

Sarah was about to thank him for her marvellous gift, when the path opened out and the children came rushing up with Merlin following closely on their heels and conversation became general again as they were able to walk in a group.

Arriving back at the house, the others went indoors while Robert and Sarah walked round to the garages, where he was able to present her gift in person.

'It really is magnificent, Robert. I am overwhelmed, thank you.' Sarah said.

Robert smiled. 'It is pure self-indulgence on my part, when you go out alone I want to feel that you have as reliable a car as possible.'

'I appreciate its finer points,' Sarah said, 'but from a purely feminine viewpoint, it is a lovely colour.'

'I'm glad you noticed that,' Robert replied, 'I chose it specially as being the nearest I could get to that wonderful blue/grey of your eyes.'

The unexpectedness of the remark took Sarah completely by surprise. It was said so casually, although sincerely, that she was left at a loss for words for such a graceful compliment. Her feelings for him, plus the effort she made not to read more into his words than was actually meant, made her as tongue-tied as a gauche schoolgirl.

Maturity came to her aid at last and she said as calmly as she could manage, 'That is a very elegant compliment. Thank you, Robert.'

He privately thought that her smile alone was enough thanks. Someday, when the time is right and there are no more barriers between us, we will be able to drop our defences, he thought. Two years at this stage seemed endless and though he had enjoyed the last four months with Sarah, more than he could say, he desperately wanted to put their relationship on a more secure and permanent basis, if Sarah would allow him to do so. He realised that many men would despise him for his restraint and many women would be more than willing to anticipate their freedom but he considered that Sarah was in a minority there. It was that difference in her that he found so appealing and, anyway, how could he be sure that she would accept his advances. Robert did not want to spoil what they had at the moment and must allow time to heal the wounds caused by what had obviously been a very traumatic experience, so that Sarah could learn unquestioning trust again.

They went indoors to join the others and as they walked through the door of the red drawing room where everyone was gathered, Sarah thought the whole scene would make a very attractive Christmas card with the drawing room lending itself to the colours of Christmas.

Patrick was lying on his front on the floor, absorbed in constructing something with the latest edition to his special building bricks.

George was sitting on the arm of Lauren's chair, flirting outrageously with her in the usual harmless fashion that he employed with any attractive woman.

Sophie was being charming to Robert's brother, Richard, her father-in-law, and young Richard was being attentive to his mother.

But the sight that brought a lump to Sarah's throat was Adrienne sitting back in one of the huge armchairs with Alexandra in her lap. The child was gazing up into Adrienne's face, utterly intent on the story that she was narrating of the first Nativity. For once, Adrienne had shed the aura of impregnable glamour that she usually wore and was totally engrossed in her attention of the lovely little girl in her arms.

With the accidental similarity of their colouring, they could have passed for mother and daughter and Sarah's heart ached as she recalled Robert's saying, 'Her lasting regret is that she did not have a child.' Sarah felt doubly lucky and almost a trifle apologetic that she had Lauren and her children.

It seemed a shame to break up the tableau and Robert must have felt the same as they both hesitated in the doorway.

Alexandra looked up and suddenly abandoning her place on Adrienne's lap, she hurtled across the room to Sarah, babbling in her baby way about the story to which she had been listening.

Sarah hugged the child and over her head, looked at Adrienne who was puzzled by the expression on Sarah's face. She looked almost – what was it? – apologetic.

The conversation which had ceased at their entry, started up again and under cover of the general hum, Sarah said to Adrienne, 'I am so sorry we broke up your story. You looked so comfortable and absorbed.'

So that was it! Adrienne realised. What a nice person she was – no resentment about her precious granddaughter being monopolised by a stranger. Adrienne said with a great deal of feeling, 'She is such a lovely child.' And in case she sounded too serious, she added, 'They are nice at that age, beyond the nappy stage.'

Sarah smiled understandingly. What a pity Fate and Nature together did not always manage things very successfully. She had thought often that some women did not deserve to be mothers and on the other hand there were people like Adrienne whom Fate had deprived of the chance of having a child of their own to whom they could give a warm, loving, stable background.

Adrienne was thinking how strange it was that she had known Sarah only a few weeks and yet seemed to have known her all her life. She became aware for the first time that one could fall into instant friendship at first sight in the same way, but much more comfortably, that one could fall in love. She said to Sarah, 'I like your daughter, she has a great sense of humour.'

'She is gorgeous, isn't she?' Sarah agreed, with no false modesty where her daughter was concerned. 'My lovely golden girl. I don't know how I would have existed without her.' Then on a lighter note, she added, 'She says she doesn't know how I managed before I had her. She considers she taught me all I know about life and living!' and she and Adrienne laughed together, the way friends do who have known each other all their lives.

Hearing them, Robert felt glad that they were so compatible, even though they were as different as chalk from cheese. Sarah must have missed the friends with whom she grew up. He spent a moment in idle speculation of how different things might have been if Philip Hamilton had survived the war and Robert, himself had been lucky enough to meet Sarah when she was eighteen. It would have been quite possible when he was in London on leave – they could so easily have had mutual friends. There might have been another six or seven grown up sons and daughters between them to keep Lauren company today.

Robert gave himself a mental shake. It was not like him to dwell on the 'might-have-been'. At least Sophie and young Richard were much the same age as Lauren and the three of them got on well together.

Robert's thoughts were interrupted by the announcement that Christmas cakes and tea were being served and they all trooped into the dining room. For the next hour or so the silence was punctured by the sound of crackers being pulled, accompanied by a great deal of laughter and groans as the inevitable mottoes and jokes were read aloud.

Soon afterwards, it was the children's bedtime. Robert shook hands with Patrick, saying, 'Goodnight, old chap, sleep well,' and laughed as the boy answered,

'Goodnight, Uncle Robert, but I am only four.'

Robert hugged Alexandra and she batted her eyelashes at him in an outrageously flirtatious fashion as old as time, that made Adrienne comment to Sarah, 'I feel sorry for the local lads when that one grows up. At eighteen months she can get away with it, but eighteen years...?!'

Lauren took the children upstairs where she found Lizzie/Elizabeth waiting and hoping to be allowed to help at their bathtime and soon afterwards the guests dispersed to their various rooms to have a rest and change for dinner.

CHAPTER TWELVE

All too soon Christmas was over for another year and all that remained was the children's party in the village hall, which was the following Saturday.

Lauren and the children, unfortunately, could not be there to watch the children having fun as Tom was expected home in time for the New Year and Lauren wanted to be available to fetch him from whatever part of the country he was disembarked.

Robert and Sarah planned to spend at least some of the time at the party, watching the children receive their presents and play the games organised by the indefatigable helpers. As generation succeeded generation they seemed to enjoy almost the same ritual, having heard about it from their older siblings and the more outspoken were quick to demand that something should be repeated, if they thought it had been left out. In vain did the helpers try to introduce a more modern theme to vary the changes – if it wasn't exactly as they had heard about, from the time they cut their teeth, they felt cheated.

Robert had been talking to the vicar of the little local parish church and Sarah was standing at the other end of the hall, having been helping the vicar's wife, who was in the throes of sorting and distributing the presents. At that moment she was alone and Robert was about to join her when he noticed a small girl approach her with a box roughly the size and shape of a shoe box in her hands and start a conversation with Sarah.

From where he was standing, he could not hear what was being said, but he saw Sarah squat down on her heels to bring her level with the child, who was holding out the box to her.

Sarah took a doll from the proffered box and proceeded to remove the lilac-coloured dress and matching hat that it was wearing and replaced them with some other garments that the box contained. The doll then appeared in a fluffy, snowy-white coat and matching hat trimmed with little black buttons.

The child could look straight into Sarah's face from her crouching position and was obviously thanking her as Robert decided to approach. As he got within earshot, the child reached out her hand, gently stroking Sarah's hair, saying, 'I like your hair, it looks like silver and feels like silk.'

Sarah smiled at her and replied, 'Your hair is pretty, too, like the colour of new horse chestnuts,' winding one of the child's curls round her finger.

At that moment, a young woman rushed up saying sharply, 'Come here, Heidi,' and apologised to Sarah, as she dragged the child away looking over her shoulder, obviously reluctant to lose her new friend.

Sarah called to the retreating figures, 'It was no bother at all, I'm glad she liked her doll.'

As Robert joined Sarah, he considered how much easier it was for a four-year-old without any inhibitions to speak her mind. If she thought that someone's hair was pretty and looked like silver silk, she could not only express her opinion on the subject, she could also reach out without any qualms and touch it. He said, 'You seem to have made a new friend.'

Sarah laughed. 'They are so uncomplicated at that age. She probably thought that, even though I am virtually a stranger to her, I am with people she knows so it is quite safe to talk to me.'

'Can you bear to tear yourself away?' Robert asked, smiling, as they returned to Heronshurst.

The following day being Sunday, as well as New Year's Eve, they spent it quietly with Richard and Helene, staying up only long enough to toast the New Year in champagne. Young Richard and Sophie had returned home to dress for the New Year's Eve Ball and Adrienne very reluctantly and much against her personal inclinations, had felt obliged to join the friend who had originally invited her to spend Christmas in Europe. The one saving grace as far as she was concerned was that they would be able to get in some skiing.

As they drank the toast to the New Year, Robert was thinking that by the time the next year arrived, there would be only nine more months before he could approach Sarah about becoming his wife. Surely by that time, with care and understanding, she would have recovered from any in-built reluctance to marriage. In some respects time flew but in others it seemed to pass on leaden feet, he mused, pondering on one of the enigmas of life.

A few days later when Robert and Sarah were going through their mail, Robert handed her a card saying, 'There is some news for you.'

It was an announcement from Sophie to tell them that she and Richard were expecting their first child, possibly the first week in June.

Having read it, Sarah handed it back, saying with a happy smile on her face, 'That is wonderful. I hope it is a boy.'

'Why?' Robert asked.

'Because he will be another heir for Heronshurst, ensuring the continuity of the line. They can have a girl later.'

Robert laughed. 'What a very sexist remark to make. It is a good thing the Women's Rights Movement can't hear you.'

Sarah regarded him shrewdly. 'I don't expect the thought even entered your head, did it?' she asked and Robert was forced to admit that it was his first reaction, too!

Sarah looked at the card again, inside it was addressed to both of them. 'It was nice of them to include me,' Sarah remarked.

'Why shouldn't they? You are part of the family and they are very well aware of it,' Robert replied firmly.

Bates came in and announced, 'There is a call for you, my lady. Will you take it here or in your room?'

'Thank you, Bates, I will take it here,' she said, glancing at Robert to see if he had noticed Bates' slip of the tongue.

Robert grinned at her. 'You see, even Bates recognises the fact, too, so you can't get away from it!'

Sarah was saved from the need to reply by having to speak on the telephone. It was wonderful to be so considered but confusing after the long period she had spent being either ignored or denigrated since making such a badly misjudged decision all those years ago. It would be terribly easy to misjudge such kindness, as well, and read more into it than was actually there, she thought as she picked up the telephone.

Adrienne's voice came over the line, 'How about meeting me in Town for lunch,' she enquired, 'then we can have a "girls together" afternoon in my flat, so that we can have a good gossip and really get to know each other better.'

'I'd like that,' Sarah told her. 'What day do you propose? Yes, that will be fine, I'll see you then.' She replaced the receiver thoughtfully. She would enjoy getting properly acquainted with Adrienne.

As she joined Robert again, he remarked, 'There is another person who is very happy you came into our lives, she really approves of you.'

'That is very nice,' Sarah replied. 'I do enjoy her company – and she can tell me all about you when you were young,' she added mischievously.

'You should have been there with us,' Robert said seriously, 'where were you?'

The atmosphere was a little tense and Sarah was again saved from replying by Lizzie/Elizabeth coming in to clear breakfast. It was one thing to get that strange vivid impression of *déjà vu* herself – she was used to it – but she had always kept it to herself and found it strange that Robert accepted it. In the past she had been ridiculed if she unwittingly revealed any psychic tendencies. She was toying idly with her napkin ring and suddenly noticed something slightly different about it. Most of them bore just the Heronshurst crest engraved in the silver but as she turned it round she noticed the other side had the name 'Estelle'. A slip in laying the table? She laid it down for Lizzie/Elizabeth to retrieve when she finished clearing, without making any comment, glancing at Robert to see if he had noticed.

He was watching her with a slight smile on his lips. 'I told you that Bates knows everything about this family and he never makes mistakes,' he told Sarah as though reading her thoughts, in a tone that suggested there was nothing more to be said on the subject.

After nearly four months she could still feel bewildered at the way Fate seemed to have taken over and decided to say nothing.

Robert's voice broke into her rather turbulent thoughts. 'What do you think about our holding a Valentine's Day Ball?' he asked her. 'With fancy dress, each couple representing a famous pair in history or fiction. In view of the occasion, preferably lovers.'

Sarah looked up, 'That sounds a fascinating idea, there are plenty to choose from. I wonder if we will get any duplicate pairs?' The thought was engendered by an incident in her school-days when she and a friend decided to go to a fancy dress party as Mickey and Minnie Mouse. She was so pleased when she thought of the idea and not having a mother to help, had worked hard at adapting and making the costumes herself, her friend being one of those people happy to fall in with a scheme but very lacking in practical help. She had been quite satisfied with the results, especially the heads made of crêpe paper over cardboard. They had changed in the girls' cloakroom and walked into the corridor leading to the main hall, only to find that the very first couple they encountered were dressed as Mickey and Minnie Mouse, wearing authentic outfits hired from a theatrical costumier's. How deflated Sarah had felt. It just had not occurred to her that it might happen and she rushed back into the cloakroom, tearing off her home-made effort and had gone back to the party in her ordinary clothes, her friend meekly following suit.

Telling her father about it afterwards, he had said, very gently, 'You should have braved it out. It is quite possible that the costume you designed and made for yourself would have had more impact on the judges than a professionally made one easily hired from a costumier's.'

Sarah knew he was right – he usually was – but at eleven years of age, the disappointment had hit hard.

Robert was speaking. 'How about our going as Estelle and Robert? Somewhere in a trunk in the attic, I believe Estelle's gold dress and Robert's dress uniform are still preserved. They would probably fall to pieces if handled, but we can get reasonable copies made from the pictures.'

Sarah looked doubtfully at him. 'I am a lot older than Estelle was then. You don't look much older than Robert – even up to Edwardian times and after, men in their twenties seemed to look as old as men in their forties do today and the age gap would not be noticeable, but even if I wore a wig made up like Estelle's hair, it would look ridiculous at my age.'

Robert said very tenderly, 'Don't underestimate yourself, Sarah. If a four-year-old thinks you look lovely, with hair like silver silk, what grounds could our contemporaries possibly have for thinking otherwise?'

Sarah couldn't help smiling. 'You are very good for my ego,' she told Robert.

'Then you agree? One thing is certain – no one else would try to duplicate us.'

He couldn't know how well-timed was that remark. 'Yes, I agree,' Sarah said.

'Good, I'll try to get the costumes copied as soon as possible.'

The following Wednesday, Sarah met Adrienne for lunch during which they spoke only of generalities, but later in Adrienne's spacious and elegant apartment they settled down to what she had called 'a good gossip'.

At first, they discussed the proposed fancy dress ball and as

Sarah expected, Adrienne and George were going to pair up but Adrienne laughingly refused to reveal the identity of the couple they were going to impersonate and, likewise, Sarah omitted to mention Robert's idea.

Adrienne said, 'Tell me if I'm intruding but, as you are aware, I have known Robert all my life and I don't need to tell you that there have been many women who would have given their eyeteeth to have married him. I've always felt that he was waiting for, this may sound fanciful, his Fate, Destiny, call it what you will, then eventually you came into his life and that seems obviously what he was waiting for. What I don't understand is, why it took so long. Where were you?'

There was that question again, the one that Robert himself had asked.

Adrienne continued, 'Didn't you ever feel that you were in the wrong place, when you should have been here?'

Sarah considered her question and thought how odd it was that, as a comparative stranger, Adrienne should go straight to the heart of what Sarah had felt was her own private confusion. How can one explain logically without sounding melodramatic, those sudden fleeting glimpses of another world that seemed more real than the one she had inhabited so long.

All her life, she had been aware of knowing things about which no one had told her, she had not read about them, but nevertheless, the knowledge existed. It was not only the past, long before she was born, that opened up to her, sometimes the future did also.

Adrienne was still waiting patiently for an answer. She said now, 'Everything seems to have come right at last, even I can see that, so what is keeping you and Robert at arms' length?'

Sarah said bleakly, 'I am still married to someone else and won't be free for at least another eighteen months.'

'Oh,' said Adrienne, the modern woman, 'is that all it is? Do you want to tell me about it?' She watched Sarah's face and the expressive eyes that at this moment were reflecting anything but happy memories.

'Not really,' Sarah said, slowly. 'I don't even want to think about it. It is like a very bad dream that seems to go on forever and when you wake up, you are afraid to go back to sleep again, in case it comes back and even when you find that everything is all right, you can't be really sure that *that* isn't a dream, too.'

Adrienne was at a loss for words, but under that sleek, sophisticated shell, there still lurked the twenty-year-old who had had her dream of a happy life with Philip shattered, as so many other young women had, by the fortunes of war and his death at the early age of twenty-two, leaving her with only the memories of a shared childhood and adolescence to sustain her.

She had been young enough still to retain the mental and emotional resilience of youth but Sarah ... it seemed her nightmare had lasted thirty years.

Adrienne waited quietly, while the woman who, in such a short time, had become as dear to her as the sister she had always wanted, struggled with the past that was threatening to engulf the present.

Sarah spoke at last. 'Like you, Adrienne, I had grown up with someone whom I had hero-worshipped as a child and with whom I later fell in love for the first time with all the abandonment and compulsion that one does at seventeen. He, too, wanted us to marry before he went to France, but I considered I was too young. I wanted to develop into a person in my own right, not a carbon copy of him, as I was in danger of becoming. It didn't occur to me – it doesn't at that age, does it? – that he would not come back. You don't need me to tell you how it feels. You went through it, too, as did so many of our contemporaries. There were other men who would have been willing to help pick up the pieces. One, whom I considered to be a good friend, even said when he heard the news, "Now perhaps the rest of us will get a look in." I would never have believed he could be so crass or so imperceptive and I didn't want to speak to him again – things are so black and white to one at that age, aren't they? I dropped out of socialising but one day befriended a young soldier who was terrified in one of the London bombing raids. Because he was not one of my regular circle of friends, it was easier to communicate on a casual level and we struck up a friendship, but he became very clinging and gradually, I found that I was seeing less and less of friends of long standing. You know how difficult it was during the war, although one met and mingled with all walks of life in a way that didn't happen in peacetime, it was still taboo, as far as the Services were concerned, for other ranks to mix in public with commissioned officers when they were in uniform. My regular friends would not have given it a second thought but my newly acquired acquaintance was very uncomfortable. As I said, he was clinging and possessive, becoming very dependent on my company. It didn't seem to matter to me at that time that I was losing touch with everyone else – nothing seemed to matter very much, least

96

of all the constant bombing. Looking back, it's frightening how much one is at the mercy of one's emotions in one's teens, isn't it?'

Adrienne remembered only too well. 'I'm glad one learns to have more control over them, as one gets older,' she said, 'though sometimes I think it would be nice to experience that glorious euphoria that one felt about the exciting things that can happen.'

'I know what you mean,' Sarah said, 'I suppose it's like life in general – you can't have everything.'

'How did it happen that you actually married him?' Adrienne asked.

Sarah tried to remember just at what point she had committed herself. It was difficult to recall the thoughts and feelings of the young girl she had been all that time ago. 'He came from a family who considered that if you went out with someone more than three times, you were as good as engaged. I suppose I should have done something drastic at that point but I drifted along, unwilling, I suppose, to hurt anyone's feelings. Then I discovered that his mother was already arranging the wedding – "because you have no mother of your own". Each day I felt I should extricate myself from the situation, but what was the alternative? At that time, there was very little indication of the personality problem that existed, although looking back there were one or two incidents that should have warned me but I made allowances for a different outlook on things. Hindsight is a wonderful thing, isn't it?'

Adrienne understood so well how it could have been.

'I had grown quite fond of him. I didn't want to go through life without any children but, on the other hand, I did not want to feel that all-consuming passion of youth again that makes one feel as though one person held all the rhyme and reason for living in their hands. I thought I could help him face life with more confidence and we could have a good marriage and I would have a purpose in mine. He didn't say that he did not like children, thought them intrusive and didn't like their demanding the attention that he saw as rightfully his.'

Adrienne remembered with a pang in her heart how she and Philip had discussed having a family 'as soon as the war is over'. Life had never been fair, had it?

Following her train of thought, Sarah said, 'Things weren't too bad while the war was on and we saw each other only on leaves, but settling down to domesticity afterwards was quite another thing. He was unable to appreciate that he had come through the war without a scratch and back to a fully-furnished home, while many men had broken bodies or found no home when they returned – either literally, through the bombing or metaphorically because their wife had found someone else she preferred. He developed into a morose and sullen person who seemed to resent my very existence and constantly vented his inadequacies on me.'

'Why didn't you leave?' Adrienne asked.

'That would have been the obvious thing to do but I was reluctant to give up so easily – I'd always believed in the "better or for worse" bit of the marriage service and considered that people gave up too easily. I thought care, patience, understanding and sympathy would eliminate the mental and emotional scars left by his neurotic mother, but I was wrong. I won't bore you with the details, I don't even want to think about them any more.'

Adrienne could imagine how it was. She had met all types during her war service with the Wrens and wondered, as Robert had, that it appeared to have had so little effect on her personality, except perhaps to make her even more compassionate.

Sarah said musingly, 'I cannot regret those apparently wasted years, they brought me Lauren and her children, even though he deprived her of brothers and sisters, which she finds very hard to bear. His only reason for consenting to have her, I think, was because he suspected I would leave if I didn't have a child. With another father, Lauren herself would be different and I wouldn't change her by an iota.'

Adrienne hoped that making Sarah speak out had had a cauterising effect on what must be emotional wounds suffered over the long years. Now she wanted to bring back the serene unclouded expression to her eyes that, thankfully, had become the norm since her arrival at Heronshurst. Sarah was back in her rightful place now, of that Adrienne was certain and the best way, she felt, was to bring her back to the present. 'I must order a taxi for you or you will miss your train and Robert will not forgive me for making you late.'

Sarah smiled, the tension and strain fading from her eyes at the thought of returning to Heronshurst and Robert, just as Adrienne had hoped it would.

'I will come with you to see that you get the train and I can be sure you are on your way. I take it that Frazer will be meeting you?'

'Yes,' Sarah replied, 'I told him which one I would be travelling on.'

As she was seeing Sarah off, Adrienne said quietly, 'It had to work out that way, Sarah, don't you see? Or you would never have reached the point where you arrived at Heronshurst.'

Sarah regarded her friend with something like awe. How uncannily perceptive she was! She was right, of course.

Just before the train drew away, Sarah leaned down from the window and kissed Adrienne's cheek. 'You are a good friend,' she told her, 'I'm so glad we met.'

'Me, too,' Adrienne said, rather ungrammatically, 'I always wanted a sister and you are the nearest I will ever get to having one.'

Sarah felt overwhelmed with gratitude for the turn life had taken as the train drew away, taking her back to Heronshurst – and Robert.

CHAPTER THIRTEEN

Settling back in her seat on the train, Sarah went over her conversation with Adrienne. Never before had she opened up her heart in the way she had to her and there was no doubt, it had cleared away a lot of the cloud and depression in her mind.

Adrienne was right about one thing – if events had taken another turn in any one aspect, Sarah would not have arrived at Heronshurst. There were so many points at which she could have taken another direction. The thought was rather sobering.

Whatever had happened in the past, ceased to matter any more, she was happy now, so that just waking up in the morning seemed a great adventure, as it had when she was small.

She remembered again the man who said, 'This job is not really for you' and, 'Don't feel rejected, you have so much to offer.' His words had restored a confidence in herself that had been sadly shaken and gave her a fresh heart and a determination to aim high and not take just any job. Once again, she blessed him for giving her back her belief in herself. It was strange that Robert had used almost the same words about the original post for which she applied at Heronshurst.

Dear Adrienne, she thought, what a comfort she is. But was she, Sarah wondered, completely right about how Robert felt? She recalled saying to Adrienne that she did not want to feel that any one person held all the rhyme and reason for living in his hands, but here she was more deeply committed emotionally to Robert, with all the strength of her maturity, than ever she had been at seventeen and in love for the first time. It was the very strength of her own feelings that made her reluctant to believe that Robert could possibly feel the same way. True, he had been exceptionally kind, generous and considerate, but should she read more into that than the fact that he was a kind, generous and considerate person? It was miracle enough at the moment that he should not only understand her strange feeling of *déjà vu*, but share it and consider that she belonged to Heronshurst. It could be that he just recognised the legend and accepted it, no more than that.

It was no good dwelling on it at this stage. She was, to all intents and purposes, still not free and he was an honourable man. Adrienne, with her modern outlook, could decry such scruples, but wasn't it part of what made him such an appealing person to someone like Sarah who had suffered from someone's lies, deceit and disloyalty for far too long?

Sarah had told Robert that she was taking each day as it came for at least two years and that was the way it had to be. She, too, believed in honour as her father had done and taught her to do. He was the most honourable man she had ever met until she met Robert, though it was considered old-fashioned these days. It was a pity they lived so far apart, they would get on well together, she meditated.

Glancing out of the carriage window, she saw the lovely countryside around Heronshurst silhouetted against the sky that still held traces of light towards the west where they were heading. The train began to slow down as it approached the station and glimpsing her reflection in the darkened window of the carriage, Sarah decided that she would pass muster without the need to tidy up before reaching home.

As the train came to a halt, she noticed Frazer waiting patiently. How reliable he was! He saw her framed in the doorway and hurried to help her down, leading her out to where he had parked the car and making sure that she was settled in comfortably. As the car drew up in front of Heronshurst, Robert came out to greet her. 'I have waited tea for you, Sarah, I expect you would welcome a cup. I know Adrienne is a coffee person.'

'Thank you, Robert. Yes, a cup of tea would be very acceptable.'

On the way in, Sarah found an airletter that had been delivered by the second post. It was from her father, which did not surprise her at all, as she often received one from him when she had been thinking particularly about him.

At tea, she said to Robert, 'My father is coming to England in March, for about a month.'

'If he has no plans to stay anywhere else, he must stay here, of course,' Robert suggested, 'and we can take him anywhere he would like to visit. Is anyone coming with him?' he asked, remembering that Sarah's father was eighty years old and travelling all the way from South Africa.

'Oh, no!' Sarah replied, laughing. 'If anyone came with him, it would be because they expected him to look after them!'

'He must be remarkably young for his age,' Robert commented.

'He is, in spite of having injured his back when he was only in his forties and often being in pain.'

'I am looking forward to meeting him,' Robert said. 'Please tell him so when you reply and also that he is very welcome here.'

'Thank you, Robert, I will,' Sarah answered, wondering at the quizzical look he gave her, not realising that he was looking forward to the time when he hoped to hear her say those last two words to him on a very special occasion in the future.

'The costume designer came today and did some sketches from the portraits of Estelle and Robert. He hoped to have the garments ready for a preliminary fitting by next week, if that is all right with you?' Robert informed Sarah. 'He thought probably on Thursday, around 2 p.m. but would telephone if there was any change of plan.'

The designer duly arrived with a female assistant and fitted the costumes to their satisfaction, then took them back to the workshop to finish.

Sarah had decided against wearing a wig made up to look like Estelle's hair and when the outfits were delivered about a week later, they had a full dress rehearsal in preparation for St Valentine's Day. The copies looked most authentic and standing by the portraits to compare them, Robert and Sarah were very satisfied with the result.

Valentine's night arrived and the guests appeared in a wide variety of guises. George and Adrienne had opted for Rhett Butler and Scarlett O'Hara and while Sarah privately considered that Adrienne looked very fetching, George hardly cut a very dashing figure as the handsome Rhett, then chided herself for being uncharitable. Young Richard and Sophie were very appealing as Romeo and Juliet and Richard and Helene were Louis XVI and Marie Antoinette.

She noticed Harlequin and Columbine, Pierrot and Pierrette and yes! even a Mickey and Minnie Mouse. Sarah thought the latter hardly qualified as great lovers, but supposed they were a pair.

There was a certain amount of interested contemplation among some guests not conversant with the Heronshurst legend, about Robert and Sarah. They recognised their attire from the portraits and speculated about their uncanny likeness to them, allowing for the obvious age difference.

Several pairs were difficult to identify from their dress, but everyone seemed to be enjoying themselves, when suddenly from the south terrace, two masked men burst in. One was carrying a sawn-off shotgun and the other wielded a wicked-looking knife.

The interruption was so unexpected that, for a second, no one realised the sinister import. Everyone was in fancy dress and while in no way could they be classed as famous lovers, the first impression was that they, too, were dressed for the party until the knife-wielding character said threateningly,

'Just keep still and no one will get hurt. We are collecting for charity – our charity. Keep 'em covered, Bert, while I relieve them of their gewgaws. You lot can all move down the other end,' he told the guests. 'The first one that makes a wrong move will get a blast from the gun – and that won't improve your looks. He ain't particular who he gets.'

Out of the corner of her eye, Sarah saw Robert start to move towards her and her heart stood still. Please don't get shot, she pleaded despairingly in her mind and then on the heels of that thought, unbidden, Merlin, where are you? I need you desperately.

The guests had already cleared the centre of the floor and were being herded together by the shot-gun thug. Two of the male guests had restrained Robert, realising the foolhardiness of his action.

Sarah had not moved and the man with the knife walked threateningly towards her. 'You, too, lady, and before you go I'll have that nice little diamond pin you're wearing,' and he reached out to pull it from Sarah's dress.

She had been thinking, please don't let me show any fear, but when the nasty little thief stretched out his grubby hand for her unicorn brooch, she saw red. Never had she been so angry and looking him straight in the eye, she said between her teeth, 'Don't you dare to touch it!'

103

The sheer unexpectedness of her reaction, the venom in her voice and the look in her eyes, stopped him momentarily in his tracks, then he pulled himself together. What could a little thing like her do to him? But the hesitation was his undoing.

Behind him, Sarah caught a glimpse of a black and gold shadow streaking through the open door from the hall out of sight of the thug. She stood very still as Merlin rose like a rocket, seizing the arm that held the knife in his jaws. Man and dog crashed to the ground and the knife went skidding across the polished floor.

'Get 'im off of me, he'll kill me,' screamed the thief as Merlin stood astride him, still holding his arm.

Sarah spoke very coldly. 'He won't if you keep very still,' she told him, her tone implying that if he moved, anything might happen.

She spoke softly to Merlin and he released his hold of the arm, but otherwise did not move.

Looking up from his position on the floor, the would-be thief found the nearness of the dog's face to his own absolutely terrifying and he remained rigid. He was convinced that his arm must be torn, not knowing that the dog could hold it firmly without breaking the skin unless he struggled.

The accomplice panicked and after an unwitting, involuntary shot which caught the edge of the chandelier and peppered the ceiling, he dropped the gun and turned to run, but several of the male guests grabbed him, none too gently, while Robert rushed to Sarah.

'I'm quite all right, thank you,' she said in answer to his frantic enquiry, feeling as if her knees were about to give way at any moment. 'Someone had better call the police.'

That proved to be unnecessary as Bates, the dependable, had done so already, having seen Merlin racing through the hall and having followed him to discover the reason.

The police arrived in minutes and hauled off the miscreants.

'They are a stupid pair,' the police inspector said, 'confused by drugs and all the more dangerous because of it. Is everyone all right?'

'Yes,' Robert replied, thankfully, 'we must be more careful to lock the doors in future. I thought we had got beyond the days of highwaymen.'

'Merlin was magnificent,' Sarah said, 'he saved the day.'

'Strange how he knew what was going on,' remarked the inspector.

'Yes, wasn't it?' Sarah agreed, smiling for the first time since the incident. How could you explain to the obviously uninitiated, that one could call a dog like Merlin without using one's voice?

All the drama having died down, Bates went round ensuring that all the outside doors were securely fastened and then announced that refreshments were being served in the adjoining dining room.

There was an animated buzz of conversation. It was not every day that such things happened, thank goodness, but now it was over, since no one had been hurt, it had been quite exciting and everything had turned out all right in the end.

Trying to be the perfect host, Robert was polite and entertaining, but he was very glad when it became time to usher out the last guest. He wanted more than anything, to get Sarah to himself and make sure that she was none the worse for her terrifying ordeal.

How proud and sure of herself she had looked, facing that odious little crook. What had she said to him that made him stop so suddenly and appear frightened? Merlin had arrived like an express train before he had time to recover. It had probably needed only a telepathic message from Sarah to bring him rushing to her rescue from the rear of the house. The dog had been her devoted shadow from the moment she had arrived at Heronshurst.

Eventually he got Sarah to himself and they were having a quiet nightcap in the small green drawing room, to relax after the excitement of the evening, prior to retiring for the night.

Robert sat sideways on the sofa beside Sarah and taking her hand in both of his, he asked anxiously, 'How are you, Sarah? Do you feel any the worse for your frightening experience?'

Sarah looked up into the handsome face, now so close to her own that she could see the fascinating gold and green flecks in his wonderful eyes. 'No, thank you, Robert, I am fine. At first I was terrified, then I didn't want to let that nasty little man see how frightened I was, but when he tried to steal my unicorn brooch, it made me so angry I forgot my fear. My worst moment was when I saw you start to move towards me and I was afraid you would get shot, then Merlin came to the rescue. He can move so fast that the crooks were taken by surprise and even if the gunman had had time to think, he would probably have missed hitting him.'

'He certainly was magnificent,' Robert agreed. 'It was obviously his devotion to you that warned him you were in danger and he acted accordingly. We owe him a lot. Were you really afraid I was going to be shot?'

'Yes,' Sarah said, as usual feeling confused by the strength of her emotions where Robert was concerned.

The anxious look left his face and he smiled in the way she had come to think of as special. They sat looking at each other and Sarah was completely bereft of anything sensible to say.

Robert leaned forward and at first she thought he was going to whisper to her, then she felt his lips brush her ear and thought that her bones would melt.

He drew back saying, 'I'm sorry, but you have a little tendril of hair that escapes and curls round you ear and I always want to kiss it.' His tone was contrite but his expression betrayed his satisfaction that he had succumbed to the temptation. He stood up, at the same time drawing Sarah to her feet by the hand he was still holding. 'After the drama of the evening, we had better try to get some sleep,' he said, hoping that he had not embarrassed Sarah.

They walked through the hall to find Merlin waiting patiently at the foot of the stairs. Sarah patted his head with her free hand, by way of 'goodnight' and she and Robert walked slowly up the stairs.

Outside her room, Robert lifted her hand and gently kissed the third finger which, although bare of rings, still bore the faint impression of having worn one for a long time.

He opened the door with his free hand saying tenderly, 'Goodnight, Sarah, sleep well. I will see you at breakfast.' He relinquished her hand, giving her a last little smile as he walked along to his room.

Sarah lay for a while staring at the ceiling and going over the events of the evening. It certainly had been frightening at first, especially when Robert had started to move towards her and she was afraid he would be shot, but her anger had overcome her fear at the very thought of that nasty little man even touching her cherished gift from Robert. Then that wonderful dog had answered her silent plea for help and raced to her rescue. Her mind moved on to the last few precious moments with Robert and with the memory and a little smile on her lips, she slid into a deep sleep.

CHAPTER FOURTEEN

Coming downstairs the following morning, Sarah found Merlin sitting where she had left him the previous night, looking as if he had not moved since then, though logic told her he must have done so.

She went in to breakfast and he followed, stopping outside the open door of the breakfast room.

Getting up from the table to greet her and noticing Merlin outside, Robert commented, 'He seems reluctant to let you out of his sight, doesn't he?'

Sarah asked, 'How old is he, two-and-a-half to three years?'

Robert thought for a moment, 'Yes, almost three years. Why do you ask?'

'He is such a magnificent creature, with a wonderful temperament, it seems a pity not to try to perpetuate it by breeding from him. Have you ever thought about it? Any breeder would jump at the chance of having him at stud and one can usually have the pick of the litter in exchange.'

'That is a very good idea,' Robert agreed. 'We will do that. I will get in touch with the kennels where he was bred. I chose him – or rather, he chose me – from all the litter. They had just been given their meal and instead of rushing in to gobble it down like the others, he looked up and came right across their quarters to make friends with me. He was a handsome animal, even as a puppy and I could not resist him, although, as it transpired, he seems to have been waiting for you!'

'I'm sorry,' Sarah sounded really apologetic, 'I did not mean to monopolise him.'

Robert laughed. 'Don't give it another thought, it is better that way, as you can spend a lot more time with him and I don't need to concern myself so much about you when you go walking or riding alone, as long as I know he is with you. It would be an advantage to have another dog like him, if we are lucky enough that at least one of his progeny inherits his qualities and perpetuates them through the years. It is a pity that dogs have such a short life span compared with human beings.'

'I agree,' Sarah replied, 'they should have at least as long as the average human life span. If turtles and parrots can live to be a hundred years old, there doesn't seem to be any reason why a dog can't, too.'

The days slid by and it seemed no time at all until the day that Sarah's father was due to arrive from South Africa. His plane was scheduled to land around 8 a.m., having left Cape Town overnight.

Several other long-haul flights were due also, within a few minutes of each other, which made the reception area very crowded, but Sarah just managed to catch a glimpse of her father and squeezed through the crowd to reach him.

He looked remarkably well for an octogenarian who had just travelled 6,000 miles overnight, alone. They hugged and made their way to where Frazer was waiting and all three headed for the multi-storey car park where Sarah and her father waited with what seemed like hundreds of other people who had been meeting all the other planes, while Frazer fetched the car from the top storey, which had been the only space available at the time.

Eventually Frazer managed to reach them, apologising for the delay.

'They were converging on all floors, madam, and one lady said, "Please let me in, my old aunt of seventy-five is waiting for me. She has come all the way from Spain alone." I hadn't the heart to tell her that I was meeting a gentleman turned eighty, who had come all the way from South Africa alone.'

Sarah laughed. 'It would have sounded rather like one-upmanship, wouldn't it?' she said.

They managed to get free of the crush and soon arrived at Heronshurst. Robert was waiting, not wanting to encroach on Sarah's first meeting with her father for several years.

Sarah introduced them, 'Father, this is Robert, Lord Falconbridge, Robert, my father, Edward Matthews.'

She had explained in letters how she had first arrived at Heronshurst but it was difficult to elucidate the strange sequence of events. Her father was very down-to-earth and she had never discussed her psychic tendencies with him, always feeling that she must have inherited them from her mother's side of the family and often wished she were still with them, so she could talk about it to her. She had no idea what her father thought about her position but he and Robert got on famously from the start and the fact that both their fathers had belonged to Household Cavalry Regiments, though in different generations, gave them common ground.

The month flew by, during which time they took Mr Matthews all around the area that he had known and loved when he was courting Sarah's mother and they dined in the little inn where he had taken her for strawberry cream teas and to which Sarah had directed Robert on their way home from Switzerland.

Two days after his arrival, they celebrated Mr Matthews' eighty-first birthday with a little family party and one or two close friends.

Adrienne had been there and having spent some time talking to Sarah's father, she commented, 'They don't make them like him anymore, more's the pity. He wouldn't like to take me back with him to South Africa, would he?'

Sarah had laughed and said, 'I'm sure he would be delighted. It's lovely where he lives at Seapoint. From his apartment he can look right across Table Bay. He still drives and could take you to some wonderful places – along Marine Drive and out to Cape Point, for instance. There is a sort of Nature reserve there and if you are not careful, the baboons will pull off the windscreen wipers and even get into the car if you are unwise enough to leave it open. The lighthouse has a million candle-power light – good job they don't have to be lit one by one! It is a very beautiful country – very different from England but I would still pine for an English spring, if I had to live out there permanently.' She felt very glad that everyone found her father so easy to know. He had always had a great deal of charm and it didn't seem to diminish with age – children loved him.

A fortnight later was Sarah's own birthday – her father always said she had been a late birthday present to him – and, as far as she knew, no one at Heronshurst was aware of the fact, apart from her father, so it came as a big surprise to find so many gifts and cards on the breakfast table beside her place.

Robert's present to her was especially remarkable, not only because he knew it was her birthday but because of the nature of the present, which was obviously a family heirloom, a heavy gold bracelet set with exquisite emeralds and engraved inside 'Estelle' with her coat of arms which included a unicorn. Sarah wondered if she had felt the same way about the mythical creature. She felt overwhelmed and found the thought behind the gift even more precious than its intrinsic value, which was clearly priceless. She mentioned the fact to Robert and he seemed inordinately happy about it.

By coincidence, Lauren's gift was a pair of earrings – emeralds set in pendant filigree hearts. Her father had bought her a heavy, antique gold necklace and Adrienne's present was a large, expensive bottle of her favourite perfume. When Sarah thanked her, she said, 'There is enough to bathe in,' and Adrienne had smiled and said in an unusually serious tone for her, 'Nothing is too good for my adopted sister,' which touched Sarah deeply.

The party, which Robert had patently arranged with the help of Mrs Bates, had much the same guest list as that for Sarah's father, consisting of family and close friends.

Sophie had less than three months to wait for their longed-for baby and was keeping very fit and happy.

All too soon, it became time for Mr Matthews to return to South Africa and Sarah could not help wondering how long it would be before she saw him again, but as he went off to the departure lounge he turned and called back to her with a big smile, 'See you next year, darling!' and she hoped that would prove to be true.

April came with the first of the primroses and Alexandra's second birthday. As the month progressed, Heron's Wood acquired a pale gold carpet, which slowly gave way to a deep sapphire blue, later paling to azure as the bluebells opened widely with the advance of May, just as Sarah had imagined it would when she saw it, ostensibly for the first time, in September with Robert on her arrival at Heronshurst.

From time to time they continued to pay their visits to the farms to check that all was in order and that the tenants were happy.

One morning, Robert received a telephone call and went in search of Sarah, asking her, 'Are you busy at the moment or can you spare the rest of the morning to come out with me?'

Seeing the expression on his face, Sarah realised that there was an element of surprise involved and she refrained from asking any questions. She smiled at him and said, 'No, I am not doing anything that can't be left and yes, I would like to go out with you.'

'We can ride, if you have no objection to changing, or go in the car,' he told her.

'It is a lovely morning, riding would be pleasant, I won't be more than ten minutes,' Sarah replied.

'Don't rush, I have to change, too, and I'm only a man,' Robert answered, laughing, knowing that Sarah would be as good as her word – if she said 'ten minutes', then ten minutes it would be.

He telephoned through to the stables to get the horses saddled ready for them and followed Sarah upstairs to change.

She was intrigued by the prospect of a surprise but did not try to guess as she considered it would spoil the fun, knowing that if she concentrated hard enough, she could divine what it was all about.

Sarah and Robert emerged from their rooms at the same moment and proceeded to the stables where Foster and the lad had already saddled Apollo and Flame.

Robert realised that as soon as they arrived at their destination, Sarah would guess the reason for going, but he hoped it would be a pleasant surprise anyway.

They reached a farm and as they neared the house, the owner came out to meet them and after they dismounted, he took their horses round to the stable, loosening their girths and hitching the reins and they all walked on to another building very similar to the stables. The owner opened a door, stood to one side and said to Sarah, 'Look over there.'

She turned to the partitioned area that he indicated and felt as if her heart had skipped a beat. There was a beautiful Alsatian bitch lying on a pile of clean straw and tumbling around her were seven or eight sturdy puppies.

Mr Chapman, her owner, said, 'You may go over and look. Faun won't mind in the least, she will know you are a friend, coming in with me.'

Sarah walked over, bending down slowly, while she spoke softly to the lovely and proud mother of the puppies. Most of them carried on either trying to feed or playfully fighting each other, but one detached itself from the throng and walked over to Sarah.

She couldn't believe her eyes, and after asking permission from Mr Chapman, she lifted the puppy gently and cradled him in her arms, turning to Robert with shining eyes. 'Look, Robert, isn't he absolutely wonderful? One doesn't need to ask who sired that litter,' and she held out a perfect miniature replica of Merlin. Robert took the puppy from her saying, 'He looks exactly like

Merlin did at the same age and also, he left the others to go to you, as Merlin did to me.'

The puppy wriggled ecstatically, trying to lick Robert's face while his mother looked on proudly and benignly.

Sarah regarded the puppy, now happily snuggled down in Robert's arms, quite content to be there. 'May I give him to you for your birthday, Robert? He looks so happy with you, I would like to do that.'

'I would like it, too, Sarah, thank you.' Robert smiled at her over the puppy's head. 'We must let him go back to his mother for a week or so longer, then Mr Chapman will deliver him. I wonder what Merlin will think of his new son?'

'He is so gentle with small creatures, he will probably be ecstatic to have him for a playmate,' Sarah answered. 'Hopefully he will be able to teach him all he knows, much quicker and easier than we could. After all, they will speak the same language!'

Robert laughed. 'We must think of a name for him.'

Sarah suggested, 'Since Merlin is his sire, why not call him after one of the knights of the Round Table and keep the Arthurian theme?'

'That is a good idea. We will decide when we have had time to consider which one might suit him best.'

On the way home, Robert remarked, 'That was an excellent notion of yours to breed from Merlin. As you say, we can continue the line from time to time and there will always be a younger dog who, hopefully, will teach each new puppy how to behave.'

Sarah looked sad for a moment, the idea of not having Merlin made her unhappy, but it was inevitable when a dog's life span is so much shorter than a human being's, as she and Robert had discussed earlier. What was it that Kipling had said? 'Brothers and sisters, I bid you beware of giving your heart to a dog to tear.' It seemed incredible to Sarah that she had managed so long without Merlin, not having been allowed to keep a dog between leaving her childhood home and coming to Heronshurst. Now everyday life would be the poorer without him, but he was still very young and hopefully had many more years ahead of him.

The new puppy would be ready to leave his mother in time for Robert's birthday on 8th July.

As Tom could not be home in time to celebrate Lauren's birthday on 3rd June, she and the children came to Heronshurst for three days to mark the occasion.

On the day of Lauren's birthday, young Richard telephoned to say that their son had been born and was to be called Robert Richard and both mother and baby were doing well.

Sarah remarked to Robert, 'Now we have a young Robert as well as a young Richard.'

Robert was very happy that they had had a boy, as Sarah had remarked, 'They can have a girl next time.'

Later in the month, they held a Midsummer Ball and Sophie was very glad to be able to wear an elegant new dress for the occasion. She had brought the baby over as soon as possible for Robert and Sarah to see and they were enchanted by him. As Sophie had remarked, 'He would not dare to arrive without the Falconbridge good looks!'

Seeing Robert holding the baby and the tenderness in his eyes, Sarah thought what a pity it was that he had no son of his own, he would have made a wonderful father. There it seemed the Heronshurst destiny would not be fulfilled in his lifetime, as the legend referred to the eldest son.

Mr Chapman delivered the new puppy at the end of the first week in July in time for Robert's birthday and Merlin was fascinated by his son, who followed him about like a shadow, even wanting to go on their long walks. For the first two or three weeks, he usually had to be carried home by either Robert or Sarah, having tired himself out. He grew rapidly, each day getting more like Merlin. As he grew more independent, he often chose to stay with Robert when he was working in his study, which pleased Sarah enormously and made her feel less guilty about Merlin's monopoly of her.

CHAPTER FIFTEEN

As September approached, Robert asked Sarah, 'Do you remember what anniversary falls next week?'

Sarah gave his question a great deal of thought, but all she could think of herself, was that it was a year since she had arrived at Heronshurst and although that loomed largely on her horizon, she could not imagine that it could possibly have the same significance for Robert. It seemed incredible that a whole year had passed and at the same time, there were more and more moments when she forgot she had ever been anywhere else. She realised that Robert was waiting for a reply and asked, 'What had you in mind?'

'It is a year since you came here on 4th September and I think we should celebrate. We have been keeping our noses to the grindstone without having a holiday. How about taking a week or two and going back to Switzerland? No work this time, just the whole time to ourselves to wander where we please.'

Sarah felt breathless, both at the idea of a wonderful week or more wandering around that lovely country with Robert and because he considered the anniversary of her arrival sufficient cause to celebrate.

'That sounds a wonderful idea, Robert, I would love to do that and thank you for suggesting it.'

He smiled that deep, warm smile that always touched her heart and made her feel that the world was a wonderful place. 'Right,' he said, 'I will make the arrangements. Do you have any preferences or are you happy to leave it with me?'

'Perfectly happy to leave it in your hands, Robert,' she replied, adding to herself, I'd happily follow you to the ends of the earth if you chose to go.

Something of what she was contemplating showed in her eyes

and Robert gazed at her for several moments without comment, wondering if it was just wishful thinking on his part.

It seemed incredible to him, too, that it was only a year since Sarah's arrival. She seemed to have been part of his being all his life and yet the next year stretched interminably. Take the days as they come and enjoy them, he admonished himself, echoing what Sarah had said in those early days.

He resolved to plan carefully over the next few days so that their holiday together would be memorable and a recollection to cherish.

He finally arranged to stay in Basel, as a base for touring the German-speaking part of Switzerland. They flew into Mulhouse and got a taxi to the hotel in Bernerhof, quite close to the railway station and the very elegant shopping area. He had deliberately chosen a smaller, more friendly little place than the sister hotel to the one he had stayed at in Geneva, which was nearby and they could see straight across the park from the windows of their adjoining rooms.

After settling in and having dinner, they decided to go for a walk and were crossing the Wettstein Bridge to the older part of the city. It was dark by this time except for the city and street lights which reflected brightly in the water of the Rhine and looking down over the balustrade at the river, Sarah was intrigued to notice a man start to swim across, pushing an enormous, plastic-covered bundle ahead of him. The river was running very fast and strongly and he had to go with the current. He was swept under the bridge and by the time Sarah had managed to cross to the opposite side, he had contrived to reach the other bank, well down the river from where he had started.

She found her imagination working overtime. What was he doing that entailed such a dangerous manoeuvre in the dark and in such a secret fashion? Was it something that should be reported and would one be believed, having arrived only that day in Basel? On reflection, she decided that while it was an odd thing to witness, it was none of her business, though she wondered about it for a long time afterwards.

Robert found it highly entertaining and said, 'I think that the poor man has been unable to pay his rent and is doing a "moonlight flit" with all his personal possessions, rather than have them all confiscated to pay his debt.'

The following morning they explored the old city, which was very elegant, beautiful and very expensive where only the wealthy could afford to live. At one point the taxi driver had to ask for a car to be moved in a narrow bottle-neck, so that they could get through. He claimed that it was normal practice for the residents to park as awkwardly as possible just for the purpose of discouraging tourists. Sarah and Robert had a sneaking sympathy for them, if they were subjected to the litter-throwing, drink can dropping type of visitor. Most cities had their share these days, although, so far, they did not seem to be much in evidence. The streets were hosed down early in the day and the city was shining clean as they strolled through from the twin-spired Minster, across the square to the City Hall and on through the well-preserved mediaeval lanes, past sculptured fountains to the Spalen Gate, claimed to be the most beautiful city gate in Switzerland.

A ferry took them across the Rhine and gave them a magnificent view of the late mediaeval heart of the city on the left bank, the steeples of the Minster, cloisters, churches, patrician homes on the slopes and narrow artisans' houses on the water front. By contrast, in the courtyard of the new School of Applied Arts, stood the notable column by Hans Arp, symbolic of a new vision of the world.

Afterwards they went to the Three Countries Corner, where Basel spreads out to France and Germany, two and a half miles from the heart of the city, at Basel's Rhine port and where they found that they could have an aperitif in Germany, a main course in France and dessert and coffee in Switzerland.

'All this sight-seeing gives me an appetite,' Robert announced. 'Let's stop for a quick lunch and see if we can hire a car to go out to the Black Forest – it isn't all that far, according to my map. You have got your passport, if necessary, haven't you?' he asked Sarah, knowing that she disliked being parted from it for any reason, when travelling.

'Yes, I have,' she assured him.

After a light lunch, they took the hire car out to Titisee, where they joined several other tourists in the car park and found a little café where they could have tea.

'What would you like to eat?' Robert asked Sarah.

She glanced through the items on the hand-written board that was displayed and smiled. 'Where are we?' she asked.

Robert looked surprised at the question, but said, 'The Black Forest.'

Sarah's smile broadened, 'What else then? Black Forest gateau – it should be authentic here, shouldn't it?'

Having explored the area around the lake, they moved off,

116

stopping at Freiburg. The huge sandstone cathedral loomed over the market place and they were able to visit it, where a guide told them about its history.

On the way back to Basel, they were held up on the German/Swiss frontier, because someone in front of them had absolutely no identification whatsoever. Their own passports were given only a cursory glance and the last they saw of the other person was his being hauled off to the office of the frontier post.

It seemed to be a day for being delayed. When they finally reached Basel, they had to wait in a traffic queue while a rather straggly Swiss army parade went through right down the centre of the main street.

After watching them slouch by, Robert commented, 'They would never make the Guards at home, would they?'

Later that night at dinner, Sarah was rather amused to find that when she was sitting down and the waiter stood beside her, they were eye to eye. It was with great difficulty that she refrained from laughing out loud, when Robert whispered after the waiter had moved away, 'When he leaned towards you in that deferential way, I thought he was going to kiss you!'

They spent the following morning browsing through all the elegant shops in Basel and after lunch, took a car through the foothills of the Black Forest to Badenweiler, spending a pleasant and sunny afternoon walking around the lovely gardens. Many other visitors had the same idea and the people in the little restaurant found that they had their hands very full trying to satisfy everyone's demands for tea and cakes when they paused for a rest. The grounds were so beautiful, the sun was shining and Robert and Sarah were together, and she felt that, as far as she was concerned, time could stand still.

When they finally left, they drove on to Auggen, where they discovered that the local wine cellar was celebrating its diamond jubilee and discovered the truth of the saying that 'the wine was flowing like water'. Guides were opening huge boxes, clearing them rapidly by taking out bottles two at a time and filling glasses by the dozen, which were emptied as quickly by the eager visitors. Sarah was not the least bit surprised when they returned to their car to see that one woman, who was trying to mount the steps of a touring coach, missed her footing and sprawled inelegantly on the steps and needed to be helped up.

Robert remarked, 'It is a good thing she isn't doing the driving – she would never find her way home in that state. Apart from being a serious danger to anyone else on the road.'

'The guides were very pressing – you would think that they were trying to empty the cellar of all its stock. I lost count of the number of times I had to refuse a glass,' Sarah commented. 'It made me feel as if I were a spoilsport and not joining in their celebration.'

Robert laughed. 'I did too,' he said, 'or I wouldn't be attempting to drive now.'

They continued on their way to Ottsmarsheim, where there was an eleventh century church associated with Charlemagne. As they arrived, a wedding party was leaving and the young bride and groom looked so happy that Sarah felt she must photograph them. As they drove off, the smiling bride looked straight at Sarah and waved her hand to her. 'I do hope she has a happy marriage and never loses that happy look,' Sarah said softly, more to herself than Robert.

He glanced at her, knowing what was in her mind, realising that she did not really want an answer, but he said gently, 'It can work out well sometimes, in fact, surprisingly often. One doesn't hear so much about the successes.'

When the wedding party had gone, Sarah and Robert were able to explore the church and then continued on to Alsace over the canal that links the Rhone to the Rhine and through Chalampe d'Alsace, getting back to Basel in time for dinner at their hotel.

The weather was still beautiful the next day and they decided to go to Lucern by train to avoid being encumbered by a car. It was only about 10.30 a.m. when they arrived and they boarded a water bus, which sped over the shining water of the lake in brilliant sunshine, with a flock of seagulls following in their wake, attracted by the food being thrown to them by several of the passengers. It was obviously an established occurrence, since the water bus was on regular service to the villages surrounding the lake. Sarah was fascinated to see the birds swoop and catch the food before it hit the water.

Far to the left, the lake stretched to the skyline, to the right and ahead of them, the mountains rose up almost sheer, curling round the lake's edge. Sarah was surprised at the size of Lake Lucern and the journey across just a small corner of it took two hours, in spite of the speed at which they were travelling.

'We can get lunch on board, if you care to,' Robert told her, 'since we are uncertain of finding a shore restaurant in reasonable time.'

'That would be a good idea,' Sarah agreed, 'travelling always did make me hungry.'

Robert looked amused, 'You have a wonderfully healthy appetite for a slim young woman,' he told her, smiling.

Sarah laughed with him, 'Thank you for the "young",' she told him. 'As you know full well, I'll never see my fiftieth birthday again.'

'You seem very young to me,' Robert said, much more seriously. 'Young, but mature and very wise at the same time.'

'That is a charming thing to say, thank you,' Sarah replied, trying, as usual, not to attach too much importance to a casual compliment. It would be so easy to get carried away.

By the time they had finished lunch and resumed their seats by the rail, the boat was pulling into a little jetty at Alpnachstad and most of the passengers disembarked. A train, reputed to be the steepest rack train in the world, was waiting to go to the summit of Pilatus Kulm, and they boarded it, managing to get seats opposite each other. As it toiled up the steep incline, they watched the valley drop away beneath them until the train disappeared into a tunnel cut in the rock and they eventually arrived at the top of Pilatus Kulm.

The views were breathtaking as they followed a path called the 'gallery', looking down on the tops of other smaller mountains, with wisps of cloud drifting in and out, emphasising the azure blue of the sky. From far below in the valley the faint sound of cowbells drifted up to them.

From time to time, where there were loose chippings and pieces of rock, Robert took Sarah's hand to prevent her from slipping and she wondered how much happier it was possible to be than she was at that moment, with her hand in Robert's, gazing at the magnificent scenery and breathing that wonderful air.

Occasionally, one of the cable-cars that would later take them back down the mountain, swung out from the top and dropped down until it was lost to view among the trees below them.

With the usual Swiss efficiency, there was an extremely attractive little restaurant perched on the mountain top, where they found some luscious hazelnut torte to eat with their tea and Sarah found some enticing gifts to take back for the family and Charlotte. Robert bought something, too, which he said would remind her of the day, but at that stage he was keeping it secret.

All too soon it was time to take the cable-car to Frakmunegg, where they alighted and transferred to a tiny telecabin which took them the rest of the way. It dropped them off by a little path that led down into the centre of the tiny village of Kriens, where they discovered a bus stop from which they could get taken straight back to Lucern and Robert was impressed when Sarah recognised where to alight for the railway station.

'It fascinates me how you return like a homing pigeon when you go somewhere completely strange and new,' Robert said, 'I never feel I have to be alert in case we get lost. It's almost as though you operate on your own personal radar.'

Sarah looked surprised, 'Do I?' she said. 'Yes, I suppose it must seem like that, but I have always done it since I was a small child.'

They found that a fast inter-city train was due in a few minutes, during which they wandered round smart shops in the station concourse. The train seemed to fly on its way back to Basel and they settled comfortably in their seats and saw an air-balloon take off as they passed through Zoflingen.

It was very hot the next day and they spent the morning in the coolness of the Fine Arts Museum. They found a delightful riverside restaurant for lunch, then crossed the Mittere bridge to Schifflande where they discovered a boat going to Rheinfelden and boarded it. Finding a pleasant, shady spot, they sat and watched the scenery slide by and made friends with a delightful Japanese family, the father of whom spoke perfect English.

About two hours later they arrived at Rheinfelden and strolled around the attractive small town, admiring its interesting architecture and the masses of bright flowers. Standing in an embrasure of a tiny stone bridge, watching the river flow by, they wondered about the amount of traffic going over – then realised it formed the border between Germany and Switzerland!

Before the boat was due to return to take them back to Basel, they were able to sit under the welcome shade of some chestnut trees where they drank tea and ate some delicious pastries. Sarah's German was still very rusty, so she was relieved and gratified to find that everything she had ordered at the counter was brought to their table perfectly satisfactorily. She was convinced that Robert would have managed it better, but he probably considered that she needed the verbal exercise, not knowing that he loved watching and listening to her. He thought she looked so sweet and serious while she was ordering and when it arrived exactly as planned, she gave such a devastating smile to the server that Robert felt it must make their day.

As they arose from their table, the boat was just drawing in to the jetty and they boarded it and settled down to enjoy the return journey.

Sarah and Robert had been told by the hotel owner, 'You must not miss visiting Bern, it is our capital.' So, because they found the Swiss railways clean, comfortable and very efficient, they opted to go to Bern by train. They both enjoyed being able to sit at their ease and talk without the problems of traffic and the speed at which they arrived at their chosen destination, still feeling fresh and unharassed.

Bearing in mind that Bern was the capital, they went straight to the magnificent and imposing Houses of Parliament, which stood high above the River Aare on a deep horse-shoe bend that, from above, seemed to make a large part of Bern into an island. The land sloped steeply down to the river and they wound their way down a twisting path that they learned later from a local was full of 'hair-needle bends'. It was a quite a climb to come back up into the town and while they enjoyed the exercise, Robert expressed the opinion, 'I'm glad that there is a cable railway up for those who are not so fit.'

Having left Basel very early in the morning and travelled by a fast inter-city train, they had seen much of Bern well before midday and decided to go on to Interlaken, situated between the twin lakes of Thunersee and Brienzersee, giving it its name and arriving in time for lunch at the West end. One of the many horse-carriages plying for hire took them to the East end at the foot of the Jungfrau-Region of the Bernese mountains, allowing them plenty of time to admire the buildings at their leisure on the way. After exploring the area and having their inevitable tea in a little café, they decided to walk back to the West station even though they could have picked up the train in the East. The weather was still being kind to them in spite of being early autumn and the scenery to the left of them was well worth the trip alone. The day owed more to mid-summer and while the gardens along the edge of the path were full of deep-red roses, there was still snow on the top of the Jungfrau mountain. Robert said to Sarah, 'If you stand beside the roses, I can get a shot of the snow-capped mountains in the background.'

When the time came for them to return to Basel, they found that they needed to change ends on the train at Bern and it confused them by going out backwards, creating the impression that they were returning to Interlaken and they thought they had mistaken the public address announcement. After a few minutes, wondering how late they would be arriving back at the hotel, Sarah suddenly caught a fleeting glimpse of one of the little stations through which they were speeding non-stop and said with relief, 'It is all right, Robert, we are going the right way, I remember coming through there on the way from Basel to Bern. It must have been one of those occasions when the train goes out of the station, apparently in the same direction that it came in and then diverts on to another line.'

Robert's laugh echoed the relief in Sarah's voice, 'Thank heavens! I would have hated to have given you the extra travelling for nothing. I was sure that the announcement did tell us to get on the rear half of the train, even though both my French and German are a little rusty.'

After the long day, they were later than usual getting back to the hotel and having had dinner, they discussed the plans for the following day, deciding to go to Zurich.

Still the beautiful weather held and the train to Zurich was very fast – it was much quicker and easier than coping with the traffic by road and they had plenty of leisure to peruse the photographs that they had taken so far of their holiday and picked up on their way to the station. Each day, when they settled for going by train, Sarah was amused that they could cut through a small lane leading from their hotel, arriving at the station in about two minutes, while cars and taxis took at least ten to negotiate the one-way system through all the traffic. They had been surprised the day they arrived in Basel to be told by the taxi driver whom they wanted to take them to the hotel, 'It will be much quicker to walk. If you go through there, it leads into the Bernerhof, the hotel is right there.'

It seemed very strange at the time – taxi drivers don't usually give that sort of advice – they are only too pleased to get a fare, but they had had their luggage with them and the driver finally consented to take them. Sarah remembered winding round streets and roundabouts, waiting for other traffic, until they drew up at the hotel and it was only later, when they had tried walking to the station unencumbered by luggage, that she realised fully the truth of what the taxi driver had said.

She had remarked to Robert, 'It was nice of him to tell us, knowing we had obviously just arrived in Basel, usually they are only too happy to take you anywhere – even just up the road,' and Robert had looked amused and said, rather cynically for him,

122

'He was probably looking for someone who had much further to travel and was disappointed our hotel was so close, even if it did take an age by road – or possibly because of that fact – it is the mileage that counts.'

After she thought about it, Sarah realised Robert was probably right, she could still be very naïve about people's motives – even at her age.

Zurich looked beautiful and elegant, bathed in sunshine as they strolled along from the station glancing in the windows of the shops as they passed. They turned on to the Limmatquai, walking alongside it until it ran into the Zurichersee and found an empty seat facing the lake, by a little jetty where some boats were moored and sat watching the sunshine dance and glitter on the water. Nearby, some children were feeding the swans and Sarah's expression softened as she watched them; they took her back to her childhood when she had fed the swans on the Thames by her home. They were such graceful, beautiful birds, no others were quite like them. She remembered, too, how the mallards had appeared as if from nowhere – almost as though they rose out of the water, the plain brown ducks and the more handsome drakes, with the light glistening on the iridescent green and blue of their heads and necks and sometimes a pure white mutation. There would be none within sight and suddenly, there they were, darting in and out among the swans for their share of food.

Robert became aware of Sarah's stillness and turned his eyes from the animated view in front of them to look at her. A small smile played around her mouth and her eyes looked very tender. He asked softly, 'What are you thinking about?'

Sarah came back to the present and said, 'I was just remembering the swans on the Thames at home – I always loved them then and I still do. There seem to be many on all the lakes we have seen so far this trip.'

Robert thought that, in spite of her losing her mother at such a young age, and the neighbour, whom she had obviously adored, when she was ten, Sarah seemed to have had a happy childhood. What a pity Fate stepped in to deal her another blow in her adolescent years, when she was vulnerable and prone to making a mistake. But he thought, as Adrienne had, that it was all part of the plan that brought her to Heronshurst.

He said, 'Are you feeling hungry? It is round about the time we usually have lunch.'

Sarah had been feeling so relaxed and happy with Robert in the lovely sunshine, that she had completely lost all sense of time.

She said, 'Now you mention it, I am quite hungry but it is so peaceful here, it seems a pity to leave, doesn't it?'

Robert had been thinking on much the same lines and he, too, was reluctant to be shut up in a restaurant, even for an hour or so, solely for the purpose of eating. He said, 'Just before we found this spot, I noticed a little place in that area like a small square, by the beginning of the lake, that claimed to sell freshly-made sandwiches and they also had plenty of fruit. We could always have a picnic without having to move very far.'

It went through Sarah's mind to wonder if eating al fresco in such a way, was suitable for Robert, but he seemed to be very relaxed and contented with the idea, as if it were the most natural thing in the world and he had suggested it himself. If he were happy about it, she would enjoy it, too.

There was a wide choice of sandwiches and they were surprisingly good, giving the impression that they catered for a lot of people with the same idea.

Soon after they had finished eating, a small water bus pulled up at the jetty, disgorging its passengers, who headed purposefully towards the centre of the city.

Robert and Sarah looked at each other and without a word, rose and headed for the little boat, which they boarded and settled comfortably in window seats. They found that they could buy tickets for a complete circular tour, which would take them to all the villages around the lake, returning in about two hours, in plenty of time to stroll slowly back to catch their train.

It was very pleasant gliding smoothly over the sparkling water and watching the passengers embark and disembark as they drew in to the little jetties of each village as they came to them. Every landing stage was bright with flowers and beautifully maintained – it was a perfect way to see many small villages that they would otherwise not know existed and there was no need to worry about where they had to disembark, since they would return to the same place they had embarked.

Sarah wondered if Robert were as relaxed and contented as he looked. It was hardly an exciting way for a man in his position to spend his time but, as with the picnic, it was as much his idea that they had mutually decided, without words, to board the little water bus. For her, it was enough just to be with him and the beautiful surroundings and lovely weather only added to her bliss.

When the boat returned to the Limmatquai, they strolled gently back the way they had come and Robert stopped at a shop selling sparkling crystal to buy a swan for Sarah, 'to remind her of their enjoyable time' by and on the lake.

The owner of the hotel where they were staying, had told them that on no account must they miss seeing the zoo. Neither Robert nor Sarah were very happy about seeing wild animals in captivity, but it was claimed that they were in lovely surroundings and free to move about at will, so they decided to stretch a point and go and see for themselves. It was distressing to see the elephants tethered by the foot on a narrow ledge beside a huge drop and it did not help that the weather had broken and it was wet and gloomy.

It was still raining after lunch, so they planned to go to the elegant shopping area to find some presents to take home and returned to the hotel with them and packed in readiness for a very early start in the morning, since they had to leave the hotel before eight o'clock to get to Mulhouse in time for their plane home.

Both Robert and Sarah felt a little sad to be leaving as it had been a happy and restful period together but it would be nice to be back home at Heronshurst again.

Their return flight was punctual and uneventful and Frazer was there to meet them, whisking them back home in time for a late lunch after their early start. Merlin and the new puppy were ecstatic to see them and each wanted to stay as close as possible, in case Robert and Sarah should show signs of disappearing again. They had decided to call the new puppy 'Tristram' as sounding more suitable for a dog than the names of the other knights.

As they were going up to their respective suites, Robert asked, 'Can you spare me a moment, please, Sarah?'

'Yes, of course, come in,' she replied, leading the way into her sitting room.

Robert took a small package from his pocket and gave it to her.

'Oh, the secret!' she said, smiling and opening the package to reveal a brooch designed in the natural shape and size of an edelweiss flower, wrought very realistically in silver, with a tiny pendant cow-bell. 'Thank you, Robert. I will remember our lovely holiday and especially Pilatus Kulm and Lucern when I look at it.'

Robert took the brooch from her fingers and shook it gently beside her ear.

'It sounds exactly like the muted sound of the cow-bells coming up from the valley when we were on top of the mountains,' Sarah exclaimed, smiling delightedly.

'Yes, it does, doesn't it?' Robert replied, 'That is what fascinated me about it. I wondered if the bell would actually ring and found, as you say, that it had just the same soft, muted sound as if coming from a distance that, even now, listening to it takes me back to the mountain top. Strange how evocative a sound can be. I'll leave you now to settle in and I will go and do the same. Having had a late lunch, do we have to miss tea?' he asked, rather wistfully, unwilling to forgo that special ritual for even a day.

'No, of course not,' Sarah said, smiling gently. 'Come back here when you are ready and I will make tea here. Though we had better not eat too much or we will ruin our appetites for one of Mrs Briggs' excellent dinners and if I know her, she will have "killed the fatted calf" for us, even though we have been away only a short time.'

Robert laughed, 'I expect you are right,' he said, 'I'll look forward to having tea here. I'll see you presently,' and he went along to his own suite.

There was a tap on the inner door to the bedroom and when Sarah called 'Come in', Charlotte appeared saying, 'Everything is sorted out, madam, do you need anything else?'

'Only to give you this, Charlotte. As usual, with my grateful thanks for all your care and attention.'

Charlotte unwrapped the gift to reveal a box of two dozen exquisitely embroidered lawn handkerchiefs, each with a design of Swiss mountain flowers in the corner.

'Oh, thank you, madam! I do like nice handkerchiefs. I hate seeing people use tissues, as they do these days, don't you?'

'I do, indeed,' Sarah smiled at Charlotte as she left to show her pretty hankies to her mother.

When Robert returned, Sarah had sorted herself out and was ready to relax and relish being back at Heronshurst.

As they reminisced about their enjoyable holiday, Sarah felt quite ready to resume everyday life. She still found it quite startling to think that Robert had planned it to celebrate the anniversary of her arrival at Heronshurst, as though it were something special to him, too. It was equally startling to realise a whole year had passed and that they were already embarking on the second one.

CHAPTER SIXTEEN

The time seemed to gather speed after Sarah and Robert returned from their celebratory holiday. Already they were observing so many annual events for the second time together. The Harvest Festival and Supper, the Hunt Ball, Halloween, Guy Fawkes Night and then towards the end of November, tragedy struck the Falconbridge family.

Helene telephoned to tell Robert that Richard had died peacefully in his sleep. He was only fifty-one and they all wondered if it would have happened, had it not been for the privations he suffered during his captivity at the hands of the SS during the war. It was something for which to be thankful that he had lived long enough to see his grandson born and develop into a sturdy, laughing baby of five months and to know that there was another heir after young Richard. It seemed strange that the baby's father would no longer bear that appellation.

Helene was naturally distraught and decided to return to her beloved France and her own people as soon as possible after the funeral and the necessary formalities had been attended to. Only being married to Richard had kept her in England for so long and she did not consider that the distance was too far for family visits, with modern facilities.

Patrick's birthday was exactly a week before Christmas and while they celebrated it at Heronshurst, it was naturally rather subdued in view of the empty places. It was an even quieter Christmas and New Year, as Lauren and Tom were entertaining his parents in their own home, since he would be on leave.

With the arrival of spring and Sarah's birthday in March, she was thrilled to get a telephone call from Lauren, 'You are going to be a grandmother – again,' she told a delighted Sarah. 'I'm doing my best to make up to you for not being able to have the four children you would have liked. The baby is due in September and, having one of each at the moment, we don't mind at all whether it is a boy or girl, as long as he or she is healthy.'

'I'm absolutely delighted for you, darling,' Sarah told her daughter. 'Take good care of yourself: I'm sure Robert will want Frazer to come and get you for my party. He considers it a long drive for you alone with two young children and no one to keep them amused. I know you are very capable and the children are remarkably well-behaved on journeys, but he is happier if you agree. You will, won't you?'

'If you put it like that,' Lauren said, 'how can I refuse such a generous gesture? It would be a relief as I have the inevitable bouts of nausea at the moment, until my system adjusts.'

'Good girl! – and thank you for my extra birthday present.'

Robert's birthday present to Sarah was an exquisitely intricate filigree necklace in platinum, 'for when you don't want to wear gold' he told her. He had perfect taste and a genius for finding something rare and beautiful, Sarah thought.

She often wondered how he had managed to remain a bachelor for so long, with all the designing females around in his circle. He was so special, she still could not be sure that she wasn't dreaming when she remembered how he had drawn her into the family from day one of their meeting and all his kindness, consideration and generosity.

Looking back over the last eighteen months, she realised that she had acquired so many little duties that had grown almost without her noticing and she took it for granted that it should be so – it came as second nature and was like resuming responsibilities from a distant memory.

Only if she stopped to think about it and compare it with the years of her life since she had made such a bad mistake, did it seem at all strange that so many people in the village, mostly women but even some men, should come to her for help and advice, as though she were Robert's deputy when he was not otherwise available. Robert was very happy about it and said more than once to her,

'This is what I saw happening – the reason why I wanted you to take this particular job for which I thought you were eminently qualified by virtue of your character and personality. Grayson is a very satisfactory bailiff – no one could do his job better – but there is a subtle difference from the problems with which he is qualified to deal and those that you take on. It is obvious that you can empathise with the tenants in a very special way.'

Looking back, Sarah realised that Robert had been very perceptive and far-seeing. She could never have pictured it happening, but now it seemed natural and right and it had grown on her imperceptibly, like serving an apprenticeship, she thought with a smile, but she had been helped by an unseen agency that seemed to belong to the past, rather than the present and something of which she was only clearly aware in quieter moments.

Even the household staff had accepted her without question and Mrs Bates took it for granted that, if Robert were not there, Sarah would make any necessary decisions. It might have been an onerous task if it were not for the inbuilt sense of familiarity with it.

Sarah recollected the early days of her being at Heronshurst when Mrs Bates had invited her to inspect the staff quarters on the second floor, after Sarah had got acquainted with the main parts of the house. She had opened domestic closets and cupboards to disclose their contents and explain their uses and invited Sarah to view the accommodation.

By chance, the first two rooms were unoccupied but when Mrs Bates said, 'This is Lizzie's room,' Sarah had stayed her hand on the door handle, saying,

'No, Mrs Bates, I will go into Lizzie's room only if she herself invites me.'

Mrs Bates had regarded her very intently and then smiled, 'Very well, madam, as you wish.'

It might have been a coincidence but it was not long afterwards that both Lizzie and Charlotte invited her separately to see their rooms, of which they were inordinately proud, especially of the wonderful view. As Charlotte had said, 'Because we are a floor higher than the other rooms, we have an even better view,' and looking from the window at her bidding, Sarah realised that she was not exaggerating. 'We are allowed to choose our own decorations as long as they are not too way out,' Charlotte had announced proudly.

Sarah had been pleased to see the rooms and assure herself how comfortable and suitable they were for two young ladies approaching adulthood and to know that they had a bathroom for their sole use.

Easter came in mid-April and at the beginning of Holy week, the local children received their palms on Palm Sunday. Heronsbury was one of the few places where the shops closed all day on Good Friday. No one found it at all inconvenient and considered it as important as Easter Sunday, when the church was full of both wild and garden flowers, primroses, narcissi, daffodils and pussy willow as well as the more conventional lilies.

At the end of afternoon Sunday school, Sarah had arranged for the distribution of chocolate chickens, sitting on sponge nests full of sugar eggs for the girls and large chocolate rabbits for the boys. She had asked Robert if she might do this and he had said, 'I think it is a lovely idea and could become a tradition founded by you.'

The children had great fun on Easter Monday rolling hard-boiled eggs down the long gradual slope that Sarah had first raced up on Apollo the second day that she had arrived.

A few days later, Alexandra was three years old and it seemed no time to Sarah that they were celebrating her second birthday. The primroses were out again in Heron's Wood and although Merlin looked as young as ever, his son, Tristram, was almost as big as he was, though not yet quite fully mature.

In May, Robert needed to go to Geneva again and this time he did not hesitate to ask Sarah to accompany him and was over-joyed when she agreed immediately, asking his secretary to make the necessary arrangements.

As before, they were able to spend most of the latter half of the day together and when Robert's business was finished, he hired a car again and they drove to Chamonix, going via Annemasse, over the French border at Chuses, famous for its watchmaking and halfway to Chamonix, then through Megeves with its ski slopes.

In Chamonix they took the cable-car to Le Brevant, changing to a tiny telecabin holding just four people to cross Le Vallee Blanche for about three miles to L'Aiguille du Midi. The incredible silence fascinated Sarah when the telecabin was halted for them to be able to photograph the snowy valley with the tiny pin-point figures of skiers and the towering face of Mont Blanc.

Far below, the skiers were being watched over by a hovering helicopter, on which they could look down but even that could not be heard in the awesome silence. The cable seemed to stretch as fine as a spider's web and Sarah marvelled at the feat of engineering that had produced it and taken tens of thousands of people to and fro.

She and Robert wandered about at the top, feeling as if they were in a different world, viewing every angle and exploring an ice-tunnel that was reputed to run close to the Italian border. Eventually they had to decide to return to earth and when they reached the cable-car, it was already packed with people and the operator suggested that they caught the next one. It did not run for another hour, and Robert remarked to Sarah, 'There goes our lunch! I booked at Le Taverne for one o'clock.'

The operator overheard Robert's remark and could understand English. He shouted to the conductor of the cable-car and after a discussion in French, the conductor motioned them to climb aboard. It was an extremely tight fit, being so packed and out of all the nationalities in the world, Sarah found herself next to a girl from Wales and they were able to talk.

The lunch at the 'Taverne' was delicious, prompting Robert to say, 'I'm glad we made it in time – I would not have liked to miss it.'

Sarah agreed wholeheartedly, 'I loved the big iced confection, appropriately called Mont Blanc, it would make a wonderful sweet for a dinner party. I wonder if it is among Mrs Briggs' many accomplishments?'

Robert laughed. 'I wouldn't be surprised, but would some of the women we know appreciate the calorific value?'

Sarah laughed, too. 'I didn't think about that – it was so gorgeous.'

Robert eyed her, 'I really don't know where you put it all,' he said, smiling.

After leaving the 'Taverne', they explored Chamonix, always aware of the wonderful backdrop of the real Mont Blanc and when they were ready for a rest, they sat at a little pavement café table and had tea before leaving for Geneva, passing an enormous glacier and the steepest ski run on the way. Robert felt that the short time that they spent to themselves after he had finished with his business more than made up for his having to go to Geneva and when they arrived home he felt thoroughly refreshed and ready to tackle his many daily problems.

June arrived with Lauren's birthday and Robert Richard was one year old. He was an enchanting, sunny-tempered baby, already with a limited vocabulary and looking as though he would walk any minute. To avoid any confusion of names while he was young, Sophie and Richard called him 'Robbie'.

The day after the dual family party for Lauren and Robbie,

Robert went to Sarah and asked anxiously, 'Have you seen my gold pen? The one you gave me our first Christmas together.'

'No, Robert, I'm sorry, I haven't, but don't worry about it, it will come to light unexpectedly, I'm sure.' She regarded him intently and asked, 'Do you remember where you were when you last used it?'

'Yes, clearly. I was working at my desk in the study.'

Sarah stood very still, looking intently into Robert's eyes, closed her own for a moment, then opened them and said, 'It is in the spine of the file on which you were working.'

Robert was intrigued – how could she sound so sure? But after nearly two years' experience of her powers, he was quite prepared to believe her wholeheartedly. 'Please come and help me find it,' he begged her.

They walked along to his study, 'I was working on a forward projection file,' he said, taking it out of a drawer in the filing cabinet. He stood it on its edge and tapped it gently on the desk and as he lifted the file, the pen slid on to the blotter. Robert was so relieved that he hadn't lost it that he held on to it very tightly. 'Sarah, you are a witch!'

Sarah laughed. 'Only a white one,' she assured him, then added more seriously, 'There is a very simple explanation. When people mislay something, they are not conscious of its having disappeared, but their subconscious registers where it has gone. Most people are aware that the subconscious remembers every-thing and keeps incredible records of one's experiences, but only a few can take advantage of it. When I asked you where you had it last, you remembered quite clearly and probably pictured it in your mind. All I had to do was to switch into your thought processes and pick up the part that was in your subconscious, i.e. when the pen slid between the pages of the file and disappeared into the spine. You had not noticed it consciously, but your subconscious registered it. With a little concentration, I could latch on to that moment and "see" it in my mind.'

Robert was fascinated. 'You make it sound a lot easier than it is, I'm sure,' he said. 'If it was that easy, couldn't everyone do it?'

'Probably,' Sarah agreed, 'if they cultivated it from an early age, although I expect it comes more easily to some than others. I have been able to do it since I was about nine years old, that I remember and if other people are to be believed, even younger than that. I have always encouraged it as it can be very useful.' She forbore to mention that it was the least complicated of her psychic tendencies.

'It certainly is useful,' Robert said. 'It could have been days or even weeks before the possibility of finding the pen in the file.'

'It is very simple if you think about it,' Sarah told him, 'just pictorial thought transference of something about which you were not consciously aware. What is sometimes referred to as ESP. Many people scoff at it mainly, I think, because it can be commercially exploited, which is why I would only discuss it with someone who would try to understand. If animals could talk, they would tell you that they can pick up what you are thinking. How else do you suppose that Merlin came to my rescue when we were rooms apart?'

'It really does sound simple when you put it like that,' Robert said, thoughtfully. 'That is a valid point about Merlin. How else could he have known that you were in danger, apart from a telepathic message from you? Even Bates had no idea what was happening until he saw Merlin racing through the hall into the ballroom.' He smiled, 'But I still say you have someone helping you.'

'That is more than possible,' Sarah said, very seriously, thinking about the many times she had been helped in the past by an unseen presence. Especially on at least three occasions when she had faced almost certain death.

Sarah had always been aware that she had what she thought of as her 'guardian angel', but it was only comparatively recently that she had discovered it was her mother, without any doubt. It was not something to discuss in casual conversation, it was enough that it should be so.

Robert was deep in thought. There were several things that had puzzled him in his life, but he had dismissed them as figments of his imagination, now he was not so sure. If he had had Sarah to help explain them, he was convinced that they would immediately have become simple to understand. So much was becoming clearer out of the mist of the past and slowly he was beginning to comprehend the pattern.

There was no doubt at all in his mind that Sarah had had a previous existence. It was implicit in her personal knowledge of things that had happened nearly three centuries before, of which there was no actual record – only a family legend.

When his several-times great grandfather had died at Blenheim, his spirit knew where it belonged and found its way home to guide his son and his son's sons to administer Heronshurst and Robert was prepared to believe that he was reincarnated in himself. It would explain so many odd glimpses of another sphere that had vanished too soon to comprehend and why he had waited so long without being really sure why – except that it was essential.

Estelle's spirit had wandered off to find Robert and lost her way and in trying to find her way back, got nearer each time, until she could be reborn and fulfill her destiny. It would account for Sarah's wisdom and compassion that was stronger than one person could learn in a single lifetime.

Robert regarded her now, thinking how much lovelier his life had been since she found him. When necessary, she had all Estelle's dignity and bearing, but she could also be as artless and uncomplicated as a child and at home in any environment.

He recalled how happy and at ease they had been, sitting by Zurichersee contentedly picnicking on sandwiches and fruit. It was something that had not featured in his life before, but it seemed so natural and right then.

Estelle's spirit had learned a lot in her travels and was wiser, covering a far wider spectrum. Dimly, but slowly and ever more clearly, he was beginning to understand the reason he had waited. Fate was about to reveal the destiny for which he had been born.

Something of what he was thinking showed in his eyes as he contemplated Sarah. Now he understood that she bore the re-incarnation of Estelle's spirit in Sarah's being and Sarah was all he wanted in life. With all her comprehensive understanding and wisdom, she still retained the simplicity of a child who could take life as it came and make the most of it.

Robert wanted more than anything at that moment to tell Sarah what joy and meaning she had brought into his life and how much he loved her and wanted her to be his wife, but he had an almost superstitious belief that if he did not play according to the rules, he might lose her forever.

There was at least three months to wait before Sarah could finally shake off her past unhappy life that, strangely, had brought her to him and be free. He knew instinctively that she would be disappointed in him if he spoke too soon. She must feel the same way about him as he felt about her, otherwise there was no rhyme or reason in anything that had gone before.

He smiled now, 'Thank you for finding my pen, I would have been very sorry to have lost it after you gave it to me.'

Sarah returned his smile, 'Any time,' she said lightly. 'It will only ever be misplaced in similar circumstances. You are much too careful of things to actually lose it.'

134

I hope I don't lose you, he thought, with an unaccustomed little shiver of apprehension. Now that I've found you and recognise who you are. Sarah, my Sarah, her own person, for whom I have waited all my life. Sarah, with her own special qualities and also those of Estelle, that made the first Robert fall in love with her.

CHAPTER SEVENTEEN

For Robert's birthday in July, they held a small family party and included Adrienne and George.

Adrienne had been working very hard to coordinate all her branches and she and Sarah did not meet nearly as often as they both would have liked. She seemed very quiet now, but content as Alexandra monopolised her attention. The child still called her 'Drenny' as she had when she was too small to say her name properly. Adrienne would have been absolutely furious if anyone else had taken that liberty, but as far as she was concerned, Alexandra could do no wrong.

At almost three and a quarter, she was as enchanting as ever. More wilful than Patrick, who was very easy-going, but she was open to loving reasoning and intelligent enough to understand it. It was not enough to say 'Do this' or 'Don't do that' if it was against her wishes, without backing up the request with a satisfactory justification.

July slipped into August and then, with September, Sarah received a letter from her solicitor requesting her to go and see him in Elkesbury. She read it at breakfast and for once, Robert could not fathom her expression.

It was not so much guarded, he thought, but more as if she had gone away while still sitting at the table. He felt very uneasy, as though he could no longer reach her, but he was reluctant to pry. He could not know that the letter had released a floodgate of unhappy memories that she thought she had put behind her and brought back all the doubt and uncertainty that assailed her whenever she remembered them. Her natural confidence hit rock-bottom even though the prospect of regaining her freedom at last should have buoyed her up. She couldn't help feeling that it was not going to be as easy as it might seem. Something in the back of her mind told her that Hubert would be able to spoil this as he had spoiled everything that had given her the slightest pleasure in the past. Logic told her that she was being unreasonable but just the association of the letter with him was enough to depress her utterly. She found it was difficult to speak normally and her voice was expressionless as she looked up to say to Robert, 'I need to go into Elkesbury to see my solicitor, if that is all right?'

Robert said very gently, 'Of course, Sarah, would you like me to go with you?'

Sarah considered him for a moment, trying to recapture their usual rapport and for a fleeting instant, he thought she had come back to him, then she said carefully, 'No, thank you, Robert. You are very kind but it would be better if I go alone.' She rose from the table and went upstairs.

The concern in Robert's eyes smote her to the heart and she felt a great deal of compunction. How could she tell him that, at all costs, she wanted to keep the world of Heronshurst quite uncontaminated by the world she had left behind. He was so kind, she could not bear to have him worried by circumstances about which he could do nothing. She found herself trembling as she re-read the letter in her bedroom and tried to analyse her irrational fear. It was only a request from a kind and harmless little man to go and see him, hopefully to receive a precious document that would grant her her freedom. Why should she feel as if an abyss had opened up in front of her and was threatening to swallow her up?

She automatically checked that she looked tidy and pulling herself together mentally, went downstairs.

Robert had had her car brought round to the front of the house for her. She went to thank him and tell him that she did not expect to be back for lunch.

'Sarah, will you take Merlin with you, please?' Robert asked.

The unexpected request distracted her from her own thoughts and she tried to fathom what was in his mind but for once his expression was noncommittal.

'Yes, of course, if you want me to do so,' she replied.

He walked to the car with her, helping her in and putting Merlin in the rear. Merlin was ecstatic about going, too. So often, cars meant that he was left behind.

'Take care, Sarah, and come back safely,' Robert said.

'Thank you. I'll see you some time after lunch. I will get something in town,' and with a wave of her hand, she drove away.

Robert watched her go until she disappeared out of the end of the drive, his face a mixture of expressions. Although he suspected that this was the day that Sarah would gain her freedom and it was what he had longed for, he could not explain why he felt so uneasy. Maybe it had washed over from Sarah. She had seemed anything but joyful about the prospect of being free. Surely she could not be regretting it at this late stage?

Sarah drove her BMW a great deal faster than usual in her anxiety to see this business finished and arrived in good time for her appointment. Her solicitor was ready and waiting for her and after a few kindly well-meant words and some legal transactions, she held the precious piece of paper that proclaimed her freedom and walked out feeling bemused and wondering why she wasn't ecstatic.

After all, she found she had no appetite for lunch and walked back to her car deciding to drive out into the country and sit for a while hoping to regain her normal equilibrium. This should be one of the happiest days of her life, shouldn't it? So why wasn't she 'over the moon'?

As she walked towards her car, a voice she recognised that made her shrink, said, 'Hallo, Sarah, I thought I might see you if I hung about long enough today.'

Sarah turned slowly, her mind in a turmoil, trying to give herself time to recover, to face the man to whom she had been married for thirty years. The depths of depression and despair to which her spirits plummeted, left her inwardly shaking, while her normally buoyant disposition fought for supremacy. How could one voice so destroy her mental equilibrium in just a few words? She carried on walking and realised that he was following, still talking.

'You don't have to live on your own,' he was saying, 'I am quite prepared to forgive and forget and take you back.'

The sheer effrontery of the remark took Sarah's breath away. After more than thirty years, he still couldn't understand her or the reasons why she had left. It was quite incomprehensible to him that she would have preferred going out into the world alone with practically nothing, to living with him or having to fight for her share of their communal property, most of which originated from her own efforts and her family.

Anger made her refrain from speaking. She wanted to remain calm and not let him realise that anything he said or did could affect her any more. She reached her car and unlocked it, trying to control the slight tremor in her fingers and got in, but before she could close the door, he grabbed it, leaning down to speak to her. In the rear of the car, Merlin's growl sounded like a rumble of thunder. Hubert drew back, still holding the door and saying, 'Is that your dog? You want to watch him – he's dangerous!'

She had forgotten that dogs did not like him and the remark almost made her laugh. Suddenly she felt drained. Drained of anger, dislike, resentment and horribly cold and empty inside. She should have known that her wonderful life for the last two years could not continue. Life had dealt so many blows starting with the death of her mother when she was barely two, that she realised she had been living in a fool's paradise. Fate hadn't intended her to be happy for very long.

The harsh, unlovely voice was still speaking, beating on her eardrums, as it always did.

'There are hundreds of women who would be only too glad to be married to me. You never appreciated all I did for you.'

The icy calm and emptiness that had descended on her, stood her in good stead. 'I'm so glad,' she said, in reply to the first part of his remark. 'Now you will be able to line them up and take your pick. I wish you well. Now, if you don't want your arm taken off by my "dangerous" dog, I suggest you let go of my door, so that I can close it.'

He released the door as if it were red-hot and Sarah pulled it shut. As it closed with only a soft click, he noticed the quality of the car and the thought registered that, although she was quietly dressed, she looked very elegant. Sarah had never dressed flamboyantly but even with his limited intelligence he could recognise the quality of her clothes. She must be doing very well for herself, he thought. When he had had the sudden notion of hanging around the solicitor's office in the hope of catching sight of Sarah, he had not given very much thought to what would happen if he found her. He wasn't very good at thinking things out to a logical conclusion and as her car disappeared in the throng of traffic he determined to follow her and find out more about her present life without him. With his lack of imagination and the knowledge that he had caused Sarah to leave practically penniless, he had visualised her living a hand-to-mouth existence in an obscure bed-sitting room. Jobs were hard to get for a woman of fifty, when there were so many young people leaving school and unable to get work. It seemed he could have been wrong and he hurried to where he had left his car, with the express purpose of following Sarah and finding out where she lived.

There was only one road out of town the way she was heading and with any luck, the traffic would hold her up long enough for him to catch up.

As Sarah drove off, she tried to concentrate on the traffic. All she could think of was getting away and out of that town that held so many unhappy, depressing memories. The lunch-time traffic was heavy and the notorious bottle-neck near the edge of town held her up. Finally she edged free and this time she drove very slowly, trying to marshal her thoughts.

What had happened that she still felt so depressed and lost? It should have been a red-letter day but the sense of freedom and elation that she expected to feel, somehow eluded her. Meeting Hubert had unleashed all the miserable memories that she had tried to suppress. All she could remember was his spitefulness, violence and jealousy, with his unerring ability to spoil anything and everything that gave her the slightest pleasure and he would do it again if he could. He had inhibited her hobbies on the grounds that they were a waste of time when she 'could be doing something more useful', which in his eyes was perpetual cooking, cleaning and gardening. She had been forbidden to have any pets and when she had defied him, he had treated them cruelly, forcing her to let them go to a happier home. But the worst thing by far, he had denied her her birthright to have more than one child. Sarah suspected he had only agreed to one to tie her down.

Her very perceptive GP had long since guessed her problems without even being told. In the early days, when she had seemed surprised at his intuition, he had laughed and said, 'I have met the type before,' and had advised her to shout back at Hubert, but that was not her way. It made her feel out of control. Later when he was treating her for an incipient ulcer, he had said one day as she was leaving, 'It is not really my place to tell you this, but if you don't leave your old man, your health will break down. Your mind is too well-balanced to turn and your body will have to find an outlet for the stress you are under, somehow.'

Sarah had been grateful for his instinctive understanding and sympathy and it helped her to cope for years, but she had grown up with the belief in the 'for better or for worse' part of the marriage service. In any case, most of the time she understood her husband's personality problem and felt sorry for him, feeling that she could help him. It was only later, when things really blew up, that she started feeling sorry for herself and realised the truth of her GP's warning about her health, deciding to 'give it best' and live what was left of her life to suit herself. It wasn't that she needed anything spectacular to make her happy, all she wanted was to avoid being with someone who went out of his way to spoil the quality of her life and make her actively unhappy. Even that had been a struggle.

Having created the impression that her room was preferable to her company, she expected Hubert to be only too glad that she had decided to go, leaving everything to him to carry on how he wished, seeing whom he liked, but even knowing him pretty well after so many years, she had been taken aback by his reaction when she told him that she intended to go.

'You won't leave,' he had said in his usual taunting fashion, 'You know when you're well off.'

The aspect of that remark that had astounded Sarah was the fact that he really believed what he was saying. If anything was calculated to stiffen her resolve, that did it.

'You have a very bad memory for things you would rather forget,' she told him, 'and I mean what I say.'

'Oh, no!' he exclaimed, 'I won't have people saying that *you* left *me*! I'll be the one to leave,' and she had been relieved for the moment, thinking how much easier it was going to be. She could keep her job, which she enjoyed, and her friends and carry on as before – but without the exasperation and provocation.

'Very well,' she had answered, 'I don't mind which way we do it, it doesn't bother me if people think that I was the one to be abandoned, I couldn't care less, as long as I am free.'

It wasn't long before she realised that, as usual, he was talking a lot of hot air and had no intention of going. He always made the mistake of thinking that she was making idle threats, as he did, and that she would soon 'cool down' and forget all about it, carrying on as they were.

Sarah had waited six months to give him time to start making arrangements to go but nothing was further from his mind. He didn't even make an effort to be more civilised.

That was when she started looking round for another job that would take her right away and provide accommodation, since he had left her virtually penniless, even selling the lovely oak furniture her father had given them.

This time she kept quiet about it as she knew he would circumvent her every move. When it came close to the day she was leaving, she had packed as much of her belongings as she could, leaving the cases where they normally stayed when they were empty and on the actual day, she had just gone.

Sarah had always supposed there were people who would have said she should have stood up to him – even her sympathetic GP had said she should shout as he did and throw things, it was the only thing he understood – but it would only have incited more violence. In her heart of hearts she had been afraid of being provoked into unleashing her own anger, which was very slow to rouse, but she was well aware that if he had succeeded in making her lose her temper, she would probably do him irreparable damage and it wasn't worth ruining the rest of her life on his account.

Her belief in the 'for better or for worse' part of the marriage service, meant that she considered it to mean his mental health as well as his physical well-being, which was good, in spite of his hypochondria, although he would brook no claims from anyone else to feel the slightest bit unwell. His mental state was quite another matter.

Sarah glanced in her mirror and saw Merlin watching her carefully. Catching her eyes, he leaned over and nuzzled the back of her neck. She lifted one hand free of the wheel and reached back, hugging his head against hers. What a comfort he was! She was glad that he was there and had made it easy for her to get away. Had Robert had a foreboding when he suggested that she took Merlin?

Suddenly she became aware that a car had come into view about a quarter of a mile behind her and was drawing nearer. There was nothing sinister in that, was there? But the cold chill down her spine told her that it was Hubert following her. The delay in getting out of town and her own slow driving had made it easy for him.

How could she be free to carry on her own life if he was going to intrude and spoil it as he had spoiled everything else?

She had to think quickly to prevent his discovery of her present address and avoid his encroaching to cause trouble and embarrassment at Heronshurst. Was that why she had been feeling so uneasy since the letter arrived – was it only this morning? She remembered that there was a little lane up ahead on the left, with a triangular patch of grass in the mouth that enabled a car to approach and enter from either side more easily. Sarah slowed down and the other car slowed, too. As she neared the lane she was doing barely fifteen miles an hour and still slowing. With her left hand indicator showing, she swung into the lane, then wrenched the wheel over to the right, clipping the grass as she accelerated out of the lane and back the way she had come, noting that Hubert had already committed himself to following her before he realised her manoeuvre.

Fortunately there was little traffic on the country road and she was lucky that there was nothing in sight as she pulled out, but before Hubert's car could follow suit, a large removal pantechnicon loomed round the bend beyond, preventing him from leaving immediately and thereafter forming a bulky barrier between the two cars. She thanked heaven that he was not a quick thinker at the best of times.

Sarah pressed her foot down on the accelerator, knowing that on a good road she could have left the other car standing, but since it was a small country road, she was going to have to decide quickly what to do. Luckily, although the occasional bend and narrowness of the road kept her speed down, it also prevented the pantechnicon from being overtaken, especially as it was travelling as fast as possible in the conditions. Sarah assumed it had already shed its load at one of the country houses along the way and was on its way back.

Concentrating hard on her driving and trying to think at the same time, Sarah remembered suddenly that, a little way further on beyond the next bend, there was an entrance to a house belonging to some friends of Robert's. As she reached it, she swung into their drive, shielded both by the bend and the pantechnicon, now quite a way behind and followed the curve out of sight of the road, wondering what on earth she was going to say to justify her visit with Merlin and without Robert.

Sarah hated telling anything but the truth, which was impossible without involving Robert in what could be construed, by strangers to the facts, as a sordid little episode and she would die rather than do that.

She drew up at the house and rang the bell, trying desperately to think of something plausible to say. The maid who opened the door announced that there was no one at home at the moment.

Sarah breathed an inward sigh of relief and without giving her name, asked as casually as possible if she could leave by the other exit, the house being situated on the land between the two forks where the small road she had been on joined the main road that by passed Heronsbury and Heronshurst. 'It will be quicker for me to get home,' she smiled as easily as she could manage.

'Of course, madam.' The maid was fairly new to her job but

obviously the lady had been here before. 'What name shall I say, madam?' she called as an afterthought, as Sarah got into her car.

Sarah pretended not to hear and headed off round the house and on to the other road, where she drove as fast as she was allowed being a more major one, coming out on the other side of Heronsbury, where she turned back into the village and out on to the lane that led to Heronshurst.

Robert had been watching anxiously from time to time from the window of the sitting room in his suite, wondering why he should be feeling so tense. If anything had happened to her, someone would have got in touch with him, so no news was good news. He looked out just as Sarah turned into the drive and breathed a sigh of relief but stayed where he was. Sarah had been in a strange state of mind and he was reluctant to rush in and intrude upon what she so obviously considered a private matter. If she wanted to see him and discuss anything she would come and find him, in the meanwhile he would allow her space.

Sarah let herself into the house from the rear after garaging her car. Merlin went straight to his quarters and if anyone saw him, they would know she had come back. It went through her mind to wonder why she didn't think of it as 'coming home' rather than coming back. Perhaps she had already come to terms with the possibility that it might not be her home for much longer but she was too mentally exhausted to follow up that train of thought.

Running up to her sitting room, she flung herself into a chair trying to relax but she began to tremble and, having started, the more she tried to restrain it, the worse it became. She was glad Charlotte was not there and in an effort to control herself, she got up to make some tea. Sarah found a tablet which her doctor had prescribed for migraine but which he had said could be used also to combat tension, causing sea and air sickness. After a while she calmed down a little and went into her bedroom and stretched out on the bed, concentrating on relaxing. Her mind was going like a mill-race, random thoughts tumbling through her head, willy-nilly.

How could she have wasted thirty years of her life for nothing? No, that was not quite true. She had Lauren and through her, the children. With different parentage, Lauren would be different and Sarah would not want her changed an iota.

In the first euphoria of her physical freedom, anything had seemed possible and on her arrival at Heronshurst everything that had transpired then and later seemed part of a naturally ordained plan and she had accepted it without question, going along, as she had said, one day at a time, giving no thought for tomorrow. But now?

Time, it appeared in her case, had not brought wisdom. How could she possibly have thought she could risk exposing someone in Robert's position to such a situation? She must make very sure that it could not happen again. Hubert would stop at nothing to sabotage any chance of her achieving lasting happiness and if he ever found out how she felt about Robert, he would be included in the vendetta also. No, it was a risk she could not take.

While her own life was in limbo, she had loved Robert so much that it was enough just to be part of his existence, but now she was free, far from simplifying the circumstances, it had complicated them a thousandfold and she found that she could not face seeing him every day without giving herself away and he had been too kind and considerate to involve him in such an embarrassment.

Sarah realised now that in the back of her mind she had lived a Utopian dream of 'everything coming right', but today had opened her eyes to the fact that Robert could not feasibly want to get permanently entangled with someone who had got herself into such an impossible situation. He could be subjected to the sort of provocation that he had never encountered in his life before. She had got embroiled by her own faulty judgement but she must ensure that he was not dragged into it with her. Robert had avoided any sort of involvement in the past with far more desirable women than she and she owed it to him, for all the happiness he had given her in the past two years, to bow out gracefully now.

Yes, that is what she must do. It would be easier said than done. She must give herself a day or two to work out a good plan, in the meantime giving no indication until it was all settled, and she could slip away quietly with as little fuss as possible where Robert was concerned.

Sarah got up from the bed and went into the bathroom where she splashed her face several times with cold water, dried it carefully, changed into an afternoon dress, brushed her hair, dusted her face lightly with some powder and walked downstairs, with as much dignity as she could muster in the circumstances, and into the drawing room to face Robert.

145

CHAPTER EIGHTEEN

As Sarah had anticipated, tea had already been put in the green drawing room and Robert was sitting as if expecting her. So far, so good. To distract her mind and give herself something on which to concentrate, she busied herself pouring the tea. As she handed Robert his cup, he asked her gently,

'Is everything all right, Sarah?'

'Oh yes, perfectly all right, Robert, thank you. I am now a free woman.' Oh, God, she thought, I could have phrased that better. Her voice echoing in her mind sounded alien and far too flippant, but apart from giving her a rather close look, Robert didn't comment.

A silence ensued but not one of their companionable silences, more an uneasy quiet between protagonists who were very wary of each other. The word had sprung unbidden into Sarah's mind and taken her by surprise. Why should I think of Robert as a protagonist, she mused, no one could have behaved less like one in my life, it isn't fair to burden him with other people's short-comings. Just that brief meeting with Hubert seems to have dragged me back into his alien world of thought and behaviour that I thought I'd escaped.

Robert, too, was at a loss to understand why the instant rapport that had existed from the moment they first met, seemed to have deserted them. Something *had* happened to cause Sarah to lose her normal serene look and take on that strained expression as though she felt lost and uncomfortable.

He made an effort to open a conversation that would bring them back on to their normal easy footing, chatting about every-day things that concerned them both, in which Sarah made an attempt to join in.

They finished their tea and Sarah said, 'Will you excuse me

please, Robert? I have some letters to write before dinner,' and made her escape. How am I going to get through the time until I can make plans to leave, she thought, I have adjusted to the consequences of most of the mistakes I have made in the past. Perhaps it will get easier as I get acclimatised to the idea, but she doubted it.

What an idiot I was to take for granted that I could just leave everything behind and assume the wonderful new life that magically presented itself? She considered that idea for a moment and the fleeting thought went through her mind that, at the time, it did not seem so much a new life as one she had lived a long time ago and was just resuming. You are a victim of wishful thinking, my girl, she admonished herself. You should never have chanced dragging Robert into the aftermath of the sordid little life you mistakenly adopted in your zeal for crusading.

An unbidden memory came back to her of a conversation she had had with her father long ago when she was still at school. The details were a bit hazy but she remembered feeling sorry about a particular situation and insisting that she wanted to do something about it. Her father had looked at her with an expression of tenderness and said, 'Darling, you cannot take the problems of the whole world on your shoulders.' She had felt frustrated at the time, but maturity had taught her that what he had said made sense. There were limits to the lengths one should go to redress some problems – one could only create more in the process.

After Sarah left the room so precipitately, Robert stayed where he was feeling utterly bemused. What had happened since this morning? This was the day for which he had been waiting patiently for two years and now everything appeared to have gone wrong. Life seemed to have a nasty habit of dealing a body-blow just when one least expected it. He tried to see things from Sarah's point of view. He must be very patient and then perhaps she would tell him of her own accord.

He must remember how prisoners of war felt when they were released. All the time they were in captivity, their courage, mental and moral strength held out, buoyed up by the prospect and hope of seeing their loved ones again eventually, then when they were released, it did not work out rightly every time.

Richard was a case in point. After he, Robert, had managed to free him and smuggle him back to England, it had been a year or two before he could readjust to normal, everyday relationships, even with his nearest and dearest. Helene had been a tower of strength to him but even her love and patience must have been sorely tried. Poor Richard could not understand himself and that had been the biggest stress of all. He had been a prisoner for four years – Sarah for over thirty, with her family thousands of miles away and separated from her friends. How much more difficult it must be for her to adjust.

Robert vowed to himself not to bother Sarah by trying to talk things over too much and too soon, hoping that just by being there and making it obvious that he would give her help and support if asked, she would eventually free her mind of what was worrying her and they could sort the problem out together satisfactorily.

The next few days were utter misery to both Robert and Sarah. His very forbearance and quiet patience convinced her that she was right about leaving. Their easy camaraderie had died and if she left, he would be able to revert to the life he led before her unwarranted intrusion, as she now thought of it.

Sarah had lived so long with spoken or implied criticism that she had forgotten what it was like to be with people who conceded others the right to be their own person without constant cross-questioning.

Robert remembered his thoughts on the subject of losing Sarah and felt that though she was right there in front of him, he had lost her already. The hardest part was not knowing why. Something must have happened the day she went to Elkesbury to have reduced her to this state of near somnambulism, but what? She had come through so many years of what had obviously been a traumatic existence apparently unscathed, how could one day make all that difference?

Sarah was doing her best to behave normally – her duties about the estate were not neglected and the part of her that could still empathise with other people's problems continued to function. To the women – and men – to whom she gave help and advice, she appeared to be her normal, sympathetic self.

It was a pity that Adrienne had gone on a trade mission to the States and on the rare occasions that they were able to talk by telephone, Sarah could not bring herself to discuss it with her. Even all those miles away, with their telepathic rapport, Adrienne could sense something was amiss but when she asked outright, 'Is anything wrong, Sarah?' Sarah had dismissed the suggestion in such an airy fashion that Adrienne was even more convinced that all was not well. She was tempted to telephone Robert to ask him, but felt that he would consider it an intrusion in spite of their long-standing friendship. It would have to wait until she could see Sarah, then perhaps she might get to the truth.

Sarah had got into the habit of spending more and more of her leisure time alone in her suite. It was just too difficult to spend the evening with Robert as she used to do and pretend that all was well. The misery of the past was nothing to what she felt now, being in love with Robert and knowing that it could never come to anything. Her confidence was at rock bottom.

She found herself going back in time and trying to put her finger on when and where everything went wrong and wondering at which point she could have changed things. Hindsight is a wonderful thing. How had she committed herself to making the mistake in the first place?

Her mind went back to the time when she still belonged to her own world and Hubert had impinged on it. To understand how it had happened she would need to recollect her state of mind at that point. She had been very young – even for her age of eighteen. Many of her contemporaries, freed by the relaxed attitudes of war-time, had had two or three quite torrid affairs, while she was still committed to the love born of the hero-worship that had enmeshed her from the time she was fourteen.

Would things have been any better if William had survived – would they have had children and been happy? He certainly was very fond of his younger brothers and very patient with them and they adored and admired him. But then I wouldn't have had Lauren, Sarah thought, and that brings me back to the point where I wouldn't be without her or have her changed by an iota.

It had been her sense of loss and unhappiness at William's death that had made her so vulnerable to other people's unhappiness. Hubert was an only child and according to common belief, only children were spoilt. True he had not needed to share anything which could have been the cause of making him selfish, but wasn't it more the influence of his self-centred and demanding mother? He had told her incredible stories of her bid to get her own way and monopolise his father's attention. None of which would have made a very stable background for a small boy who was very nervous and unsure of himself. She had always put him down as she had tried to do to Sarah, spreading stories about her that had not the remotest basis in fact.

At about that time, when it had been assumed that Sarah and Hubert were getting married, Sarah had tried to extricate herself from the situation but Hubert had made vague threats about suicide. She had never met anyone as unbalanced as that and with her lack of experience, actually believed he might carry out his threat not knowing, as her GP had later told her, that he was too fond of himself to do such a thing. She had shelved the decision until a more propitious time but that time had never come and she sank deeper and deeper into the trap.

It was strange to think that if she had been dealing with people with whom she had grown up and whom she understood, she could have discussed her misgivings and been allowed to make her own decisions about pulling out of the impending marriage. It hadn't helped when she had met the older sister of one of her closest friends, who had said to her, 'You look as if you have seen a ghost. What is the matter?' Sarah had tried to explain haltingly and the woman had said, 'Let's go for a walk and you can tell me all about it.'

They had walked all round a large part of the area where they lived and at the end of Sarah's confused explanation, the woman had said, 'You are only suffering from bridal nerves – all women go through it at some time before they marry. I did myself. In any case if they have made most of the arrangements, you can't pull out now and upset everybody.'

Sarah could still remember that feeling of being trapped but she had gone through with it, thinking that if she concentrated on trying to make up to Hubert for his unfortunate childhood and made him happy, she would be happy, too. At that stage he had given her only glimpses of the personality problem that assailed him and when his father had said to her, 'He puts on his party manners for you, you haven't seen him in one of his really black moods, when nothing and nobody is right for him,' she had thought that it was an instance of what was later dubbed 'the generation gap' although she hadn't thought of it in just those words and had felt even sorrier for Hubert. When the arrangements for the wedding had been finalised, and they had discussed the future, he had been quite agreeable to having children. It was only later that he resented having to share even a particle of Sarah's attention.

She had also been very upset afterwards to discover that her father was hurt that she should let William's family monopolise the event. He had wanted them to be married from her home in the church in which he and Sarah's mother had been married. Sarah had told him, 'Hubert's mother said she did it because I haven't a mother – I think she was trying to be helpful.'

Her father had replied, 'I had that all planned – the local caterers were prepared to arrange everything.' He named a

150

distinguished firm who had a reputation for doing things perfectly.

It was only later that Sarah had discovered it was all part of Hubert's mother's penchant for interfering and trying to take centre stage.

Another one of the problems, Sarah thought, was our different standards of behaviour. While staying at the older Mrs Mannering's house, remembering that she was a guest, Sarah had asked her each morning if it was convenient to have the bathroom.

On the third day, 'What do you want it for?' she had asked in a truculent voice – she never asked, 'Why do you want it?' always, 'What do you want it for?'

Sarah has been surprised at the question and said, 'To have a bath.' She had been even more surprised to be told in an accusing voice, 'You had one yesterday and the day before.'

'If it is the expense, I am quite willing to pay extra,' Sarah had assured her.

'No, I just don't think that it is necessary to bath every day. You can have one on Friday – that is when I clean the bathroom.'

'What about the other days?' Sarah had asked.

'No other day, I told you, I clean the bath on Friday and I want it to stay clean until the following Friday.'

Sarah had tried to adjust to the regime by taking hot water up to her room where there was an old-fashioned washstand with a ewer and basin and washing herself as well as she could, carefully cleaning the basin and leaving it as before. That had been sabotaged as well.

'I don't want you washing in the bedroom – it might splash the walls,' she had been told.

At a loss to know quite what to do, Sarah had asked, 'Where may I wash?'

'In the kitchen – like everyone else. We don't want your fancy London ways here,' Mrs Mannering had said.

That had set the pattern for a lot of adjustment that Sarah had had to make during her life there.

When she and Hubert were first married, Sarah had rented a house near to the government office in which she worked. She had lived in London right through the 'blitz' when it was bombed every night and her own home had had the conservatory destroyed and the windows of her bedroom were blown in across the room and embedded in her pillow. Luckily she had stayed with a friend that night, not having been able to get transport home. They had been lucky all through the hostilities with only the odd incendiary landing in the garden apart from that incident. With the possibility still of raids, Sarah had considered it was hardly worth buying a house.

Then Hubert's mother had made her move again, ringing up to invite Sarah to live with them in the country. 'It will be safer for you here and Hubert won't need to worry about you in London.'

It said a lot for Sarah's naïvete then, that she considered that Mrs Mannering was being kind and, only for the reasons given, Sarah accepted. That had been her second big mistake. She was neither allowed to go out alone or even stay in alone – if Hubert's parents wanted to go out, she had to go, too, or precipitate a grand tantrum that not only upset her but Hubert's father as well. For his sake she 'toed the line' on the principle that the war couldn't last for ever – could it?

She had transferred from her job in the Government office in London to another department closer to where she was living with her in-laws. If the bus were late or too full to get on and she had to wait for the next one, she got an inquisition when she got back (she couldn't call it 'home') on 'Where have you been?' and 'Who have you been with?'

Her mother-in-law had another strange idiosyncrasy. Where most ordinary people would apologise if they realised something they had done or said was annoying and try to avoid doing or saying it again, she would give a funny little, almost mad smile and continue to do it all the more, then say afterwards in a smug self-satisfied tone, still with the same maddening smile and would-be innocent look, 'Oh, you don't like that do you? I forgot,' but not a hint of an apology. It was one of her many deliberately irritating characteristics that Hubert had inherited in full measure. He attained considerable pleasure from deliberately ruffling people's tempers, giving that same strange, little twisted smile. Sarah had long since stopped rising to the bait but controlling her irritation was only one of the many petty stresses that added up. She realised later that she had expected Hubert to move into her world, not vice versa.

At the beginning of the war Sarah had applied to join the WRNS, as Adrienne had done. After going through all the preliminaries and being accepted, she got a letter from the Ministry of Labour to say that, as she was employed by the Government, her mobility was restricted and she could not be released.

After nearly two years of being a virtual prisoner, it occurred to Sarah that, since she had married, she was now 'mobile' as it was referred to and applied again to join the WRNS and was accepted immediately with no further examinations and, after a probationary period, was posted as part of the signals unit to a Fleet Air Arm establishment. She later went on a course, brushing up her French and German preparatory to taking a commission.

Her move was not popular but there was very little Mrs Mannering could do about it without laying herself open to the charge of being unpatriotic. She dare not say the equivalent of 'Never darken my door again' as that would have meant that she would not to be able to 'keep tabs' on Sarah.

Sarah's mind quickly glossed over the next two years – even now she could not bear to think of it without hating the woman who caused her such pain and anguish. She considered that hate was a destructive emotion. If it hadn't been for that woman, Lauren would have had a sister, which she had always wanted.

Sarah came back to the present which had been so happy until her brush with Hubert. The encounter had really brought home to her the impossibility of risking Robert's being involved with any of Hubert's devious plans to thwart her happiness and try to force her to go back to him.

She had asked him once, 'If you find me so unsatisfactory and want to change everything about me, why did you want me to marry you in the first place and why can't you let me go now?'

He had looked at her in complete surprise, as if she had asked a very stupid question and replied, 'I love you, I've always loved you – you must know that by now.'

Sarah had said, 'You have a very strange way of showing it. If that is your idea of loving, I would rather you disliked me as much as you give the impression of doing.'

He had said, 'And you are a very strange person. Most women would be glad to be in your shoes.'

Sarah said wearily, 'Yes, so you have said before.' The odd thing was that he really believed it. Most women were taken in, initially – she had been, herself.

Her thoughts were interrupted by a tap on her door and Charlotte came in.

'His Lordship wondered if you would join him for a nightcap, madam. Shall I tell him you will be down presently?' Charlotte sensed that all was not well with her master and mistress and it distressed her. They didn't seem to have quarrelled – they were not the sort of people who would have a row – but the wonderful aura that they always shed when they were together seemed to have dimmed. She hoped that by suggesting to Sarah that she should go down, she could induce her to do so. Sarah very seldom refused to do anything that she was asked.

For a moment she thought that Sarah was going to decline this time, then she lifted her head, took a deep breath and said, 'Yes, Charlotte, I'll be down in a moment.'

When Charlotte left the room, Sarah went into her bedroom to check on her appearance. With having to face Robert and carry on a conversation as though nothing was amiss, she needed all the confidence she could muster. Even to her, the idea sounded strange but the sooner she could escape somewhere where she could live a neutral existence without any highs or lows, the better. The one aspect of it that would be the final straw in breaking her heart would be leaving Merlin behind. He had never really been hers and she could not possibly give him a life like the one that he enjoyed at Heronshurst.

She walked downstairs wondering how she could ever have thought that just being in the same sphere as Robert would be enough to make her happy. Even if the threat of Hubert's trouble-making wasn't hanging over them, now that she had her freedom, for some strange reason, it was unbearable to be with Robert and not blurt out how much she loved him. That really would be the end and it would be difficult to know who would be the most embarrassed out of the two of them. Hesitating outside the green drawing room, she took a deep breath, grasped the handle and walked in.

Robert was sitting in his usual place and looked up with a welcoming smile that seemed to Sarah's fevered imagination to be a little wary. Surely he didn't suspect her feelings for him and feel uneasy in her company? Why had he asked her to join him?

Perhaps, in the last few days he had come round to her way of thinking that their unusual relationship was not going to work and wanted to suggest that, after all, her presence was no longer required at Heronshurst. That would solve the problem of secrecy about her going and allow her to make arrangements openly, which would make it a lot easier from the practical point of view, even if it was harder to endure that he might agree to it without another thought. It was one thing to make a decision on her own account, for his benefit, but it would hurt unbearably if she thought he could let her go without a qualm. How illogical she was being! At least, thanks to his past generosity, she would no longer be going out in to the world practically penniless as she had two years ago.

CHAPTER NINETEEN

Robert had not, after all, given any indication that Sarah would not be at Heronshurst for all time. They had discussed the usual topics concerned with the running of the estate and he had been his usual gentle, considerate self. Sarah felt that she had never loved him so much, which made her all the more determined that she would avoid getting him embroiled in any embarrassment caused by Hubert – and herself.

She didn't feel any happier than she had done for days but she had come to terms with any regret she may have had about meeting Robert and had come to the conclusion that, whatever happened in the future, she would always cherish the memory of his kindness and concern for her and the feeling that her life had been enriched by knowing him. She slept better than she had for days and awoke with a determination to make some sort of arrangement that would enable her to leave Heronshurst quietly and with dignity.

A phone call to her bank had left her surprised at the amount of money that was available to her. She had not given a lot of thought to how the allowance that was paid in for her could mount up. That would make things a lot easier and she could determine in what part of the country she wanted to live and make arrangements for accommodation there. She could live quite comfortably for a while until she could find employment. In fact with careful investment of her funds, she really did not need to find work. The thought of Merlin came to her again. If she wanted to, she could find somewhere conducive to breeding Alsatians and perhaps, one day, produce one nearly as nice as he.

It had occurred to her to wonder if she should return the money to Robert after she had managed to get away, but realised that he would be mortally offended. He had treated her as family and they would not behave in such a cavalier fashion.

Going to her desk, Sarah settled down determined to write all the necessary letters entailed by her proposed removal from Heronshurst. It was better to bite the bullet and maybe, years from now, if she lived to be very, very old she would be able to think of Robert without its hurting so much.

When Robert had asked Sarah to join him the previous evening it was in some sort of hope that they would be able to establish what was bothering her and perhaps talk it out.

At the last moment his courage had failed him and he was reluctant to intrude into something that she was not prepared to discuss with him willingly. But this morning he felt no nearer to being able to restore their normal happy relationship and he could not settle down to work until he had.

Sarah had disappeared again immediately after breakfast – probably to her suite and he must think of an excuse for infringing on her privacy. If he could think of a good reason to call on her, perhaps in the seclusion of her room, she might unburden herself and perhaps their relationship could resume its previously happy footing.

It was quite a long way down to his study from his suite and if he could use that as an excuse to borrow one of her reference books, perhaps they could continue from there. It sounded rather flimsy, even to him but, in the absence of a better idea, that would have to do.

He walked along to Sarah's room with a great deal of trepidation and tapped on the door. Her voice called 'Come in' and he turned the handle and entered.

Sarah was expecting it to be Charlotte and Robert saw her start of surprise as he walked in.

Not a very good beginning, he thought, but decided to press on. 'Sarah, to save my going all the way down to my study, may I borrow your copy of Shakespeare, please?'

Sarah looked relieved at such a simple request and said, 'Of course, help yourself,' and turned back to her desk trying to re-establish her train of thought.

Robert took down the volume of Shakespeare and made a pretence of searching for a reference, wondering about his next move. As he flicked through the pages, a loose sheet of paper slid out and fluttered to the floor. He picked it up, intending to restore it to the book. It was obviously keeping a place but he had no idea where and was about to place it between the pages of the sonnets where the book was opened, when the heading caught his eye. He had no intention of prying but there it was, *A Sonnet to Robert*. The handwriting was Sarah's and it was signed Sarah/Estelle, with the date, September 1973.

Glancing at Sarah's back, he saw she was apparently engrossed in what she was writing and Robert decided to read the sonnet and apologise afterwards. It read:

SONNET TO ROBERT

Love came late, by Fate deferred, but coming
Relit the brave, bright flame of youth anew,
Setting my quivering heartstrings humming
A hymn of joy on golden wings to you.
Love came late, but came at last and living
Unravelled its true reason and its rhyme.
Gloried in the selfless act of giving,
Beyond all earthly space, beyond all time.
Love came late, with wisdom, truth and seeing
A heart so empty, desolate, forlorn,
Revealed to the essence of my being
Its very aim and purpose to be born.
I love you truly now, as I did then,
For all of distant time beyond our ken.

Sarah/Estelle

September 1973

Robert felt the tears pricking at the back of his eyes as he read it over again, assimilating the full import of his find and feeling both humble and proud. Here, in his hand, he held the answer to their problem and he must be very careful how he approached the next few minutes. The whole of the rest of their lives depended on his not making a false move.

'Sarah.' He found that his voice shook slightly with unshed tears and trying to control the elation he was feeling after the misery of the last few days.

Sarah turned at the unaccustomed tremor in his normally firm voice.

Robert walked over to her and drew her to her feet. 'I want to ask you two questions and it is essential that you say exactly what you feel now at this very moment and not what you think I might want to hear.'

'Very well, Robert. What are the questions?'

He was relieved to hear that she sounded almost her usual self.

'First of all, did you write this sonnet to me?'

Sarah took the sheet of paper from his hand. So that was where it went, inside her copy of Shakespeare.

She remembered the utter joy with which she had written it originally, entirely for her own satisfaction, never dreaming that it would be seen by any other eyes than hers. Robert had specifically asked for the truth. 'Yes, Robert, I did,' she said candidly, waiting for his next question.

'Do you still feel the same way, now?'

Sarah was still under the influence of the dark cloud that had descended on her the day she went to Elkesbury, creating its imaginary problems at the time of her encounter with Hubert, but she had agreed to be honest. Hesitatingly, she replied, 'Yes, Robert, I still feel the same way.'

He gave a joyous laugh and caught her in his arms, holding her as though he never wanted to let her go. 'Where have you been these last few days and why couldn't I reach you? I've been so miserable.'

Sarah gazed up at him, hardly daring to believe this was happening. The apparently chance meeting with Hubert, the flood of unpleasant memories it had released, his following her, her escape and her fear of the upset and embarrassment he could cause for Robert had completely destroyed her normally good judgement.

Sarah began to try to explain it to Robert but, once started, it all came tumbling out almost incoherently, the shock of meeting Hubert, the fear of the embarrassment he might cause for Robert if he discovered where she was living, the words falling over themselves in her anxiety to make him understand and free herself of the burden of misery that Hubert had left in his wake.

The one thing that seemed to make itself clear to Robert was that Sarah considered she could not possibly embarrass or involve him in anything as sordid as her unhappy past. If it hadn't been so nearly tragic, it would have been laughable. 'Didn't you know that I loved you? Couldn't you feel it? Ever since the moment I first saw you, when you chose to fall in love with Merlin.'

He was smiling but became aware that the tears were coursing down her cheeks. He held her closer, 'My poor darling, have a good cry, it will make you feel better.'

The unexpected tenderness and loving understanding coming then, when for years she had been unaccustomed to crying because it provoked a violent scene and she had been told, 'For heavens sake, don't turn on the waterworks!' completely shattered her emotional defences.

The last of her tenuous control deserted her and the flood of tears which followed were for all the pent-up unhappiness and stress that she had suffered in the past, but most of all for the knowledge that, through her own stupidity, she could have lost Robert before she really found him.

Having started to cry after controlling it for so long, Sarah found it was difficult to stop and Robert picked her up and sat down on the sofa holding her on his knees, his arms close around her, letting the healing tears do their work.

After a while the sobbing ceased and worn out with several sleepless nights, Sarah fell asleep in his arms.

Robert looked down at the tear-stained face against his shoulder and felt that he had never loved her more than he did at that moment. Her normally immaculate hair was tousled and the little tendril he had noticed before, had escaped and was curling round her ear. Smiling at the memory, he bent his head and kissed it again and then the tear-stained eyes, feeling happier than he had ever been and content just holding her close to him. Everything was all right now and things could take their course. When Sarah awoke, her memory would be cleansed of all the past sadness. It would be as though she had awakened from a long nightmare into a bright and sunny morning, never to be bothered by the bad dream again.

She had been so courageous for so long, the strain was bound to take its toll, but now she had given way to tears, they would help wash it all away. Robert had heard a surgeon friend of his claim that, the night before a tricky operation, he either read a sad book or went to see a sad film, giving way to tears to release the tension and help him sleep soundly.

Robert looked at the time and then down at the beloved face against his shoulder. He would have liked to sit there holding her until she awoke, but it was possible that Charlotte might come in to do her duties, so standing up very carefully to avoid waking Sarah, he carried her into the bedroom and lay her gently on the bed and covered her with a blanket.

159

Looking at her for a moment, he walked quietly back into the sitting room to telephone Mrs Bates to say that – what did he call Sarah now that she was free? He hesitated for an instant, thinking about that problem. As far as the staff were concerned, it would only confuse things for Sarah to revert to her maiden name. After all, it would be for such a short while, if he had anything to do with it, before they were having to change to call her 'Your Ladyship'. The thought brought a happy smile to his face as he picked up the telephone to call Mrs Bates. She answered almost at once and he said, 'Mrs Bates, Mrs Mannering is resting and doesn't want to be disturbed. Will you see that no one wakes her until one of us calls you?'

Mrs Bates was concerned that Mrs Mannering might be ill, but his Lordship's voice sounded happier than she had heard it for several days and she forebore to ask, merely saying, 'Yes, my Lord, I will see that no one disturbs her until we hear from you.'

Robert replaced the telephone, the Bates' really were treasures, he could always rely on them. He returned to the bedroom, drew up a chair and sat watching over Sarah until she should awaken.

When she did awake, nearly an hour later, she gave him such an enchanting smile that he wanted to pick her up again and hold her close, but he only said, 'Would madam like a cup of tea?'

'Madam would love a cup of tea,' Sarah replied, still smiling, 'are you going to make it?'

'Of course,' Robert answered. 'Do you think I can't?'

'I am quite sure you can do anything you put your mind to,' Sarah said, convinced that this was true.

'To quote our transatlantic cousins "you'd better believe it",' and so saying, Robert went in to the sitting room to make the tea. 'I have told Mrs Bates that you are not to be disturbed until we call,' he said, 'so you can either stay here or get up when you feel like it.'

Sarah gazed into his beloved face, not even trying to conceal her intense love for him that had been growing steadily stronger ever since they first met and feeling relieved that she no longer had to guard her expression. She said seriously, 'Thank you for your patience and understanding. I felt as though I were enveloped in an evil black cloud and couldn't get away. I am out of it now, thanks to you. It won't happen again.'

Robert answered equally seriously, 'You are not alone now,

your problems are my problems, whatever they are. You must never feel that you need to shield me from them again, for any reason.'

Sarah regarded him, her heart in her eyes and Robert said, 'Tell me, please, you haven't actually said the words yet.'

Sarah understood what he meant and said with deep feeling, 'I love you, Robert. I tried not to but it was already too late that first morning, when I said I had fallen in love with Merlin. I had, but much more so with you and later, I told myself you were just being kind, I could not believe that you could possibly feel the same way.'

'And I told myself that it was just wishful thinking that you might love me,' Robert smiled. 'I thought of what I would do when you were free and in my more fantasising moments, I set a scene somewhere romantic with moonlight, roses and music to ask you to marry me, but I can't wait until then and I want to ask you here and now before another minute has gone by. Sarah, my love and my life, will you marry me, please and very, very soon?'

Sarah discarded all the clever-clever answers and said very simply, 'Yes, Robert, I will.'

'Bless you!' he said happily, getting out of his chair to move near enough to kiss her.

It started as a very gentle kiss, as between people who have been close for a long time, but it grew with the measure of their love and longing for each other during the months of waiting that they had shared together.

When they finally drew apart, Robert asked, 'Do you feel well enough to come along to my suite so that we can put the official seal on our engagement?'

Sarah said, 'I have never felt better than I do at this moment. Thank you again for your care and consideration – but most of all, your love.'

Robert stood up, holding out his hand to her and Sarah took it, swinging her feet to the ground and standing up. They walked hand-in-hand along the corridor to Robert's suite.

In his sitting room, he went to his desk and came back with a jeweller's box in his hand, saying, 'This is the Falconbridge emerald that the bride-to-be of the eldest son always has as an engagement ring.' He took it out of the box and slipped it on the third finger of Sarah's left hand. It was a perfect fit.

Sarah looked at it in awe. 'Robert, it is so beautiful, what a wonderful colour, and the diamonds surrounding it look as though they have just been newly set.'

'When I thought I might have the chance of giving it to you, I fetched it from the bank and left it at the jeweller's to be cleaned. It does look well, doesn't it? That is our official engagement ring but I want to give you one that is just between ourselves that hasn't belonged to anyone else and is my private pledge to you.' He produced another ring with a huge fire opal surrounded by seven stones.

Sarah was immediately fascinated by the fact that not only were the stones different, two of them were set asymetrically.

'Do you like it, my darling,' Robert asked her anxiously. 'I had it set to my own design when we were in Switzerland, hoping to give it to you as my special pledge. It holds a message, as I am sure you are clever enough to read without my telling you.'

So that accounts for the asymetrical design, Sarah thought, that must be the clue.

She held the ring in front of her, intent on the stones surrounding the opal. Emerald, sapphire, topaz, diamond. No, that wasn't right, she turned the ring while Robert watched her intently, a little smile on his face. He would wager that it would take his clever girl less than a minute to read his message to her.

Sarah tried again, diamond, emerald, amethyst, ruby, sapphire, emerald, topaz. That made sense, she looked at Robert, her eyes smiling at him – and the opal in the middle, was that part of the message? Of course! 'That is a clever touch, Robert, it took me a while to fathom where the opal fitted in. O in tennis parlance is "love". Dearest Love. It is very beautiful just as it is but the message makes it especially precious.' She removed the emerald ring and put it in its box. 'I won't wear that all the time, but keep it for formal occasions – it is much too intrinsically valuable and irreplaceable from a family history point of view for everyday wear.' She gave Robert the opal to put on her hand in its place. He slipped it over her finger, lifting it to his lips and kissing it. As he did so, he remembered that other time when he had kissed the bare finger and hoped for this moment when he could claim her for his own.

Sarah sat looking at it, loving it both for the message and the thought that Robert had had it made as long ago as when they were in Switzerland. If only she had known then! How much anguish she would have been spared! But his integrity was much of what she loved in Robert and she knew instinctively, now, that he had wanted to give her time to gain her freedom and adjust to it. Putting her hands either side of his face, Sarah gave him a long, lingering kiss, saying at the end of it, 'I shall treasure it always. I am especially moved that you had it made all that time ago, when we were in Switzerland.'

'I should have given it to you then,' Robert said, 'I wanted to very much.'

'No, it wouldn't have been in character,' Sarah replied, thoughtfully. 'That is one of the many things I love about you, it is so special these days. Where are we going to keep the Falconbridge emerald when I am not wearing it?'

'There is a concealed safe in your room,' Robert told her. 'There is one in all the main suites. I hadn't realised that you probably haven't been told about it.'

Sarah laughed. 'Until you gave me so many beautiful things, I haven't really needed one! As the youngest of three daughters, my mother's jewellery got rather spread around. I have the pieces that I like best – her wedding ring and the ones my father had especially made for her when they were very young. Not intrinsically highly valuable but precious to me for the same reason as my lovely opal.'

'I will walk you back to your room and show you where the safe is, then I expect you will want to freshen up after your sleep. The time seems to have flown since then and we haven't had any lunch. Aren't you hungry? I know being in love is supposed to put you off your food and I hope you don't think that I am being unromantic, but I feel I need some sustenance after all the excitement, I don't get engaged every day,' Robert said, leaning over to kiss her.

Sarah laughed. 'Come to think about it, now that you mention it, I could do with a bite of something. Excitement always makes me hungry, too!'

'I'll call down to Mrs Bates and let her know we are available again. How about one of her special omelettes and a green salad to start with and we can take it from there?' Robert suggested.

'That sounds wonderful,' Sarah agreed, waiting while Robert called Mrs Bates and then getting up from her chair and walking with Robert back to her room.

Sarah was intrigued to realise that she had come so close to where her safe was situated without even knowing it was there. She would never have guessed in a hundred years and having safely deposited the fabulous emerald in the safe, Robert took her in his arms saying, 'We must decide where and how soon we can be married. I don't mind where – St Margaret's, Westminster, the local parish church or a register's office – but it cannot be soon enough for me!' He gave her another long kiss, feeling that he would never be able to make up for all the times he had wanted to kiss Sarah and restrained himself. He let her go very reluctantly and went back to his own suite to freshen up for a late lunch.

During the latter part of the afternoon, they went riding, letting their horses wander almost at will while they discussed future plans or lapsed into a happy silence. The day still held some late summer's warmth while displaying the soft haziness of autumn, the sky a pale azure, setting off the green and gold and flame of the changing trees.

After the trauma of the last few days, Robert felt reluctant to let Sarah out of his sight, feeling at times as if he were dreaming and afraid that he might wake to find that she had disappeared completely. When they had finished dinner that night, he suggested that they adjourned to Sarah's suite instead of staying in the green drawing room, to ensure that they would not be disturbed and they enjoyed their first evening together as lovers.

BOOK II

DESTINY DECIDES

CHAPTER TWENTY

Sarah awoke the next morning with the recollection that something wonderful had happened and, at the same time, feeling completely tranquil and at peace. She stretched luxuriously, basking in the sensation for several minutes before arising and wandering into her bathroom to shower and dress.

It was early still, yet she felt totally alive and refreshed in a way that she couldn't recall experiencing for many, many years. It was like being born again into the heyday of one's youth, she thought. While she was brushing her hair, Charlotte came in to make her tea.

'Oh, madam, you're up already!' she said, somewhat obviously.

Sarah smiled at her and the happiness in her expression lifted Charlotte's spirits and made her feel happy, too.

'You shall be the first person in the household to know that Lord Falconbridge and I are going to be married,' Sarah told Charlotte.

'Oh, madam, I'm so glad. Of course, I knew it would happen,' Charlotte added, being somewhat wise after the event.

'Did you? How?' Sarah asked, curiously.

'Well, it was clear that you belonged here from the start. Mum and Dad recognised it, although they refused to discuss it, so why shouldn't you and his Lordship marry? I hope you will both be very happy. I am sure you will, you make a lovely couple.'

There seemed to be no answer to such logic, so Sarah merely said, 'Thank you, Charlotte,' and, having drunk her tea, prepared to go downstairs.

She glanced at her beautiful fire opal ring which Robert had put on her finger last night and which she had been reluctant to remove before going to sleep. She held it against her cheek, the

Falconbridge emerald was superb and probably worth a king's ransom and she would be very proud to wear it but it would never touch her heart like the lovely ring that Robert had designed especially for her with such love and thought. One of the most precious features of it was that Robert had ordered the ring even before he felt he was in a position to talk about it and, though they would both have been saved a lot of anguish if he had followed his heart and given it to her then, it was that old-fashioned chivalry that Sarah found so attractive in him.

Robert, too, awoke refreshed and very content after the first really good night's sleep he had had for days. Fate sometimes had a wonderful way of working things out eventually – but why did she have to be so devious about it? He hummed happily to himself as he showered, shaved and dressed. Sarah, his lovely Sarah, for whom he had waited so long, was really going to be his wife. In spite of the traumas caused by her unfortunate encounter in Elkesbury, it was really a blessing in disguise. The incident had served to break down her stoic control and the floods of tears must have washed away all the hurt and stress of years. From now on they could start afresh, unencumbered by any unhappy associations. Robert had no idea what Sarah had had in mind that her ex-husband could do or say that would harm him, Robert, in any way, but when they were safely married, the fellow could do his worst – it was unlikely that anyone who mattered would give him credence.

Today was the first day of the rest of their life together which, DV, would be many happy years. What a red-letter day!

As Robert approached Sarah's door, he paused, wondering if she were still sleeping, it was still quite early. While he hesitated, the door opened and Sarah came out, looking radiant and happy. She closed the door behind her.

After glancing quickly both ways, Robert took her in his arms and kissed her very thoroughly, then drew back to look down at her saying, 'That is what I shall expect first thing every morning for the rest of my life!'

Sarah smiled up at him, her heart in her eyes and said demurely, 'I will do my best, sir.'

'That is as it should be,' Robert replied firmly, taking her by the hand and heading for the staircase.

As they were nearing the foot of the stairs, Bates went by below in the hall. He looked up and said, 'Good morning, my Lord, good morning, my Lady.' Sarah tried to withdraw her hand but Robert held on to it tightly, saying, 'Good morning, Bates, a very good morning. You are right, as usual, we are going to be married.'

'Yes, my Lord, congratulations and best wishes to you, my Lady. I know you will be very happy.'

'Thank you, Bates.'

'Very good, my Lord,' and Bates went on his way.

'Isn't he wonderful?' Robert remarked to Sarah, 'anyone else would say "I hope you will be very happy" – not Bates, he knows!' They followed Bates at a leisurely pace into the breakfast room, where he was checking that all was ready for them. Over their meal, Robert said, 'When we have had breakfast we will go into my study and work out the details of our wedding.' He felt very smug saying the last two words. 'That is, of course, if you haven't anything more important to do?'

'No-o,' Sarah said, deliberately sounding doubtful with an impish smile on her face, 'I don't think I have.'

'I should hope not!' Robert replied with mock severity and they both laughed.

For the first time in years Sarah felt that she was the right person in the right place, whereas, for decades she had the impression of being outside of her body, as though watching someone else going through the motions of living. Adrienne had come very close to the truth when she had asked Sarah, 'Where were you? Didn't you feel as though you should be here?'

Crying herself to sleep in Robert's arms had purged all the doubt and conflict in her mind and now she could take her rightful place in the scheme of things, confident and assured, with belief in the future as she had in her youth. It was a wonderful feeling and she hoped she would never lose it again. At this stage, she wondered why and how she could possibly have considered that Hubert could cause any trouble for Robert – how ridiculous it seemed to her now. It was a measure of how Hubert's spite, jealousy and deviousness had really got through to her without anyone of her own world to turn to.

After they had settled down in Robert's study with Tristram beside him and Merlin by Sarah, Robert said, 'First of all, we must announce our engagement. Not, I think, that it will be startling news to any of our family and friends and strangers won't be concerned.'

Sarah said facetiously, 'Have you told the dogs?'

Robert laughed. 'You don't think they need telling, do you?

Why do you think they look so insufferably smug? Nearly as smug as the face that looked out at me from my mirror when I was shaving this morning!'

'They do look disgustingly pleased with themselves, don't they?' Sarah agreed, looking from one to the other.

Both dogs wagged the tip of their tail in an identical movement as she regarded them. Really, she thought, a stranger would be unable to tell them apart, now, although she and Robert would never mistake one for the other, if only for their proprietary air towards them individually.

'The next question is,' Robert said, '(a) do we satisfy all our conventional friends and have a big, fashionable wedding in somewhere like St Margaret's, (b) do we please the household and village by having it in the local parish church or (c) do we sneak off somewhere quiet and get married quickly with only Adrienne and George as witnesses, or (d) do we do all three. If the answer is (d) I vote we get a special licence now and get married immediately. Actually, I think that is a wonderful idea.'

When Sarah had stopped laughing, she said, 'Quite seriously, you have made some very valid observations. In your position, you will be expected to have a fashionable wedding, especially since you have kept everybody waiting for it for so long. On the other hand, it would be nice to have it in our little local parish church. Would it be possible to combine (a) and (b)? – (c) is a nice idea, too,' she finished. 'That wasn't very helpful, was it?'

'Yes, it was,' Robert replied enthusiastically. 'That is a wonderful idea to combine (a) and (b). We will limit the invitations to our closest relatives and friends, leaving room in the church for the household and any villagers who may want to come. We will make sure we reserve enough seats for the household and it will be a case of "first come, first served" for anyone else who wants to attend. In the meantime, we will get a special licence, round up Adrienne and George and pop off to the nearest available Register Office. Do you think you could stand getting married to me twice?' Robert asked, half-seriously.

Sarah smiled, 'I can stand it if you can,' she replied, thinking how wonderful it was to be discussing it all in such a light-hearted fashion, when she remembered falling in love with Robert against her own advice the very first day they met and only a little while ago she had seriously considered that, for his sake, she ought to leave. But that was over now.

'At least I will make sure of you that way,' Robert told her, 'and by the time we have had a quiet wedding as a rehearsal for the big one, I shall know what to do and be able to enjoy it without being nervous.'

The idea that Robert 'wanted to make sure of her' gave Sarah a warm glow inside, but she found it hard to imagine his being nervous in any circumstances.

'That seems to have our priorities sorted out,' Robert said. 'Now we must draft a list of the wedding guests, so that as soon as we have a definite date we can get the invitations printed and dispatched. I vote we ask Adam Carter to do the printing, don't you?'

'Yes, he makes a wonderfully elegant job of invitation cards,' Sarah agreed, thinking about the first time they had used his services.

'Tomorrow,' Robert continued, 'I will arrange our quiet wedding as soon as possible. It should not be too much of a problem, then we can plan the church ceremony leaving plenty of time for everyone to fit it in to their calendars. We must not forget that Lauren's baby is due towards the end of this month – as if you would! – so if we plan for latish October, that will give her plenty of time to recover and we can buy her a lovely outfit. Either Charlotte or Lizzie can take care of the new baby for the short time that Lauren will be in church. Patrick and Alexandra can accompany her, they are usually very well-behaved in spite of being so young. Who are you going to have as attendants?'

'I thought about Lauren and Adrienne as matrons of honour and Alexandra as bridesmaid and Patrick as page. I am sure, as you said, they are old enough to behave well. If we are planning for the benefit of the guests, we might as well do it properly.'

'I could not agree more,' Robert said, 'and if the news does leak out to the national paparazzi, we might as well give them something worth photographing. Your father will be able to give you away, won't he?'

'I would think so, all being well. I must write to him and tell him about it so that he can make his travel plans in time.'

'Yes,' Robert agreed. 'If you invite him to come over immediately, he will be on hand whatever date we arrange, that is, if he can get away and he can stay as long as he pleases. I must go and see the vicar and you must start looking at dress designs! I have waited a long time for this and I'm going to make the most of it,' Robert concluded.

'Aren't you the tiniest bit chary, Robert?' Sarah asked.

'Not the smallest iota, I can't wait,' he replied. 'The one consolation is that, if all goes according to plan, we will be married by then and able to enjoy the encore as seasoned troupers.' He stood up and sat down on the arm of Sarah's chair, leaning down to kiss her. 'I don't think we have left anything out – except of course, where we are going for our honeymoon. Do you have a secret longing to go anywhere in particular?'

'Yes,' Sarah answered promptly.

'Where?'

'Anywhere you happen to be,' she replied returning his kiss.

Robert laughed. 'You are very accommodating and I have an idea if you agree. It will mean postponing our honeymoon until the spring, but if you have no objections, I always thought I would like us to find a small hotel on Lake Geneva, somewhere quiet and pretty – and secluded.'

'That sounds lovely – and romantic,' Sarah replied. 'When did you think about that?'

'Ever since we stayed in that other stream-lined, gold and chromium-plated hotel the first time we were in Switzerland together.'

'Did you, now?' Sarah said, smiling.

'Oh, yes,' Robert said airily, 'I was planning our honeymoon then.'

Sarah still had to pinch herself to make sure she wasn't dreaming when she realised that all the time she had lost her heart to Robert and thought that he was just being kind, he had been feeling the same way she did.

'Vevey in late spring/early summer is a pretty place, what do you think?' Robert asked.

'That sounds lovely. As you know, I adore Switzerland.'

'And me, too, I hope,' Robert said.

'Oh, yes! and you, too, most definitely,' she said, pulling his head down to kiss him again.

'I must telephone old George and give him the news and you had better ring Lauren and Adrienne, before they read the news of the engagement in the newspapers. They would never forgive us if they found out that way,' Robert said, reaching for the telephone on his desk.

'There is just one thing I don't relish telling,' Sarah remarked. 'How are we going to inform either Lizzie or Charlotte that she is going to be the one to stay at home on the day of the wedding? Much as they love babies and young children, this time could be

172

the exception, don't you think? The answer would be to get a professional in but even if Lauren were prepared to leave her brand new baby in the care of a complete stranger, however competent, I wouldn't be too happy about it.'

'That is certainly a point that needs careful consideration,' Robert agreed. 'We must give a great deal of thought and try to come up with a suitable solution, so that everybody is happy, most of all the bride – I don't want to think that you are not giving me your undivided attention on that particular day!'

Sarah laughed, as Robert meant her to. 'I will go and make my calls from my room,' she said, 'They are both liable to be rather lengthy if I know my daughter and Adrienne!'

'While you are on the telephone, why don't you ring your father – it will save so much time and you can answer any queries he may have on the spot,' Robert suggested as Sarah was leaving the room. 'Tell him he is welcome to come over as soon as convenient to him and stay as long as he wishes.'

Sarah turned at the door intending to say that calling to South Africa in the middle of the morning was very expensive, then she realised that, to Robert, it was a mere bagatelle and if he was at all bothered about it, he wouldn't have mentioned it in the first place. Not like people who suggested one thing one minute and then complained bitterly about it afterwards, disregarding the fact that it was their idea.

With his infallible intuition where Sarah was concerned, he said, 'Don't worry, darling, we can afford it!'

She blew him a kiss and left the room, thinking as she went of all the times she had been made to feel guilty for talking to her family, even to Lauren, who was only eighty or so miles away. It had happened to such an extent that she had almost ceased to use the telephone. She dismissed the memory as not being worthy of recollecting, that sort of thing couldn't affect her ever again.

She telephoned Lauren and gave her the news. 'Robert has suggested that we leave the church wedding until you have had time to recover from having your baby and then we will go out and choose a stunning dress for you.'

'He really is a wonderful person, mother, I'm glad you are so happy,' Lauren told her.

'You will be my matron of honour, won't you?' Sarah requested. 'With Alexandra as bridesmaid and Patrick as page.'

'I would love to,' Lauren assured her. 'It will be nice to look forward to it.'

After exchanging a few more words they cleared the line and

Sarah called Adrienne, who answered the telephone almost immediately. Sarah repeated the news to her and she said,

'I'm over the moon about it, Sarah, but it was only a matter of time, wasn't it? Are you happy?'

'So happy, Adrienne, I can't tell you how much.'

'That's as it should be, have you settled the date?'

Sarah explained about the two ceremonies and asked, 'Can you stand as witness at the civil one, Adrienne, please? Lauren is too close to when her baby is due for it to be wise for her to attempt it.'

'Just try and stop me, Sarah! I will make sure I keep the next few days free.'

'Thank you and bless you! Goodbye for now.'

'Goodbye, Sarah, I'll await your further instructions with baited breath.'

Her father was delighted with the news and promised to come over as soon as he could make the arrangements. As Sarah had been, he was conscious of the cost of overseas calls on her behalf, so after an exchange of news, he rang off.

A few days later, Sarah asked Adrienne to accompany her to choose her wedding outfit for the civil ceremony, although she did not need a lot of persuading.

'We must get yours, too,' Sarah said. 'I insist on providing it since you are virtually my matron of honour, as you will be for the church ceremony, though, of course, the choice is yours entirely.'

'What colour were you thinking of having, Sarah? I don't want to clash with you.'

'I don't think that will be a problem, as I hope to wear ivory for both occasions. Something like a silk suit for the civil one and a dress for the church wedding,' Sarah told her.

'Why exactly, are you having two ceremonies, Sarah?' Adrienne asked.

Sarah smiled. 'If you believe Robert, it is one for us and one for "them". He wants us to get married as soon as possible, but realises he must conform to convention and provide a pageant for the village. He says that knowing we are safely married already will make him relaxed and able to enjoy what he calls "the encore".'

Adrienne burst out laughing. 'That sounds just like Robert! He never did anything like everyone else.'

'After we have settled on the outfits for the civil wedding, we will go and choose the designs for our other dresses and order them to be made up in time for the church wedding. We have about six weeks maximum. If we leave choosing them till the end of this month, Lauren may be able to join us for that trip.'

CHAPTER TWENTY-ONE

Marriage

Robert and Sarah slipped off and got married by special licence as planned, with Adrienne and George as witnesses.

Robert had asked Sarah if she would like a few days away, but they both decided to start their married life at Heronshurst. He had given her the choice of keeping her own suite or sharing the enormous one designed for the head of the family, which was situated over the main entrance hall and leaving it to her whether they had twin beds or a king-size double one.

For once, since she and Robert had got engaged, she was doubtful about how he felt, bearing in mind he had been living alone for so long and it was just possible he liked having a bed to himself. She tried to explain what she was thinking rather hesitantly.

'You are pulling my leg, aren't you, darling?' Robert had asked, wrapping his arms tightly around her. 'If it is all the same to you, I would rather like to know that you are there beside me if I wake in the night, otherwise I might think I am dreaming,' and that more than convinced Sarah.

For herself, she could not imagine anything that would make her happier than, like him, to know he was there beside her if she awoke in the night.

The main suite was vast, with dressing room, small den and bathroom on one side of the huge bedroom and another bathroom and sitting room off the other side.

'When we are settled down, you must have your own choice of colour-scheme and decoration for the suite. It can be done while we are away on our belated honeymoon,' Robert told Sarah.

Sarah hugged him. 'I love you and you spoil me utterly,' she said.

'Nothing would spoil you, my darling. I just want everything to be perfect for you,' Robert replied, holding her closely.

The civil wedding was somewhat lacking in glamour, but the Registrar was a kind little man who tried to make it as pleasant as possible in the circumstances, feeling that it wasn't every day that he had such an attractive couple and wondering what lay behind their decision to marry in a Register Office.

Adrienne and George had returned to Heronshurst with them for a champagne lunch, both finding a reasonably convincing excuse to leave before evening.

It had been essential to tell Mr and Mrs Bates and the staff about the civil wedding to allow for the necessary changes to be made to their accommodation. Robert particularly avoided putting any stress on the confidentiality of the information, knowing that he could rely on their discretion.

Bates felt that it was typical of his Lordship's trusting nature and Robert and Sarah's suite had been thoroughly prepared for their occupation and needed only the transference of their personal effects on the day of the wedding.

After Adrienne and George left, Robert and Sarah went to inspect their mutual accommodation and Sarah was overwhelmed by the masses of flowers in their sitting room.

'They are so beautiful!' Sarah exclaimed, 'where did they all come from?'

Robert tried to look off-hand. 'I did not know which flowers to choose that would look best for the colour-scheme, so I ordered all they had in the shop. They mix in a garden so I thought, why shouldn't they mix equally well indoors.'

Sarah laughed. 'You are wonderful!' she told him, 'You never do things by half, do you?'

'Not if I can help it,' Robert replied, smiling, 'that is why I want to marry you twice – I want to make sure of you.'

'That deserves a kiss,' Sarah said.

Robert held out his arms and she went into them for the first time since they had been married. They felt the passion rising as they embraced but by mutual silent consent, considered that it was too precious to be rushed and they could take all the time they needed later, so after a long, lingering kiss they reluctantly drew apart to return to the more mundane. 'Like having tea,' Robert said, 'for the first time since we have been married and the first time here. There are going to be a lot of "firsts", then we will become an old married couple saying, "Do you remember when...?"'

They had dinner together as they had many times before, but never in the past had they retired to the same room. How often Robert had wished that he did not have to say 'Goodnight' to Sarah and leave her at her door. Now his dream had come true, they were husband and wife at last.

When their wedding day came finally came to an end, Robert took Sarah in his arms and kissed her, gently at first, then on a rising tide of emotion that engulfed them both and swept them along until all their love and longing and need for each other over the past two years was assuaged in a crescendo of passion.

'I love you, I love you, I love you,' Robert murmured against Sarah's hair as she lay in his arms. 'You are everything I want, all I will ever need.'

Sarah lifted her head and kissed him again. 'I love you, too, "for all of distant time beyond our ken."'

'Darling, that will forever be my favourite sonnet. You wrote it just for me and it brought you back to me.'

Sarah sighed happily and contentedly nestled even closer in Robert's arms as she floated into a blissful sleep.

He stayed for a while watching her sleeping face, remembering the first time she had fallen asleep in his arms, just happy to hold her and to know that she belonged to him 'beyond all earthly space, beyond all time.' Then he, too, drifted to sleep.

Sarah awoke the next morning to find Robert leaning over her and gazing at her with utter love in his eyes. She smiled sleepily at him and reached up to trace his features with the tip of her finger. 'I fell in love with your fascinating eyes and then your complete kindness and consideration the first day we met,' she told him dreamily.

'Was that before or after you fell in love with Merlin,' he asked teasingly, although he took her remark anything but lightly.

'Oh, before!' Sarah answered, 'the other was just a smokescreen to prevent your thinking that I was just another dizzy female.'

Robert smiled and said quite seriously, 'It would have saved a lot of time and heartache if I had known,' but he realised in his heart of hearts that what they had between them needed to grow slowly and strongly.

'I did not know then that your devastating good looks, charm and consideration were wrapped up in such a gorgeous package,'

Sarah continued, running her hand down his cheek and neck and gently stroking his deeply-muscled chest and taut, hard stomach.

At her touch, his senses flamed and the warm love for her that filled his being overflowed and he took her in his arms and loved her completely.

Lying there contentedly relaxed in their utter delight in each other, Robert said, 'Sarah, you are all woman. I loved you the moment you walked into my study, but I didn't know how much till now,'

'And I am in love and married to a real man,' she replied. 'I did not know such happiness existed.'

'Neither did I, but it was worth waiting for,' Robert answered.

They lay there holding each other closely, unwilling for some time to let the outside world intrude, until they had to make an effort to return to more mundane matters, like showering, dressing and going down to breakfast.

Gradually they slipped back into their duties while looking forward to their second wedding in the pretty little parish church of Heronsbury.

Life went on and Lauren's baby was born on the twenty-fifth of September. It was a girl and Lauren told Sarah that they wanted to call her 'Estelle Lauren'. 'You don't mind, do you, mother?' Lauren asked, 'as you won't want to use the name.'

It was a loving, innocent remark but caused Sarah a deep pang of regret, reminding her that she and Robert would not have children of their own.

She talked to him about it and he said, 'Sarah, my darling love, you are all I want, all I will ever need. If I had felt strongly about having children, I would have married years ago, but I wanted to wait for you.' The heartfelt conviction in his voice went some way to allaying her own regrets. If she had him, he was more than enough and she had Lauren, who had made her previous life worth living and, through her, her children.

Robert had arranged with the local vicar, the Revd Mr Holman, that he and Sarah would be married on 26th October, considering that a Saturday would be most convenient for all those people who might want to attend.

They went through the normal formalities of having the banns read and it was announced from the pulpit that anyone from the village would be welcome.

The vicar was, in certain circumstances, reluctant to marry divorced people, but having met Sarah soon after she arrived at Heronshurst and got to know her well, he felt that although there were two sides to a marriage problem, she had taken the vows seriously enough to persevere for thirty years. People who made mistakes in law very seldom paid so high a price and Sarah was entitled to a second chance.

Sarah, Lauren and Adrienne went to London to choose designs for their wedding outfits and have them made up. When Sarah met Adrienne in Town normally, she often went by train as it was so convenient. It obviated the necessity for Sarah to find somewhere to park the car, which was often a nuisance, or of her monopolising Frazer and causing him to have to wait around, but this time Robert insisted that they went in the Rolls as it was not long since the baby had been born and Lauren must be fatigued as little as possible.

Sarah, as always, loved him for his consideration. It would certainly make travelling much more relaxing and pleasant on what Robert insisted on calling, 'the girls' day out'.

She ordered a deceptively simple-looking dress in ivory velvet with a little matching tricorne hat. Adrienne chose coral which went well with her still-dark hair and Lauren chose a delicate azure blue which blended beautifully with both and set off her honey-blonde hair and very blue eyes.

Robert was not allowed to accompany them as he was not supposed to see the bride's dress before the wedding, which, in the circumstances, they all found hilarious.

The problem that Sarah had raised with Robert about the care of the new baby while they were in church, had been neatly solved by Mrs Bates, who had suggested, somewhat diffidently, that since Estelle was still so young, it might be better if she took care of her. Her daughters were good girls but they had had very little experience of very young babies and it meant that they could both go to the wedding in all their finery and enjoy it. When Sarah had said, 'But that means you will miss the wedding, too, Mrs Bates. We will get a professional nanny in,' Mrs Bates had almost snorted. 'I would be less happy for the little love to be left with a stranger than with one of my girls, your Ladyship, if you'll pardon the liberty. She will be fine with me and I will see you all dressed before you go and be here when you get back, don't you fret about it.'

Sarah had looked doubtful until Mrs Bates had added, 'I shall look forward to having her to myself for a while. It is a long time since my girls were babies.' She was so firm in her assertion that Sarah had been convinced. 'Thank you, Mrs Bates, I'll certainly feel a lot happier leaving the baby with you than anyone else,' and the matter was settled, leaving Lauren very relieved and grateful.

Robert and Sarah's wedding day dawned mild and misty, but sunny and Sarah was surprised and delighted to find that it felt as exciting as if it were their first. The age-old service still sounded as important when applied to her marriage to Robert and she found it thoroughly moving. Walking up the aisle on her father's arm and seeing Robert standing there, it was as if it were happening for the first time and when he turned and smiled at her, she felt she was falling in love with him all over again.

Robert, too, felt that this was a new, fresh experience. He had wanted to be married to Sarah as soon as she was free and the civil ceremony had accomplished that, but now the wedding in the little parish church which had featured in a large part of his life and the life of Heronshurst before him, would set the seal on their commitment to each other and make it feel that it was truly for ever. When the organ announced Sarah's arrival, Robert turned to enjoy the precious moments of watching her walk towards him to receive the church's blessing on their marriage.

The church was packed on both sides, with people having to stand at the rear on either side of the font, but he saw only Sarah walking up the aisle on her father's arm, looking radiant and lovely in her simple ivory dress. He smiled at her and her answering smile made him catch his breath. He knew, without a vestige of doubt in his mind that this is what he had waited for since he was first a man and that moment and what lay ahead of them was more than worth the waiting. As Sarah came to him, she handed her small bouquet of cream roses to Lauren and stood beside him. He reached down to touch her fingers, feeling the ring she was wearing and, glancing down quickly, he was touched that she had chosen to wear her opal ring, rather than the more spectacular Falconbridge emerald.

The traditional service started and in a few minutes it was time to replace the wedding ring that Sarah had needed to remove temporarily, this time to stay on forever. As many other brides and grooms had done in the past, witnessed by the little church, they sealed their vows with a kiss.

After the usual formalities in the vestry, they emerged into the still-sunny day to find both sides of the path to the lych-gate were packed with people. While standing for the wedding photographs, Sarah noticed Foster in the front, looking slightly less comfortable in his best suit than he did in his riding breeches. He was holding a paper bag in his hand and either side of him, sitting ramrod straight, were Merlin and Tristram.

The photographer finished taking his pictures and Robert and Sarah had to stand for several moments longer while other people dodged this way and that, trying to take pictures of the wedding party without intruders and all getting in each other's way, but it was all very amicable. Finally, as everyone seemed satisfied with their shots, Foster removed something from the bag he was holding and gave it to Merlin to hold, repeating the action for Tristram. At a quiet word from him, both dogs moved swiftly and easily towards Robert and Sarah. Merlin stood in front of her holding a ribbon in his mouth from which hung a 'good luck' card in the shape of a silver horseshoe filled with orange blossom. Tristram waited patiently for his turn while Sarah took the horseshoe from Merlin's mouth, then presented her with his own card in the shape of a lucky sweep.

She spoke softly to the dogs and they returned to Foster, who gave a half-salute, half-wave and turned away with both dogs following him. She remarked in an undertone to Robert, 'There is another perfect example of an animal understanding by telepathy. The order Foster gave Tristram to deliver the card is not a regular instruction to which he is used, but he brought it straight to me, as Foster wanted him to do, instead of you. In the normal course of events, he would have delivered anything he had to you, as his master.'

'Yes,' Robert agreed, 'it was not a normal order like "sit" or "stay" that a dog would recognise and it is not as if Tristram belongs to Foster, but he is used to him and could understand him when Foster told him specifically to deliver the card to you. Just another instance of how a they can interpret human thought. Of course,' he added, 'they are rather exceptional dogs!'

Sarah laughed, 'Naturally – they are ours, aren't they?!'

They walked down the path and through the lych-gate to where Frazer was waiting in the Rolls to take them the few yards to the small hotel, The Heron's Nest where they had chosen to hold the reception. The little hotel was practically bursting at the seams but luckily they had an annex which was used to house the larger functions, where the huge bottom tier of the three-tiered wedding cake was placed, with wine and beer laid on, for all the village people who had not received a formal invitation card.

After the fiasco at the Hunt Ball two years previously, it was considered that, with the publicity concerning the wedding, it would not be wise to leave Heronshurst unguarded while the staff and all of the village were celebrating the wedding. Grayson had organised half a dozen men who were willing to patrol Heronshurst while all except Mrs Bates were away. She was a lot happier, not just for herself, but for the young baby who was in her charge. It would have been too tempting a target for all the villains around to think that it was completely empty.

For a small establishment, The Heron's Nest produced an excellent, extremely well-arranged buffet meal in the dining room for the invited guests. Speeches had been cut to the minimum and after the toast had been drunk, Robert and Sarah cut the cake, circulated among the guests, receiving their congratulations and best wishes, until it was finally time for them to leave.

Standing outside the small hotel, Sarah surveyed the sea of faces smiling at her until she located Lizzie and Charlotte standing together and tossed her bouquet of cream roses towards them. Being an inch taller, Charlotte managed to reach up and catch it, holding it close to her and smiling more broadly than ever. Sarah smiled in return, hoping that it did not cause any friction between the sisters. It was as well that the elder one caught the bouquet, she thought, and they were really very good friends, as well as being sisters.

Robert and Sarah drove back to Heronshurst to relax for a while before changing to go to London for dinner at their favourite restaurant to which they had invited Adrienne and George, both of whom would remain in London afterwards, returning to their own homes.

Lauren chose to stay at Heronshurst with the children, since Tom was not with her. Mrs Bates and the staff would take good care of them.

Robert and Sarah were quietly happy and perfectly willing to share the evening with their friends. They had the rest of their lives together and, if the legend were true, that was going to be a long time.

CHAPTER TWENTY-TWO

Robert and Sarah found it hard to believe that they were already celebrating their third Christmas together. Life had settled happily into a pleasant mixture of work and play and each day was especially precious to them, since they were rather more mature than most newly-weds.

Christmas that year was a happy, family occasion apart from the sad absence of Richard, and of Helene, who had chosen to stay in France. Tom was able to get home on leave and he, Lauren and the children came for Christmas and the New Year, as did Adrienne and George, providing all their favourite people to help them celebrate.

In May, Robert arranged the honeymoon that he had promised himself and Sarah and they went to Vevey as planned late in the month, staying at a little lakeside hotel in view of Chillon and the Dents du Midi, which they found much more congenial than the bigger, more impersonal hotels.

Robert was enchanted to find how much Sarah had broadened his outlook and perception of life, while at the same time, being completely at home and fitting perfectly into his sphere.

He smiled to himself sometimes, when he remembered how Sarah had agreed with him when he suggested that he expected a lot from a woman. That she should be efficient, glamorous and have charisma. How trebly lucky he was that Sarah was undoubtedly efficient and, when she chose, could look very glamorous, while possessing great charisma, of which her warmth and tenderness formed a large part combined with her complete lack of awareness of her own charm and to crown it all, she loved him enough to consent to be his wife.

They found the small hotel at which they spent their delayed honeymoon, charming and comfortable, with all the necessary facilities and the food was excellent without being too elaborate. The view from their room across the lake was idyllic and they could see Chillon and the Dents du Midi beyond Montreux.

One morning, soon after their arrival, Sarah was sitting up in bed, idly watching Robert heading for the bathroom, clad only in his pyjama trousers and she said conversationally, 'You know, you really are a magnificent looking creature. It would take a Michael Angelo to do justice to your physique.'

Robert turned at the door and studied her face for a moment, smiling. He tried to match his voice to her conversational level and asked, 'Are you, by any chance, trying to tempt me?'

Sarah returned his smile, 'I was merely making a passing comment, but if you choose to interpret it as being tempted, you are more than welcome.'

Robert walked back to the bed saying, 'I was going to shave, but to quote Oscar Wilde in *Lady Windermere's Fan*, "I can resist everything but temptation"!' and he joined her in bed, making her feel very glad that she had spoken.

It was quite some time later that he finally got his shave and Sarah marvelled for the hundredth time how so much happiness could depend on the small action of applying for a job, encouraged by a total stranger who wished her well and gave her back her self-confidence. So much had hinged on sheer chance – or was it? There was the accident of Robert's finding the sonnet that she had written originally for only her eyes to see – he could have borrowed any number of her reference books and he had chosen the Shakespeare. She had forgotten leaving it there after she wrote it, thinking only to put it away safely.

Sarah mentioned something of what she was thinking to Robert and he said lovingly, 'It was all part of Destiny's decree, my darling, working towards fulfilling the legend.'

'You really believe the legend yourself, don't you, darling?' Sarah asked.

'Of course, don't you?' Robert asked her. 'It did seem far-fetched to me and a figment of someone's vivid imagination when I first heard it repeated when I was very young. Then, as I got slightly older, I experienced fleeting glimpses of what some-how seemed to be another world, but they vanished in a second before I could pin them down and later, I felt as though I were waiting for something very special to happen. The years went by and as I got set in my life, whatever it was that I was expecting, didn't happen – until the day you walked into it. I realise now, that you were almost unaware of speaking about Estelle. The

185

portrait had triggered a memory in your subconscious and when you talked so knowledgeably about not being able to see the statues now the woods are thicker, I nearly dropped the paddle, which would have marooned us in the middle of the lake. If I hadn't already recognised you as the woman for whom I was waiting, that would have enlightened me.'

Sarah was amazed how well he understood the effect that her glimpses into the past had on her, but if he had had them, too, it was only to be expected.

'Too much has already fallen into place to think otherwise,' Robert said. 'What seems to be random chance is anything but an accidental happening.'

Sarah considered the legend for a while, but she did not mention her doubts on how it could be fulfilled, since she and Robert would not be able to have children. The child had to be a Falconbridge, so adoption was out of the question apart from the fact that, in law, an adopted child could not inherit Robert's title. It was difficult to see how it could work out even though, as Robert had said, so much had already fallen into place.

They spent several peaceful, happy and relaxing days walking, going to visit other places on the lake by boat, sightseeing and generally just enjoying being together, returning to England in time for Robbie's second birthday.

Ever since he was born, Richard and Sophie had been considering moving into the country rather than bringing him up in London. Robert had an idea that he put to them one weekend when they were discussing it on a visit to Heronshurst.

'The Dower House is empty, why don't you move into there? It would be ideal for Robbie, he can be brought up among all the people for whom he will be responsible one day, the new generation of staff that are growing up now.'

'That sounds a wonderful idea, Uncle Robert, are you sure that it would suit you?'

'Of course, it would ensure that the house doesn't deteriorate being empty and I would rather you were there than a stranger. It will be quite simple for you to commute to London by train, the service is good, instead of having to sit as long as you do now in a traffic jam, trying to get to your office and arriving feeling stressed before you start. I will get Grayson to inspect the house and you and Sophie can spend a weekend or two here deciding how you want it redecorated and Sarah and I can keep an eye on it while it is being done.'

186

'That is very kind of you, Uncle Robert. How can we refuse such a generous offer. It would certainly solve the problem of deciding where we want to live. Then we would have to find a suitable place. The Dower House is ideal from all points of view – it is charming, in lovely surroundings and, as you say, Robbie will grow up among the people for whom he will one day be responsible. It is not something I have ever considered before and I hope it is many years before he needs to accept that responsibility. I would like to think that we will see you open the telegram from the Queen on your hundredth birthday at least.'

Robert laughed, 'It's a nice thought. We will be well into the next century by then.'

By the middle of July, Richard and Sophie's town house had been sold. Robert and Sarah had been supervising the redecoration of the Dower House and it was finished just in time for the young couple to move in after vacating their old home. Sophie was much happier when they went out for the evening and could leave Robbie with Sarah, who had suggested that they could leave him overnight with her and Robert so that they need not worry about what time they returned. It was very reassuring to Sophie to know that he was in Sarah's care, Robbie adored Sarah, as most children did, and he found it fun to stay in 'the big house' while Mummie and Daddy went 'out to play', knowing that they would come and fetch him or Sarah would take him over the following day.

When Robert had first made Patrick's acquaintance, he had been fascinated to find how self-reliant and what intelligent company a four-year-old could be. He had never had anything to do with very young children since he and his brother were small. Robbie was already developing in a very similar manner to Patrick, although they were not related. It augured well for the future of Heronshurst.

Patrick was now seven, but still very easy-going and on family occasions, when the children got together, he was very patient with Robbie, building models for him, which Robbie usually immediately dismantled again.

Alexandra, too, enjoyed Robbie as a playmate, although she was not as patient as Patrick and Estelle, who was a roly-poly nine months old, sometimes objected to anyone else monopolising her big brother.

Seeing them together, Robert frequently thought they looked like one family.

September came and Robert and Sarah were already celebrating the first anniversary of their civil wedding and again in October for their church wedding. As Robert said, 'It was not everyone who has two anniversaries a year!'

In late November, Richard and Sophie wanted to visit friends in Oxford for a few days' pre-Christmas celebrations as they would be staying at Heronshurst for the festivities and they decided that Robbie would probably be happier with Sarah and Robert than in a strange house with people he didn't know.

On the day they were due home, the telephone rang in the late afternoon and Bates took the call. His voice sounded unusually solemn to Sarah as he informed Robert that someone wanted to speak to him and her stomach seemed to turn over. Sarah watched Robert's face change to an expression of profound shock and her heart sank. She waited in fear and trepidation while Robert said, 'Yes, yes, of course, I'll come at once.'

He replaced the telephone and walked across to Sarah, taking her in his arms and saying as gently as he could, 'That was the hospital in Oxford. Some drunken lunatic driving on the wrong side of the road has hit Richard and Sophie's car head-on. Richard was killed outright and Sophie died on the way to hospital. I shall have to go there at once, they need formal identification.'

'Oh, Robert!' She put her arms round him. He held her closer, resting his cheek against her hair. 'First Richard and now young Richard, I'm so sorry.' Sarah couldn't think of anything to say that would comfort Robert and she felt devastated for the young couple cut off from life so soon and the lovely little boy, so suddenly bereft of parents and for Helene who, not so long ago had lost her beloved husband and now her son and for Robert who had so few of his own family. She even felt a pang on her own account, as she had become very fond of them and considered them her family, too.

'Shall I come with you, Robert?' she asked.

'No, my darling, you stay with Robbie – he is all alone now. Somehow we are going to have to tell him that his mummy and daddy are never coming back. I am needed for identification purposes. Come up with me while I change into something more suitable. Where is Robbie now? Is he still having his afternoon nap?'

'Yes,' replied Sarah, 'Charlotte is standing by for when he

wakes up. I will ask her to keep him occupied until you get back home.'

'I must telephone Helene. It is a good thing she is with her family. After all the traumas she went through during the war and the worry on Richard's behalf and losing him so early in life two years ago, she has had more than her fair share of sorrow. It must be much more devastating to lose a child than a parent later in life. One expects to outlive one's parents, but not one's children.'

Sarah was moved by his perception, especially as he had no children of his own.

Robert checked his appearance quickly in the mirror and taking Sarah in his arms, he kissed her tenderly, saying, 'I will be back as soon as I can, then we must tell Robbie, as he is expecting to see them later today. Take care of yourself and try not to grieve too much.'

'You take good care of yourself, too, Robert,' Sarah replied, thinking that Richard had been a very good and careful driver. 'I will wait until you return.'

After Richard had left, Sarah was left alone with her thoughts. Oh, Robbie, I know so well what it is like. I was your age when I was told that my mother was not coming back and I can still feel that sense of loss even now.

It was the longest afternoon that Sarah ever remembered since she had been at Heronshurst. Her impulse was to run up to the nursery and hug Robbie to her in an effort to shield him from the hurt that life had dealt him, but she was aware that her own grief and anxiety would convey itself to him and it was better to leave him with Charlotte until Robert returned home. That, at least, was something that figured regularly in Robbie's routine when he was staying with them, before Sarah and Robert went upstairs to fetch him down.

Sarah would have liked to go for a long walk with Merlin but the idea was impossible, apart from the fact that Robert might need to get in touch with her before he was able to get home, Robbie might get fretful with a young child's ability to sense trouble and Charlotte be unable to pacify him, in which case she would need Sarah there.

The long hours dragged slowly by and Robert returned looking devastated. It had been a harrowing experience and having to tell Helene, as well, had been horrendous for him.

'She was so brave,' he told Sarah, 'and asked if we could take care of Robbie at least for the present until she can get over here and decide what arrangements will be best to make for him. I told her he was welcome to stay with us for as long as it was needed, forever, if necessary. She seemed very relieved and grateful and said we could discuss it when she comes over for the funeral. Is that all right with you, darling?'

'Of course, Robert, you know you don't need to ask. I wonder if Helene will want to take him back to France with her?'

'Legally she is entitled to do so, Sophie's parents are too old to cope with a young child. Sophie was born late in life to them and her mother is not at all well. But Helene has not seen much of Robbie and although he might appear to be a replacement for Richard, I think she may feel he is better off with people to whom he is accustomed.'

'Oh, Robert! I do hope so. Apart from how we feel about him, it really would be better for him to be brought up with his inheritance, as Richard and Sophie had planned, wouldn't it?'

'Yes, my darling, it certainly would and, hopefully, that is how Helene will see it. Now we must break the news to Robbie that his mummy and daddy are not coming home after all.'

It was very difficult for Robert and Sarah to keep a calm, reassuring demeanour when Robbie looked up at them with his remarkable Falconbridge eyes and asked, 'But why can't Mummy and Daddy come home?'

Robert lifted him on to his knee and said very gently, 'They wanted to come back to you very much and they would have done if they possibly could, they loved you very much, but they had to go and live with God.'

'Like Grandpa did?' Robbie asked.

'Yes, Robbie, just like Grandpa,' Robert answered, wanting to weep for the small boy in his arms. He was trying to anticipate Robbie's next question so that he could have a ready answer, when Robbie said, 'I expect Grandpa was lonely. You won't go away to be with him, too, will you?'

'No, Robbie, we don't have any plans to go away, we want to stay here and watch you grow up at Heronshurst.'

Robbie looked thoughtful, trying to absorb the change in his young life. 'Will Patrick and Alexandra and Estelle be here, too?'

'Not all of the time, Robbie, as they live quite a long way away, but certainly for as long as possible in the school holidays.'

'Oh, yes, they have to go to school, don't they? And I will have to go to school at the same time soon, won't I?'

'Yes, Robbie, in a year or two you will start school.'

Robbie looked round for Sarah and held his arms out to her, 'You will look after me, like you always do when Mummy and Daddy are away, won't you?'

Sarah moved over to where they were sitting and knelt beside Robert so that she could hug Robbie and said as steadily as she could manage over the top of his head, with silent tears streaming down her face, 'Yes, darling, of course we will take care of you like we always do.'

Robert and Sarah hoped that they would never have to live through days like those again. Robert made all the necessary arrangements for Helene and when she came over to see Richard and Sophie laid to rest together, they had a long discussion about Robbie's future.

Helene had typical French practicality and being aware that she had not seen much of Robbie since his birth, she realised that his best place was at Heronshurst with Robert and Sarah, especially since he was now Robert's heir and it would be an advantage all round, as Sarah had said, for him to grow up among the people for whom he would one day be responsible. Another consideration was the fact that now, sadly, he would never have any brothers or sisters and it would help him to adjust to his loss if he were to be close to Patrick, Alexandra and Estelle, whom he patently adored.

Robert made the point as tactfully as he could that he would be totally financially responsible and Helene gracefully accepted, knowing that it would not be a burden on Robert and Robbie would be in good and loving hands. She also agreed, if the law allowed, for Robert and Sarah to adopt Robbie legally.

With the emotional resilience of the very young, Robbie settled in permanently at Heronshurst and Robert and Sarah aimed to spend as much time as possible with him in the early days of his bereavement. Tom and Lauren brought the children to stay for Patrick's birthday, a week before Christmas. They remained until after the New Year so that Robbie would have as happy a time as possible.

The New Year started bright and sunny, though cool and crisp, gradually warming up to a pleasant spring and turning to an unusually hot summer. For Robbie's third birthday, Robert bought him a pony and Sarah took him to be fitted with his riding outfit. He was absolutely ecstatic and once on the pony, it was difficult to persuade him to come in for meals. While he was at home all day, he often joined Sarah or both her and Robert on their rides round the farms and became a great favourite with the families, enjoying the company of their children and seeing their pets while the adults talked.

Watching Robbie at times with Patrick, Robert often thought how like brothers they were and was glad for Robbie's sake. They both had the same devastating honesty, sometimes being more truthful than polite – especially to Alexandra. Both Robert and Sarah hoped that he would learn to temper truth with tact as he got older.

From the first, Robert wanted to arrange to adopt Robbie legally and he was somewhat abashed when he was told that normally he would be considered too old. Circumstances were in their favour – both he and Sarah were in superb health and Robbie had been left permanently in their care by his legal guardian and next of kin and they could see no real reason to refuse their application. It was irrelevant that an adopted child could not inherit the title, as Robbie was already the natural heir, being the next in line.

The authorities responsible for making the decisions always bore the welfare of the child in mind and were very careful not to make a hasty judgement. It seemed a long time to wait for Robert and Sarah and there was a certain amount of discussion regarding the necessity to adopt in the circumstances, but with the consent and approval of both grandparents, no other objection was raised.

After attending the High Court hearings and holding their breath, Robert and Sarah were granted an adoption order and acquired a son of their own to nurture and cherish for Heronshurst. As Robert had said previously when discussing the legend with Sarah on their honeymoon after she had asked him if he believed in it, 'Too much has fallen into place already to think otherwise,' and Fate had added another link in the chain of events that the legend foretold.

CHAPTER TWENTY-THREE

A Son for Heronshurst

For some time Robbie found it difficult to adjust to the fact that his mummy and daddy were not coming back and sometimes gave the impression that he thought he was just staying at Heronshurst on a visit and that they would soon come and fetch him. But gradually the present took over and by the time that Robert and Sarah were in a position to explain to him, very gently, that they had adopted him and he was now their little boy, he had looked at them with a wisdom far beyond his three years and said, 'So you are my mummy and daddy now?' His expression was so serious that it was difficult for Robert and Sarah to assess if he were glad or sorry about the arrangement.

Sarah said, 'Yes, darling, we are your mummy and daddy now.'

Robbie climbed onto Robert's knee and looked gravely into his eyes, 'Are you pleased about it?' he asked anxiously.

'Yes, Robbie, we are very pleased and happy about it.'

Sarah looked at the two pairs of eyes regarding each other and was struck anew by the strange quirk of heredity that had given Robbie those wonderful green and gold flecked hazel eyes that she had loved in Robert, when Richard's eyes had been brown. They, as much as anything, proclaimed their kinship and with Robert looking so incredibly young for his fifty-six years, any stranger would automatically assume that they were father and son.

Robert looked up and caught the expression on Sarah's face which made him feel that he was the luckiest man on earth. He smiled at her, his eyes full of love and looked back down at Robbie, waiting for his next question and hoping that he could answer it satisfactorily. But with a child's practicality and swift change of thought he brought them back to more mundane matters. 'I'm hungry,' he announced, 'is it teatime yet?'

As the days passed, Sarah sensed that Robbie was feeling more of a permanent feature of Heronshurst and their lives. She tried as far as possible to keep to a regular routine to engender a feeling of security in him that must have been severely shattered with the tragedy of losing both his parents together, especially being so young.

The household had taken him to its heart completely, partly out of sympathy for an orphaned child, but mainly for his charm and friendliness. Lizzie and Charlotte especially adored him and would find any excuse to do things for him.

Several days later at breakfast, Sarah asked Robbie if he had had enough to eat.

'Yes, thank you, Mummy,' he replied, making it sound as natural as if he had always used that name for her. Sarah wanted to jump up and hug him, especially when he continued, 'Are we going riding this morning, Daddy?'

'Yes, Robbie, we are going riding,' Robert replied and to Sarah his voice sounded a paean of gladness.

They exchanged delighted glances, each knowing that the other was sharing the joy and relief that a small boy had accepted them as parents and seemed very happy and content with the situation. At least that problem had been solved.

Sarah had thought after her marriage to Robert that she could not be any happier but she felt she had reached the pinnacle of content, having achieved the apparently impossible and acquired a son. She loved Robbie as much as if she had given birth to him but she was more glad for Robert than herself that he had not, after all, been deprived of one. There were times when she shed a silent tear and said a prayer for Richard and Sophie in gratitude for her happiness and vowed to herself that she would try to make as good a life for Robbie as they would have done. He was, after all, Robert's flesh and blood and that was a major part of the miracle.

When Robbie was four years old, Robert and Sarah sent him to nursery school. He had already experienced mixing with other children while having Patrick, Alexandra and Estelle frequently staying with him, but they considered it would be a good idea to acclimatise him for full-time school later on.

Having had such a drastic change in his young life already, rather than send him to a prep. school, Robert and Sarah decided to send him to the village school, where Mrs Grayson was still headmistress and he could come home each day. Robert considered it would be an advantage to grow up with the people with whom he would spend most of his life. He himself had been sent away to prep. school and had not particularly enjoyed it although he had accepted the situation, but he hadn't had his world torn apart before he was three.

Robert had recently converted to using computers to facilitate the keeping of records and make the work of administration easier generally. He started to teach Robbie how they worked and was amazed how quickly and easily he assimilated the knowledge and bought him one of his own for his seventh birthday, which Robbie used both for his schoolwork and for recreation.

The following month, July, Robert had his sixtieth birthday. He looked at himself rather more closely than usual when he was shaving, wondering if he appeared to be any different from the day when Sarah walked into his life nearly eight years ago and decided that, if he had changed, there was nothing he could do about it now and carried on, dressing with a little more care than usual out of deference to Sarah, who always made a special occasion of birthdays.

He walked into the bedroom, where Sarah was sitting in front of her dressing-table brushing her hair and he bent down to kiss her neck.

She looked at him in the mirror, smiled, then rose and went into his arms, saying, 'You are looking particularly handsome this morning, birthday boy.'

He held her closely, wondering if it was possible to love her any more than he did at that moment.

Sarah reached into a drawer of her dressing-table and took out a beautifully wrapped package which Robert unwrapped at once. He opened the box it contained and exclaimed, 'Sarah, it is beautiful! Did you design it yourself?'

'Yes, I did. They have interpreted it rather well, haven't they?' It was a paperweight, sculptured in silver, of old Neptune by the stream. Somehow the artist had managed to convey its age, in spite of the new sheen of the silver. Robert's memory went straight back to the first time he took Sarah on the lake. The accompanying card read: 'When you look eye to eye with Neptune, you will see how much I love you.'

Robert noticed that the eyes were made of crystal and he held the figure to his face, looking through one of the eyes. 'Sarah, it is incredible! I can read every word.'

At the back of the eye, every word clearly visible by the magnification of the crystal, was the sonnet that Sarah had written about him, not realising at the time that he would ever see it, and which had been the means of bringing them back together again, clearing up all misunderstanding.

'It is unbelievable,' Robert said, 'What artistry and workmanship! Thank you, my darling, when I am bored working at my desk, I shall just pick it up and read it.' He took a long time thanking her properly, which made them rather later than usual for breakfast.

While there was still plenty of daylight left after school hours, Sarah and Robbie liked to meet and go home through the woods, accompanied by Merlin and, occasionally, Tristram if Robert thought he needed the exercise. Sarah made a point of not waiting at the school gate as she thought Robbie probably considered he was too big to be met, so they had their special rendezvous in a little shop-cum-café where they would have an ice-cream.

Sarah really enjoyed being able to show Robbie all the woodland creatures and he especially delighted in watching the squirrels, sometimes persuading them to feed from his hand, as Sarah did. One day when they were walking back from his school, he said, 'I have to learn a poem for English. Which one can I learn that no one else is likely to recite?'

'Lauren was in that position once when she was about your age at school,' Sarah told him, 'and I wrote one especially for her. It is about a squirrel, would you like to learn that one?'

'Oh, yes! Mummy, that would be super. No one else will be able to say it.' Robbie was delighted with the idea.

'As soon as we get home, I will write it out for you,' Sarah promised him.

'Can you remember it to say now while we are walking home, please?'

'Yes, of course,' and Sarah recited the poem that she had written especially for Lauren, going back to the time when she was seven.

THE SQUIRREL

Two bright eyes in the thicket there
And a whisk of silvery tail,
Where a busy squirrel takes good care
His food supply won't fail.

Rustling leaves and a cracking stick
Betray his busy feet,
Search – and he's gone with tail aflick
And movement swift and neat.

To bury all his hard-won hoard
In one place, he's too wise.
No pirate's treasure better stored
Away from prying eyes.

'Oh, Mummy, that's great!' Robbie enthused with the current schoolboy vernacular.

As soon as they arrived home, Robbie went rushing to Robert saying, 'Daddy, Mummy is going to give me one of her poems to say at school. She wrote it for Lauren when she was my age – no one else will know it.'

'That's fine, Robbie. Mummy writes very special poems for special people,' Robert answered, smiling at Sarah over the top of Robbie's head and she knew he was thinking about his sonnet and gave him a warm smile in return.

Robbie enjoyed school, he worked hard and he played hard and was popular with his schoolmates, not just because his father was the local landowner, rather in spite of it. He had fleeting recollections at times of his young parents, but they did not trouble him, being more like the passing memory of a dream on waking. If he ever thought about Robert being older than the average father, he dismissed it as something not worth even bothering about, since Robert could keep up with any of them in physical prowess and was a lot more understanding than some of his friends claimed their fathers to be.

When it came time to move on from the village school, Robert expected that he would go to public school as he knew that Richard had entered his name at birth, so he was astounded when Robbie announced that he wanted to go to the County Senior School, where many of his friends were going.

197

Robert tried to understand how Robbie felt. Being in the RAF and later, Intelligence, had widened his own circle considerably and he knew one could be great friends with people whom, in other circumstances, one would never have met. Times had changed a great deal in the aftermath of the war and continued to change.

He tried to imagine what Richard would have said, if his son had faced him with the problem of his unexpected opposition to going to the school where he and Robert had been sent, that had been a Falconbridge tradition for generations and he felt he had probably precipitated the dilemma by sending Robbie to the village school, instead of prep. school. At the time, he had been unwilling for Robbie to have to make yet another major adjustment so soon in his young life and he wondered, too, if he were not subconsciously pandering to his own and Sarah's desire to keep the boy as part of their everyday existence, having acquired a son so late in life.

Robbie's voice broke in on his thoughts, unaware that their minds were running on similar lines. 'You would like me to be at home every day, wouldn't you, Mother?' he asked.

'Yes, of course I would, darling, and so would your father, but that is not the real issue, is it? You will inherit great responsibilities when you are older and, in this instance, I would not dream of contradicting his decision. After all,' Sarah added, trying to lighten the atmosphere, 'I did not go to Public School so I am in no position to judge.'

Robert shot her a grateful glance. Sarah, of all people, was aware of hereditary responsibilities over generations and yet could blend readily into any environment. He considered her remark, 'I did not go to Public School.' He and Richard had. Were they particularly happy there and, more importantly, did they cope with life any the better for it?

He looked at his son, bequeathed to him by the untimely deaths of both Richard and young Richard. Robbie stood tall and straight, already possessing great self-confidence and a passionate love and concern for Heronshurst, its people and their welfare. He would be a more than worthy successor, wherever he went to school, it was bred in him and he would not fail.

'Very well, Robert,' Robert senior said at last, acknowledging, by calling him by his full name, that his son was a person in his own right and old enough to make his own judgements. 'I will not stand in your way, but I trust you will continue to work hard and, at least try for university.'

198

'Thanks, Dad. I won't let you down,' Robbie answered, unashamedly hugging his father. Robert and Sarah regarded each other over their son's head, both of them feeling immeasurably proud of him. They were secretly relieved that he would be with them daily for at least another six or seven years, all being well, and that time would be so very precious.

When Robert and Sarah were in their own room later, he took her in his arms and held her closely, wondering as he had a thousand times, how he could be so lucky. 'I love you more today than I did yesterday, but less than I will tomorrow,' he told her, kissing her with all the passion he had felt when they were first married.

'You have a wonderful way of expressing yourself and I love you more than I thought possible,' Sarah answered, wondering how she could have decided that she did not want ever to fall in love again all those years ago, when she was too young to know any better. How earnest one was at seventeen, there were no half measures, everything was so black and white and intensely dramatic. It was a painful experience growing up and learning to make compromises, it really was true, in some cases, that love was wasted on the young, although looking at the young people in her circle, they did seem to be a lot wiser and more certain of their goal in life. Perhaps we were too sheltered, Sarah thought, until we were pitchforked into a major war which threw our whole lives out of balance at an age when youngsters these days enjoy complete freedom to do what they want and go where they will. At all events, life now was as wonderful as she had ever hoped it would be and she was eternally grateful to her stars.

Whenever she felt remotely depressed about the past and the wasted years, she remembered Adrienne's words in those early days of their friendship and what Robert had reiterated later, 'It had to happen that way to bring you to Heronshurst.' Now here she was with a handsome husband whom she loved more than life itself, who loved her and entrusted with a handsome and lovable son to rear.

'You are looking very solemn, my darling,' Robert's voice broke into her thoughts, 'Is the weight of your responsibilities as a wife and mother weighing heavily on you?'

Sarah laughed, as he had intended she should and said lightly, 'No, I was just counting my blessings.'

'I hope I figured among them,' Robert said, semi-seriously.

'Oh, you did!' she assured him, 'you were right at the top of the list.'

Robert held her closer, 'We have been married nearly nine years and I still cannot believe my luck,' he told Sarah.

It was not just his friends at Heronsbury that Robbie was reluctant to leave by going away to Public School. It would also mean that he would see less of Patrick, Alexandra and Estelle at weekends when they often exchanged visits. They always felt as close to Robbie as if they were his brother and sisters which more than made up for the fact that he would never have any of his own.

Alexandra was two years older than he and treated him with a mixture of affection and imperiousness that she felt was warranted by virtue of her advantage in age and being a girl. She was happiest on horse-back and they often went for long rides together when she was at her most relaxed and charming and with no one else around, they settled into a comfortable comradeship.

She had always been a beauty, even at an age when most children go through a plain stage, but one of her most endearing characteristics was that she was the only person he knew who did not think she was attractive, even after the Mayor and Corporation of her home town had chosen her to reign as Carnival Maid for a year when she was only twelve years old.

Sarah sometimes remembered what her father had told her that the people in her mother's village had said about her family. 'Their greatest charm was that they were completely unaware of it,' and she often thought that Alexandra had inherited that quality in full measure.

CHAPTER TWENTY-FOUR

In accordance with their earlier plans, Robert and Sarah sent Tristram to stud and for Robbie's tenth birthday, they let him have his choice from the litter.

As they had done with Merlin and Tristram, Robbie chose the puppy that left the litter to go to him. But there the physical similarity ended. Although the new puppy proved to have inherited the intelligence and superb temperament of the other two he had quite different colouring and would be easy to distinguish when he grew as big as the others. He had a lot more gold around his neck and chest and where the others were so dark as to be nearly black, he was a much lighter brown.

Robbie called him 'Maximus', because he said he 'was the greatest', Max for short, and the dog was already a year old by the time that Robbie left the village school and was preparing to go to Senior School in the autumn after the summer holidays.

It was around that time that Sarah awoke very early one morning feeling completely sad and bereft. She knew long before the telephone call arrived from South Africa that her beloved father had died. He was ninety-two and he passed away very peacefully in his sleep. Robert wanted to accompany her to Cape Town for his funeral but Sarah thought it was unwise for both of them to make the visit together. It was very unlikely that any- thing would go amiss, flying was the safest transport in the world, but she did not want to take the chance and leave Robbie alone in England, putting six thousand miles between him and both his parents, even though he would be well cared for by the staff.

Her elder sister was taking care of the formalities and she stayed only long enough for the service. Her family had chosen to have the poem read at the service that she wrote for her father, to tell him how much she appreciated his love and care after their mother died and expressing her love and gratitude to him. Her flight there and back was uneventful as it happened and she remembered little of the journey after she returned, only being aware that she would never see her father again.

It was only a few days later that she again awoke to the feeling that something was amiss and like a person sleepwalking, she got out of bed and hastily dressed. The clock showed six-thirty and Robert was so peacefully asleep she hadn't the heart to wake him but, almost without volition, she hurried down to the stables.

Foster heard her footsteps and came to meet her. 'Oh, my lady, I am so glad you're here. I did not want to disturb you so early but I thought you ought to know that Merlin has had a seizure of some sort. He is in their quarters.'

Sarah ran in and found Merlin lying on his side. She bent over him, and laying a gentle hand on his head, she asked, 'What is the matter, boy?'

He lifted his head with a great effort and looked at her with all the affection he felt for her in his eyes, gave a little sigh, lay down his head again and went to sleep for ever.

Sarah thought she would choke on her tears. Her lovely, handsome Merlin, her constant companion from her first day at Heronshurst, her rescuer from the armed thief, would no more roam the fields and woods with her or welcome her back when she returned home. He was fifteen years old and it was inevitable but it was still hard to bear and he had seemed so young still.

'My Lady,' Foster's voice penetrated her misery and she looked up.

He wished he could do something to take that sorrowful look from her face. 'My Lady, I will take care of him now, there is nothing you can do, he had a wonderful life.'

Sarah tried to pull herself together, Foster was right, Merlin had had a wonderful life and his presence would always remain with her and he lived on in Tristram and Max.

'Thank you, Foster. I had better go back to the house. His Lordship will wonder where I have gone.'

A soft, warm muzzle pressed against her face as Tristram tried to comfort her. She hugged his head against hers as she had done once with Merlin when she was unhappy and he had tried to convey his sympathy.

She stood up and he followed her as she walked dejectedly into the house and he stayed at the foot of the stairs as she went up to her and Robert's suite.

Robert was just waking and seeing her already dressed, he looked surprised, then he saw her face. 'What is it, my darling? What has happened?'

'Merlin has died. I think he just came to the end of a long and happy life,' Sarah said as steadily as she could manage.

Robert leaped out of bed and caught her in his arms. 'Oh, my darling, I am so sorry. I know how much you loved him.'

Sarah struggled for composure but broke down and wept in Robert's arms. Finally she managed to regain her equanimity and said, 'Thank you, darling, you are such a comfort. I had better go and shower and get properly dressed.'

She wandered into her bathroom, thinking, it is strange, I did not cry that much for my father, it went too deep for tears and I cannot believe he is not still on earth, but sometimes when I am quiet, he is closer to me here than he was when he was alive in South Africa and she remembered the times when she had felt that if she turned her head, he would be standing there.

After Robbie started school, Sarah and Max kept each other company. They walked the woods and fields together as she had done with Merlin and though it was said that animals have no soul she felt that his spirit walked with them.

Robbie had insisted on travelling independently and the Senior School bus picked him up every morning by the gates at the end of the drive after coming from the village with all his friends that he had known in Junior School.

Sarah always knew the moment the bus was approaching their gates at the close of the school day. Max would suddenly streak down the drive to meet Robbie and walk back with him, bouncing up and down beside him in an effort to express his pleasure at Robbie's return.

When Robbie was sixteen he went along to Robert's study and tapped on the door. Robert knew at once by his expression that he had something serious on his mind, but he only said, 'Hallo, son, sit down,' and waited for Robbie to speak.

After a while he said, 'Patrick, Alexandra and Estelle have always been close and are like my brother and sisters, but we are not actually related are we?'

'No, Robbie, Lauren was Mummy's daughter by a previous marriage, so you are not related.'

There was a long silence, eventually broken by Robbie.

'Alexandra is going away to Art School and I want to ask her if she will keep in touch with me by writing when I go up to university. I was fairly sure that although they are family, we are not actually related, but I wanted to be certain.'

Robert was being very careful not to tread on Robbie's young dreams, so he only said, 'I am sure she will be only too glad to keep in touch, Robbie. The two of you have always had a great rapport.'

Robbie suddenly looked very happy. 'Do you really think so, Father?'

'Yes, I do, Robbie,' Robert replied, 'and there is no reason why it should not continue all through your lives.'

'Thank you, Father. I hope I did not interrupt your work?'

'No, son, nothing is important enough to take precedence over talking to you or your mother. I am always available if you need to discuss anything.'

'Thank you, again. I will see you later,' and Robbie left the room, looking a lot happier than when he entered it.

After he had gone, Robert looked thoughtful. So that is the way the wind is blowing. It is early days yet but if what I am supposing, should happen, nothing would make me happier.

Alexandra, who had always been especially close to Sarah, had been discussing her future with her, too. Since she had been in her early teens, she had often spent some of her school holidays in London with Adrienne, going with her to the various establishments which she owned and subconsciously absorbing a great deal of knowledge of the aims and methods of administration of the company. Alexandra had never lost her childhood affection for 'Drenny', as she sometimes still called her, and if anything they were closer than ever. While being careful never to poach on Lauren or Sarah's preserves, Adrienne enjoyed having Alexandra around, feeling that she compensated a little for not having had a daughter of her own. As Robert had informed Sarah many years before, she greatly regretted never having had any children and ever since she had lost her heart to the lovely little toddler, Alexandra had gone a long way to filling the void in her life.

It was an especial joy to her that Alexandra was obviously so artistically gifted and passionately interested in interior design and it often occurred to her that she could do a lot worse than groom Alexandra to be her successor when the time came, providing she was agreeable. She also wondered whether her own daughter, if she had been lucky enough to have one, would necessarily have taken after her and understood the business as well as Alexandra or whether, by a quirk of heredity, she would have been completely alien to it. Adrienne was eternally grateful to Lauren and Sarah that neither of them resented her 'borrowing' Alexandra. They were both only too well aware that love engenders more love and by giving it to one person did not mean that it had to be taken from another.

Alexandra adored London and was thoroughly happy in the high-pressure atmosphere of Adrienne's business. She had inherited Sarah's artistic ability in full measure and wanted to go straight to Art School at eighteen, rather than pursuing an academic life at university and she felt herself to be very fortunate to have been accepted by a very prestigious School of Art.

As Robert had predicted to Robbie, Alexandra was only too happy to keep up a correspondence with Robbie. He had done very well with his O levels and worked hard to obtain at least three A levels at a good grade for entrance to university and he chose Oxford as being the most conveniently situated to Heronshurst.

Four months before he was due to go up, Robbie celebrated his eighteenth birthday when Sarah and Robert organised a coming-of-age party for him. It was the first time for a long while that he and Alexandra had been able to get together again and, after the first slight constraint when Robbie's breath was almost taken away by her sheer beauty and she was jolted out of her usual sophisticated self-confidence by finding that the good-looking young friend of earlier days was now a devastatingly handsome young man who towered over her 5' 9", they found that they had not lost their easy camaraderie. The two years age difference no longer seemed of any significance and his height made him appear to be the elder.

There were moments when they both had instants of self-doubt. Alexandra, who was completely unaware of the effect of her beauty, combined with considerable charisma, on Robbie, thought that there must be hundreds of girls ready to prostrate themselves at his feet, not only for his undoubted charm but because of his potential title. Robbie, who subconsciously compared every other girl to Alexandra to their detriment, had never really been aware of their presence in his young life and could not believe that she would choose him, when there were so many older and more worldly-wise men just longing to claim her as their wife.

Alexandra was disconcerted to find that it was impossible to treat Robbie with the same imperious casualness that she used to employ when they were young and with which she treated other men, while Robbie found that just the sight of her lovely face left him tongue-tied and breathless.

Robert and Sarah looked on with affectionate amusement and awaited developments. On comparing notes very privately and confidentially, Robert mentioned that Robbie had remarked, 'Alexandra must be a lot like Mother was at her age, they have the same charismatic charm.' Sarah divulged Alexandra's remark, 'Robbie must be a lot like Uncle Robert when he was young, they are both so charming and considerate and have the same fantastic eyes.'

'Robert, would you object if they were serious about each other and wanted to marry?' Sarah asked him one day.

'I would be delighted,' Robert replied, 'Robbie is right, Alexandra is a lot like you and if she makes him half as happy as you have made me, I could not ask for more on his behalf.'

Sarah showed her appreciation of the compliment in a way that completely put an end to any further discussion on the subject for quite a long while.

Just under ten months after Robbie's coming-of-age, Alexandra had her twenty-first birthday and although, like many other young people, she had celebrated her coming-of-age at eighteen, like them, she still attached as much importance to being twenty-one as the older generation had done. There was still a faintly magical air about being twenty-one.

To the world at large, Alexandra was still footloose and fancy free and continued to correspond with Robbie regularly, but each time a letter arrived he dreaded opening it to read that she had become engaged to be married.

They both wrote casual, newsy uncommittal letters to each other and Alexandra wondered each time she received one whether a fellow student might have captured his heart, after all, the girls there had the advantage of propinquity, while she saw him but rarely on an occasional weekend when they both happened to be at Heronshurst.

By the time Robbie was twenty-one, he had attained his B.Sc. with honours and was able to acquire an extra ticket for Alexandra to attend his graduation with his parents.

They were naturally all very proud of him and he looked handsomer than ever in the sombre black cap and gown relieved only by the touch of light blue and white on the hood, but Alexandra was slightly disconcerted by the number of attractive young female graduates who swarmed around him. They completely ignored her and she found herself wanting to scream at them, 'Keep your hands off him, he belongs to me.' The thought confused her more than ever – to be fair to Robbie, he had never in any of his dealings with her, given her any cause to think that they were anything more than very good friends – and they had been brought up almost like brother and sister. In fact there were times when he was positively off-hand with her.

With the intuition that existed between them, Sarah could feel her distress. She considered that, because of their very similar colouring, the girls probably thought that she was his sister and mentioned this casually to Alexandra in the hope that it would pacify her.

Eventually they managed to get away and return to Heronshurst, where Mrs Briggs had excelled herself producing a superb meal in honour of Robbie's graduation. It was a merry occasion and now that Alexandra had Robbie to herself, her naturally buoyant and wickedly witty sense of humour came uppermost. Sarah noticed that, for the most part, Robbie was content to sit and gaze at her, relaxed and contented now he was at the end of his university life, with a fairly decent result.

The meal had been magnificent, Sarah thought, and wondered how much longer they could count on Mrs Briggs as a cook. She was turned sixty years old and many women retired at that age, though, thankfully, she seemed very happy at the moment to carry on. She still enjoyed cooking, even after all the years she had been doing it and sometimes gave the impression that she would be lost without a family to cook for. She had been a widow for years, had very comfortable accommodation in the staff quarters and belonged to various organisations in the village with many friends. Mr and Mrs Bates were in much the same position. Nothing lasted forever and Heronshurst would seem very strange without them. It occurred to Sarah that Charlotte or Lizzie might like to take over from their mother as housekeeper. They were now forty and thirty-eight respectively and had been well-trained by their mother. Charlotte's daughter, Emma, was about the same age as her mother had been when she first came to Sarah as her maid and if she did not want to pursue another career, it was possible she might like to take over from her mother if Charlotte became housekeeper. Oh, well! Time would tell and it was frightening how quickly it passed.

Robert's voice broke into her thoughts, 'You are looking very serious, my darling. Is anything worrying you?'

Sarah smiled, 'I was just feeling the passage of time – it goes so fast one can almost feel the breeze as it passes,' she said lightly.

Robert laughed. 'I know how you feel, it seems only yesterday that this handsome young couple here were only babies.'

Robbie raised his wine glass, 'This baby would like to propose a toast of thanks to his revered parents for all their love, care and understanding.'

Alexandra repeated, 'For all your love, care and understanding,' and the two young people clinked glasses and drank to Sarah and Robert.

Robert raised his glass and said, 'Thank you, we are very proud of you and here's to your long and successful future.'

Tonight is yet another milestone, Sarah thought, it is already 1994. I wonder what will have happened by the turn of the century apart from, hopefully, our Silver Wedding.

Robert said as they prepared to leave the dining table, 'It is still a lovely evening, if you young people want to enjoy it, we will excuse you.'

Robbie grinned, 'Thanks, Dad, we will see you later,' and he and Alexandra made their way out into the glorious summer garden, where the golden sun was throwing long shadows as the evening was preparing to draw to a close.

CHAPTER TWENTY-FIVE

As Robbie and Alexandra walked out onto the west terrace, heading towards the lake through the garden, Max joined them. Robbie put his hand on to his head, remembering how Max had come to him as a small puppy on his tenth birthday and all the loyalty, love and companionship he had brought him since. At eleven years old, Max was still very active and Merlin and Tristram had lived to be fifteen years old, while Caesar and Brutus, Max's son and grandson were there to carry on the line.

Robbie transferred his full attention to Alexandra, how lovely she was looking tonight, but then she always looked lovely. She had been in his life from his earliest memory and had grown up a part of him. He thought of the long hours they had spent riding around Heronshurst. It went through Robbie's mind that there was a parallel there to his parents. A large part of their lives was spent doing that in the course of their daily duties to their tenants. Robbie just couldn't visualise a life that did not include Alexandra in it.

Feeling his eyes on her, Alexandra turned her head to look at him, quite unaware of the unguarded expression of admiration and adoration in her eyes.

It made Robbie feel ten feet tall, combined with the confidence of his newly acquired honours degree and the knowledge that his father had given him that he was to hand over much of the administration of Heronshurst to him now that he had graduated. He decided it was a perfect moment in a perfect setting to propose marriage to this lovely girl who had been part of his life since he was born. He remembered his father telling him how he had planned to propose to his mother in a romantic setting with moonlight, roses and music but when the moment came he had proposed to her at home. There was no moonlight yet, but the slanting golden sun from a sky of apricot, turquoise and palest blue was quite as beautiful, the roses were not far away and the music was provided by the last trilling notes of a blackbird singing his little heart out on a tree nearby.

Do it right, he admonished himself, guiding Alexandra towards the rose garden.

They sat on a seat in view of the lake, which was gilded by the setting sun and taking Alexandra's hand in his, he said, 'You will marry me, won't you, darling?'

She looked into his eyes and smiled that impish smile he had always loved and which had enslaved him ever since he could remember and said, 'Would it sound forward if I said I thought you would never ask?'

'Oh, my love!' he hugged her to him. 'You will? You really will?'

'Yes, I really will,' she answered, wondering how you could know someone as well as they knew each other, always feeling that they were destined to be together and yet find it all so strange and new and wonderful.

They sat happily close to each other, watching the sun drop behind the purple hills beyond the cornfields the other side of the lake. The sky was turning a deeper apricot and rose with streaks of pure turquoise.

'How beautiful it is,' Alexandra said dreamily. 'As though Beauty was born here, has remained here and will be here forever. As one of Grandma's poems says right at the end, "Where else does Beauty seem as real, so close to touch on either hand? Our England's gentle quiet appeal can vie with any foreign land."'

'It has been like this for nearly three and a half centuries,' answered Robbie. 'I would like to think that it will go on another three and a half, hopefully with our children and our children's children and their descendants still caring for it.'

'Our children,' said Alexandra dreamily. 'How many shall we have?'

'At least four,' answered Robbie. 'If that is all right with you? Are you sure you will be happy as a farmer's wife living here and only occasionally visiting London?'

'Yes, I am sure. Everything seems so real here, I feel I am the right person in the right place,' she added, unconsciously echoing what Sarah had felt from the moment she arrived at Heronshurst.

'It will be dark soon,' Robbie said, 'let's go and tell Mum and Dad we are going to be married.'

'Do you think they will be very surprised and will they approve?' Alexandra asked.

Robbie laughed, 'No to your first question and Yes to the second.' He stood up, pulling Alexandra up with him and they went in to tell the news to Robbie's father and mother. On the way, Alexandra said, 'We are going to tell four people.'

'How do you make that out?' Robbie asked.

'To you, they are Father and Mother but to me they are Uncle Robert and Grandma.'

Robbie laughed, 'Don't get technical, darling, you are confusing me! If you want to be strictly accurate, he is my great-uncle, too, but he has always been more of a father to me than a lot of boys are lucky enough to have and since he adopted me legally, in law he really is my father.'

It was no real surprise to Sarah and Robert when they broke the news of their engagement and in anticipation of the event, she had asked him, 'What do you think about giving Robbie the Falconbridge emerald for Alexandra? It is meant for the eldest son and it would look at its best on a young hand. I have my lovely fire opal, that is my real engagement ring.'

Robert smiled at her lovingly, she had always valued things for the thought and love that went into them rather than by their intrinsic worth. He remembered all those years ago on their wedding day in the little parish church of Heronsbury being touched that she was wearing her opal rather than the priceless emerald. 'I think that if you are happy to relinquish it, it would be a wonderful idea, my darling. I will go and get it.'

When Robbie announced their news, Robert and Sarah congratulated them and wished them both well.

Robbie was touched by the gift of the fabulous emerald and Alexandra was completely overwhelmed by the gesture on Sarah's part. Emeralds were her favourite stones and she had never seen one more beautiful than the Falconbridge ring. She hoped when it came time for her to relinquish it to her elder son's future wife, that she would do it as graciously – but that was a long time away and in the meantime she would enjoy it and appreciate the loving thought behind the gift.

'If you care to take over the Dower House, Robbie, I will see that it is refurbished to your requirements and later on, when your family comes along, we can talk about exchanging houses.'

'Oh, no!' Robbie and Alexandra exclaimed in unison. They looked at each other and Robbie continued, 'We would love to be able to live in the Dower House and it is plenty big enough for at

211

least four children, but you mustn't dream of leaving Heronshurst, it must be yours for all the time you need it. We will be very happy and contented in the Dower House, won't we, Alexandra? And it is equally convenient from the point of view of the administration of the estate.'

'Yes, very happy,' Alexandra agreed, 'you must not think of leaving your home for us.'

Robbie said, 'We are thinking of marrying next Easter. Normally it would take place in the bride's home town, but if Lauren and Tom are agreeable, Alexandra and I would like to be married in the parish church in Heronsbury as you were. Because it happened to be convenient at the time, Lauren and Tom were married in his home town, so we are not creating a precedent. Since it would not be remotely practical for us to be married where they were, we thought it would be nice to be married where you were.'

'It is a nice thought,' Sarah said, 'and it would be much easier, since the whole village will probably want to come as they did for us, not to mention the household. We would never be forgiven by them if we had Robbie's wedding so far away that they could not easily get to see it. It wouldn't carry a lot of weight with them if we said it was traditional to hold it in the bride's home town. As you said, you are not creating a precedent – we were married from here, too. If we held it here, there is more than enough room for us to accommodate any number of guests that Lauren and Tom may wish to invite, to avoid any long-distance travelling on the day.'

Robert said unexpectedly, 'No, the precedent was set as long ago as 1701 when Estelle got married from here because she was an orphan and her guardian was too old to be able to cope with such an event. If I know anything about our family, the then Robert's mother would have been only too glad to take it all on, she loved grand occasions and she adored Estelle so it would have seemed utterly logical to her, never mind about protocol!'

A little shiver ran down Sarah's spine as what she had designated 'the breeze of time passing' swept over her. For a second she had a fleeting glimpse of the long ago about which Robert had been talking, before it was gone. Yes, the brides of the Falconbridges did seem to defy convention, she thought. She was sure Lauren would not make a fuss about where Alexandra was married as long as she was happy. After all, she could do as much or as little as she liked as the bride's mother. Heronshurst would be at her disposal as easily as her own home.

212

'You must discuss it with them first, of course, as I am sure you intended to do, Robbie, but if they are perfectly content about the idea of having the wedding here, we would be more than happy.'

Christmas that year provided a good opportunity for a complete family council on the forthcoming wedding. They sat around the red drawing room after dinner on Christmas Eve and discussed all aspects of it. As Sarah had expected Lauren and Tom were perfectly agreeable for it to take place in Heronsbury parish church.

'That is, of course, if it is convenient to you and Robert, Mother, and doesn't create any problems for you,' Lauren remarked. She was thinking about the upheaval a wedding caused in most houses and she did not want to upset Sarah and Robert's household, although she knew from times past that they seemed to cope with any grand occasion with complete equanimity, and even seemed to enjoy it. I suppose that is what comes of the generations growing up together, she thought, they were really like one large family and everything ran on oiled wheels. Unlike some families she had known!

'Estelle cannot wait to be a bridesmaid,' she remarked to the company at large, 'and no doubt Patrick will enjoy it, too, as it is not the first time he has been a best man and it won't seem too daunting for him.'

Sarah was aware that Robbie had hero-worshipped Patrick as a small boy when he used to demolish Patrick's models and the latter patiently built them up again without getting cross with him. He had always thought of him as 'his big brother' and no other friend would have stood a chance of being best man if Patrick was willing to oblige.

They discussed having the wedding reception at Heronshurst but Robbie and Alexandra thought it would cause less disruption if they followed Sarah and Robert's example and had it at The Heron's Nest.

'You won't get caught up in any problems then, Mother, and you can just concentrate on enjoying the wedding and being the most elegant mother of the bridegroom. There is going to be enough for you to contend with, taking care of all the guests who will be staying. Apart from family and their friends there will be some of mine from scattered places round the world to whom it would be nice to give hospitality if you are agreeable. But we must remember that Bates, Mrs Bates and Mrs Briggs are not as

213

young as they were, even though they would probably not appreciate my saying so, and even with the reception being held at the Nest there will be a lot for them to cope with as it is.'

Sarah smiled at him and blew him a kiss. Alexandra was right, he really did resemble Robert in his care and consideration of people, but since his natural father was Robert's brother's son, it was not really so surprising. It was a pity she hadn't known Richard before the war had taken its toll. He was probably a lot more relaxed and carefree then.

Robbie was right about the number of guests who would need to be accommodated. Apart from Lauren, Tom, Patrick, Estelle and any of their friends, there would be Helene, Adrienne, probably old George and all Robbie's and Alexandra's friends who lived at a distance. It was going to be quite a houseful. Sarah considered how wonderful it was to be contemplating the wedding of the son that she had once thought they would never have. Not only that, but he was marrying her darling granddaughter. She smiled to herself, the relationships were going to confuse some people and her smile broadened as she thought, especially the press who were going to report it.

'What's the joke, Mother?' Robbie asked. 'Do share it with us.'

Sarah touched lightly on what she was thinking and they all laughed and Alexandra remarked, 'We were talking about that on the way back to the house the evening we got engaged. It seems quite normal to us because it happened gradually over a period of time and we got used to it at each step, but to outsiders it could sound a bit like that funny song, where the man ends up being his own grandfather!'

'That's stretching it a bit, darling,' Robbie protested lightly, 'it's not that complicated!'

Alexandra laughed, 'Sorry, darling, no it isn't, is it?'

Robert was smiling, too, but he said quite seriously, 'It's the way it had to work out according to the legend. When I was young, I thought it was far-fetched but as I said to your mother a long time ago, "Too much has fallen into place not to believe it." '

Alexandra looked contrite, her zany sense of humour was going to get her into trouble one day! 'I'm sorry, Uncle Robert, I didn't mean to be rude.'

He smiled at her in such way that she knew he wasn't cross with her and said, 'I know you didn't, darling, but you are going to confuse people even more when you and Robbie are married, if you continue to call me Uncle Robert when I have become your father-in-law.'

Sarah giggled, 'Strangers really will have a problem if you call Robert "Father" and me "Grandmother" in public,' which convulsed everyone. When they had recovered, Alexandra said, 'I shall just have to remember to call you "darling" – I decline to refer to you as "mother-in-law" – it has too many unpleasant music hall connotations and I flatly refuse to call you and Uncle Robert by your Christian names, even if you allowed it, which might have solved the problem. It may be modern and I like to think I am up-to-date most of the time but I draw the line at that. It sounds so disrespectful.'

Robbie leaned over and kissed her, 'That's my sweet little old-fashioned girl,' he said teasingly, much to everyone's amusement.

Robert stood up, 'I don't know about the rest of you,' he said, 'but I have had a long day and I am going to bed. My mother always told me when I was small that if I didn't get to bed on time, Father Christmas wouldn't be able to wait for me to go to sleep and he would move on to the next little boy. Things like that make an impression – and I don't want to take the chance of his missing me.'

Everyone laughed and started to make a move, it was getting late and tomorrow would be a very full day. They all said 'goodnight' to each other and departed for their rooms. Robert rang through to Bates to tell him that everyone had gone to bed, so that he would know he need not wait up any longer and could go round checking everything as he did usually before going to bed.

Sarah had waited while the others left and she and Robert went slowly up the stairs with their arms round each other's waist and when they reached their bedroom, Robert took her in his arms and said, 'Do you remember our first Christmas together, darling? So much has happened since then. It was tragic to lose Richard and young Richard and Sophie so early, but most of it was happy. They left us the legacy of their son who became ours and that is something we never expected but has made us both very happy. I told you once, and I really meant it, that you were all I needed. It was a wonderful bonus to have a son as well and I am sure it has made you even happier, too. Now he is a man about to embark on a family life of his own. It's frightening how time flies, isn't it? But if we are lucky enough to be as happy in the future, I shan't mind growing old with you. It will be nice to be grandparents together and to know that Heronshurst is safely in the family for another generation.'

Sarah sighed as she leaned her head on Robert's shoulder, 'It was – is – a wonderful life, I hope it just goes along the same way.'

'Amen to that,' Robert said fervently.

BOOK III

DESTINY FULFILLED

CHAPTER TWENTY-SIX

Silver Wedding – A New Heir – Estelle Returns

Christmas brought all the usual fun, frivolity and mayhem that usually follows in its wake in most families.

By the time it had arrived, Robbie was settling down to administrating quite a large part of his father's business, while Robert retained as much as he felt would keep him occupied for at least part of the day. It felt strange to him to relinquish the reins but he had great faith and trust in Robbie's ability to carry on the Heronshurst traditions. He was of an age when many men had been retired for some time but he was still mentally and physically very active. Although he was somewhat older than most of the fathers of Robbie's friends, Robbie had always been so proud of him at school functions, when he could easily outshine men ten years or more younger than he.

Robbie wondered if it was his parents' overwhelming love for each other and their family that kept them both so youthful and hoped it would work for him and Alexandra. His parents still rode and his mother walked the dogs for miles sometimes. Caesar was seven and Brutus three but they were often glad of a rest when they returned!

As soon as New Year arrived, Robbie felt that it was not too long to wait for the wedding. It was 'this year' now instead of 'next year'. His mother, Alexandra, Lauren, Estelle and Adrienne had all gone for what his father always insisted on calling 'a girls' day out', to see about their wedding finery. There was one thing to say about the women in his family, Robbie thought, they were all very decorative and showed off the clothes they wore to their best advantage. It was going to be a very picturesque wedding.

Alexandra was still Adrienne's second-in-command and working hard, but since she had decided to become, as she put it borrowing Robbie's phrase, 'a farmer's wife' and would not be in a position to take over permanently from Adrienne, the latter had decided to sell the whole business. 'I shall invest the money and probably spend the rest of my active life globe-trotting. When I get decrepit, I shall sit on the deck of an ocean liner going round the world and let it pass me by. By that time, there will probably be space travel for all and I might even try that – who knows!'

Alexandra had laughed and said, 'I could see you doing just that – you have so much energy still, nothing would surprise me!'

She and Robbie had discussed the situation and when she quoted Adrienne, Robbie had said, 'Where do their generation get all their energy? They seem to have more "get-up-and-go" than people half their age. I hope it runs in the family and we will be equally active at a time when many people want to sit back and do nothing.'

Easter came at last, bringing the wedding and, as it had happened when Sarah and Robert were married there over twenty years ago, the whole village turned out to wish them well.

Robbie could not believe the vision walking towards him up the aisle on her father's arm had really agreed to spend the rest of her life with him. He imagined that was how his father must have felt and thought himself doubly lucky that he had not needed to wait so long. Alexandra had always been there and, please God, they would still be together when they were his parents' age.

The service had finished and they were all being organised into a proper group for the wedding photographs, when Lauren whispered an old family joke to Sarah and they were still laughing when the photograph was taken.

It was still nice to have a traditional wedding album as well as a video cassette of it, Sarah thought. One could sit and linger over it so much more comfortably. She smiled, you are getting hopelessly old-fashioned, she admonished herself.

The photographing session was over and as the group broke up and everyone started to move away, Sarah caught sight of a little, old man leaning heavily on a stick. It wasn't anyone she recognised readily from the village but there was something about him that seemed familiar and she tried to remember if he had been one of Robert's outdoor staff. He turned away as Robbie and Alexandra walked down the path and through the lych-gate to the Rolls to go the short distance to The Heron's Nest.

In the usual mêlée which followed, with everyone discussing

the wedding and saying how lovely it had been, Sarah temporarily forgot the minor incident.

The reception had been underway for quite some time and it was the moment for Alexandra and Robbie to cut the cake. As they were toasting the happy pair, Sarah's memory was jolted suddenly into action. Good heavens! she thought, it was Hubert. It was not really surprising, the engagement and wedding plans had been widely reported in the local press as well as the society magazines and columns in the national newspapers. It was natural that he should be there, even though they had not been in touch with him for years and it was a long time since the least vestige of a thought of him had occurred to Sarah. The idea that amazed was, he is the same age as Robert and he looks at least a generation older! She felt a momentary pang of pity for him, he had always been his own worst enemy and his life was what he had made it. After all her years of happiness with Robert she felt she could forgive as well as forget the misery he had caused her.

Sarah shook off the slight depression that just the brief glimpse of him could generate in her and returned to the present, watching the happy young pair at the start of their life together.

With his acute intuition where she was concerned, Robert sensed that something had troubled her. 'What is it, darling? Is anything wrong?'

Sarah smiled reassuringly at him. 'No, Robert, nothing is wrong – everything is wonderful.' She indicated the bride and groom, 'Don't they look happy? I hope all goes well for them. They stand as good a chance as any young couple starting out in life, they have seen each other in all their moods from the time they cut their teeth.' She was being strictly truthful, everything was wonderful, it wasn't necessary to drag up the deeply buried past to Robert on this lovely day of all days.

As Alexandra hugged Sarah before leaving, she whispered, 'I always knew you were nice enough to be two people, and now you are! You are the nicest mother-in-law I could hope to have.'

Sarah laughed, 'And I couldn't hope for a more charming and delightful daughter-in-law!'

Robbie and Alexandra flew off to the States for their protracted honeymoon, combining the opportunity to pursue some business contacts.

Seeing them starting off at the beginning of their life together, made Robert momentarily aware of the passage of time. Did it gather momentum as one got older? he wondered. He supposed he should feel envious that they had had the chance to start so young, but he could not find it in his heart to have any regrets. Time had been doubly precious to him since Sarah had walked into his life just when he least expected it and even now, after all the years they had been together, she lit up a room for him whenever she entered it. It was the quality not the quantity of the time they had had that counted.

The house seemed very quiet when he and Sarah got back, as all the guests had returned to their own homes. It was a serene and tranquil quiet as though the house were just having a breathing space.

Robbie and Alexandra had been busy just before the wedding, choosing the decor and furniture for the Dower House, which was to be installed while they were away. Robert had insisted on settling any expenses incurred in refurbishing the house as one of their wedding presents, for which the young people had been very grateful.

Sarah and Adrienne were to supervise the work and undertake the arrangement of the furniture according to the plan that Alexandra had drawn out and Robert was to stand by to deal with any practical problems that might arise. As 'the children' said, 'With the three of them to take care of everything, what could possibly go wrong?'

Robert and Sarah were very happy with the way events had transpired and enjoyed the pleasure of seeing the house come alive again, according to the young people's design. It was going to be a very pleasant house to start their married life.

Thinking about all the work that would be going on in the Dower House and the new furniture, fittings, carpets and soft furnishings made Robert say suddenly to Sarah, 'Did you mind not having the whole of the house redecorated when we married, Sarah?'

She gazed at him in astonishment and her laugh was genuine, 'Good heavens, no!' she exclaimed. 'I loved Heronshurst just the way it was, it felt like coming home and apart from our own suite being refurbished to suit us, I would not have changed a thing.'

Robert put his arms around her, 'You were coming home, my darling, I knew it from the first moment you entered my study. I had never been more certain of anything until that day. I knew I had to keep you there, but not as an employee, but I did not want to frighten you away. It seemed the most normal thing in the world that you should take over being the chatelaine, as though you were just resuming your natural place in the scheme of things. If I had had any doubt at all, which I hadn't, it would have been instantly dispelled by the unquestioning way the Bates' accepted you as one of the family. No one needed to suggest that you were – they assumed it at once. I did wonder at the time if you might be suspicious of my motives, but luckily the memories of the past took hold of you and it seemed as natural to you as it did to me. As I said at the time – what anyone outside thought about it had no significance at all. I think in other circumstances I would have proposed marriage to you on the spot and that would have startled you and probably made you think twice about accepting my invitation to stay for a few days. It gave me time to establish in my own mind just how to work things out for the best.'

'You were very correct and circumspect,' Sarah smiled, 'and I fell hopelessly and helplessly in love with you from that moment and hoped you wouldn't guess and think that I was a silly, romantic, middle-aged fool and be frightened off. At that time, I was prepared to do any job that would keep me near you. It was the feeling of *déjà vu* that stopped me thinking logically about how it might seem to outsiders.'

Robert kissed her, tenderly and lingeringly, 'I still feel as certain and love you even more now that we have shared all the years together,' he told Sarah.

She sighed happily in his arms. 'I would like to think that we could go on just like this together for many more years to come, watching our family grow and prosper.'

Robert echoed her sigh of content, 'That sounds good to me,' he answered.

Robbie and Alexandra returned from the States at the end of July and were thoroughly delighted to find that their house had been refurbished exactly as they had planned down to the last detail. They organised a house-warming party, inviting all Robert and Sarah's friends as well as their own and were inundated with gifts for their newly acquired home and they settled down to married life, English style.

They had enjoyed their honeymoon, sightseeing from New York, across to Los Angeles, up to San Francisco and back to New York, during which time they made several useful contacts. Alexandra loved the sophistication of New York and they were wined and dined by many influential people, but she enjoyed it in a detached way, aware that it was not a lifestyle she would want for ever and always in the back of her mind was a picture of the beauty and peace of the grounds of Heronshurst and her own little corner of it in the Dower House.

While they were away, Adrienne had negotiated a very successful deal for her chain of establishments, but the new owners were rather anxious to have the benefit of Alexandra's knowledge of the business and professional expertise to ease them over the transitional period until new personnel were fully conversant with their mode of business in which the clientele/management relationship was very personal and of paramount importance and to reassure the existing clientele that they could rely on the excellent service to which they had been used.

'You see, darling,' Adrienne had explained to Alexandra, 'if they (the clientele) think that it is being taken over by strangers who are not completely *au fait* with their personal tastes, they won't be very happy and I would hate to think that the business would deteriorate. Could you possibly consider supervising everything until they are used to our ways and, what is more, keep our customers happy?'

Alexandra gave the idea some thought. It was not quite what she and Robbie had planned but he would be very busy on his own account and it surely wouldn't affect their life too much, just for a year? She talked it over with Robbie and though he was disappointed at first, he tried to see it from Alexandra's point of view and it would have the advantage of easing her into her quieter life gradually. He loved her to distraction and could never really refuse her anything if it made her happy.

'All right, darling,' he told her, 'if that is what you want, I won't stand in your way, but you will be home at weekends, won't you?'

'Yes, of course, Robbie,' she said, kissing him, 'It will only be for a year or so – it will soon pass.'

But it was nearly three years before Alexandra finished fulfilling her obligations and retired gracefully from the scene, to Robbie's intense relief. Sarah was secretly a little disappointed that there was still no sign of their starting a family. It was no business of hers, she was the first to admit to herself, but her passionate love for Robert and Heronshurst made her yearn for an heir for the future.

It was a great relief and joy when, soon after Alexandra finally gave up working, she and Robbie announced that by early September they hoped to be parents.

Robert and Sarah always considered that they had everything they could possibly want or be entitled to, but the news lifted them to the pinnacle of happiness. Having Robbie had been touched with the sadness of his losing his young parents, although adopting him had brought them extreme joy and their love and pride in him could not have been greater had he been the issue of their own union. Being born of Robert's nearest family and the natural heir to Heronshurst, had made him as close as a son of their own would have been. To know that his child would, hopefully, soon be with them, realised a dream.

When they were alone later that day, Sarah looked at Robert with shining eyes and said, 'Isn't it wonderful, darling? Another heir for Heronshurst.'

'I suppose you are going to say you hope it will be a boy and they can have a girl later?' Robert said, smiling broadly and feeling quite as pleased as Sarah.

Sarah's answering smile was tinged with sadness. 'Yes, I remember I did say that before Robbie was born, didn't I? We could not possibly have guessed then that there would not be another child. They were so young.'

Robert realised that his teasing remark was not as tactful as it might have been. 'My darling, one makes these remarks in good faith, don't blame yourself for it.'

Sarah loved him as always, for his intuitive understanding.

'Robbie says that they want at least four children. I hope all goes well for them and that they get their wish, all in good time,' she told Robert.

'They are normally healthy young people and medical technology has improved vastly over the years and is continuing to do so all the time. Do you realise what else is due about the same time as the baby?'

Sarah looked amused. 'You don't think that I have forgotten our Silver Wedding, do you?' she asked.

'Twenty-five years!' Robert mused. 'Twenty-five happy, memorable years. Sometimes I wonder what I did to deserve so much happiness.'

'I do, too,' Sarah agreed. 'Awe-inspiring, isn't it? You look just as handsome and are even more charming than the first time I saw you.'

Robert gave her a little bow, 'Thank you, my Lady. I am considerably greyer, so my mirror tells me.'

Sarah said, 'That only makes you look more distinguished and I was grey when we met, so that was one thing I did not need to worry about as I grew older!'

'Your hair is a beautiful silver, not grey,' Robert objected.

Sarah laughed. 'You have been listening to Lauren. She always corrected me like that when I said my hair was grey and claimed that her contemporaries spent a fortune trying to get their hair that colour. It seemed to be the fashion then for women in their thirties to anticipate going grey. Sorry! silver.'

'Do you remember the little girl at the Christmas party who said your hair looked like silver and felt like silk?' Robert asked.

'Goodness! What a memory you have! That was years ago, even before we were married. That "little girl" must be nearly thirty years old now,' Sarah commented.

'It always stuck in my mind,' Robert said, 'like a small cameo fixed in time, because I was envious of a four-year-old who had no inhibitions and could admire and stroke your hair with impunity.'

'It would have been nice then to know that you wanted to do so,' Sarah said, going back in time herself.

'I still do,' Robert replied, coming back to the present and moving over to sit on the arm of Sarah's chair so that he could suit the action to the words.

'It still makes me feel as if my bones were melting,' Sarah said, dreamily, leaning against Robert. 'Do you think we should act our age?'

'Not if it means I cannot show you how much I love you,' Robert replied, very firmly.

'We will be finishing the decade and the century in memorable style,' Sarah remarked. 'That is, if one counts the year two thousand as the beginning of the twenty-first century. Strictly speaking, I suppose it is the last of the nineties decade, counting one to ten inclusively.'

'Yes, that is a moot point, but I don't think anything on earth is going to stop people observing the year 2000 – nothing will make them wait until 2001 for the celebrations. Nevertheless, as you say, 1999 should prove to be a memorable year for us, all being well. I suppose it is in the lap of the gods whether the baby arrives to upstage our Silver Wedding celebrations or vice versa.'

'As long as it arrives safely and both mother and baby are well and healthy, I don't expect it will bother us if he/she comes right in the middle of our party, do you?' Sarah asked Robert. 'The whole idea seems so wonderful that sometimes I am almost afraid to think about it until it actually happens. Although the circumstances were sad, it was miraculous to find that we had a son and now that he is about to have one of his own. Looking back, I find the way that everything worked out awesome.'

'Yes, it is, isn't it?' Robert agreed, 'but it was all ordained a long time ago and we were merely following the natural plan.'

'That is the aspect of it that I find so astounding,' Sarah said.

CHAPTER TWENTY-SEVEN

Robert and Sarah were having a discussion about domestic matters in the privacy of their sitting room one evening after dinner and Robert said, 'I talked to Bates again today on the subject of his retirement and the conversation went something like this:

"Bates, have you considered yet whether you would like to retire and take life easily?"

Bates: "No, my Lord, I am very happy the way I am, that is, if you are satisfied with my work."

Me: "Yes, Bates, I am very satisfied with your work and I really cannot imagine Heronshurst without you but, although you are ten years younger than I, you have given yeoman service for a long time and I wondered if you had considered a rest."

"No, my Lord, not unless you want me to retire."

"No, Bates, I do not want you to retire but, I feel you are entitled to do so, if you wish."

"Thank you, my Lord, but if it meets with your approval I would like to carry on until I am no longer capable of giving entire satisfaction."

"Very well, Bates, as you wish."

"Thank you, my Lord. Is that all?"

"Yes, Bates, that is all, thank you." '

Sarah laughed, 'I had a similar conversation with Mrs Bates and her reaction was much the same. Although she is a year or two younger than her husband, she is still at an age when a lot of women are ready to put up their feet and do as little as possible. Many of the women in the village who are her age or even younger, have been retired as far as work outside is concerned and are happy spending the time they are not taking care of the house, socialising and playing bingo, or just resting.'

228

'Like you do, darling?' Robert asked, referring to the last phrase of Sarah's remark.

'I haven't had so much to worry about,' Sarah said, laughing.

When spring brought the primroses again, Sarah felt it was as fresh and new as if it were happening for the first time and it was made even more memorable when Alexandra announced that there was a possibility that she was going to have twins. Lauren was over the moon about it, she couldn't wait to be a grandmother.

'Darling! How exciting, I do hope they are right in the diagnosis,' Sarah exclaimed, when she was told. 'That is, of course, if you are happy about it.'

Alexandra looked like the cat that swallowed the cream, 'Robbie wants at least four children,' she told Sarah, 'can you think of a better way than to have them two at a time?'

Sarah laughed, 'Only by having quadruplets and I would imagine that is rather uncomfortable towards the end.'

'At least, if I am having two, I might get a look in with at least one of them, as far as mother is concerned,' Alexandra said. 'She is getting quite broody.'

'I've never known her pass a pram with a new baby in it without stopping to look,' Sarah told her.

By the time the bluebells had changed the woods from pale lemon to deep sapphire, the possibility of Alexandra's having twins was confirmed. She was asked if she would like to know the sex of the babies, but she refused, saying firmly that she would rather wait until they were born.

'Lauren can't wait to be a grandmother,' Sarah remarked to Robert. 'We always laughed about the idea that she would completely monopolise the baby but, as Alexandra said, with two perhaps she will get one of them at a time! I had resigned myself to the fact that I would have to take a back seat.'

Robert and Sarah spent considerable time discussing the plans for their Silver Wedding and remembering all the people from the past whom they most wanted to help them celebrate it.

Adrienne had arrived back in England after a protracted trip around the world. There was nothing on earth that would have kept her away from Heronshurst during the anniversary festivities. Sarah had telephoned to ascertain whether she was in the country, to remind her and give her plenty of notice of the event. 'You will be able to come, won't you?' Sarah asked and Adrienne said, as she had years before on the occasion of the first wedding, 'Just try and stop me!'

Sarah was surprised how the number of invitations had mounted up and as soon as they were received, presents started to arrive and continued daily.

'When people have been married as long as we have, there are very few things that they haven't acquired for their home,' Sarah remarked to Robert as they unwrapped yet another gift, 'but I continue to be surprised by the originality shown by our friends. We will soon run out of places to display all the lovely ornaments – even in a house this size. There seem to be even more presents than we had on our original wedding day. Strictly speaking, I suppose to a lot of people our anniversary falls in October since that was the public wedding, but since we first exchanged our vows at the civil ceremony, for me, that was the beginning of our married life together and the church wedding confirmed and blessed it.'

'Me, too,' Robert said, rather ungrammatically. 'I wanted us to be married just as soon as possible, hence the civil ceremony. You don't think we ought to have another celebration in October, too, do you?'

Sarah laughed. 'And get another batch of presents?' she suggested. 'As far as other people are concerned, apart from our nearest and dearest, they would remember our getting married but I doubt very much whether they would recollect the date unless it had personal significance for them, so the fact that we are celebrating in September rather than October, won't even register with them.'

Alexandra was getting close to the time when the babies were due, but so far, it looked as though the Silver Wedding day would arrive first. She looked very blooming and happy – approaching motherhood suited her and Robbie thought she had never looked more beautiful. He went around with an almost smug, self-satisfied grin permanently on his face.

The main plan for the party was a formal dinner, followed by dancing for the young people and anyone else who cared to participate.

Sarah looked in to the dining room at the last moment on the day in question and became aware that something had been added to the table. It was an exquisitely chased silver rosebowl, filled with roses that she recognised as 'Sterling Silver'. How lovely they were and how beautiful their perfume! She was just wondering how they got there when Bates came in to check every detail of the table and seeing Sarah looking at the roses, he said, 'Excuse me, my Lady, the whole of the staff wanted to contribute to such a special and happy occasion as your and his Lordship's Silver Wedding and we chose the rosebowl. I hope you approve the inscription. Young Harris, the new head gardener, has been nurturing the roses for weeks past to bring them to perfection on the day. I hope you and his Lordship will forgive the liberty.'

'Bates, they are absolutely beautiful, thank you. I shall be writing to thank everyone in due course. How kind and thoughtful you all are. The bowl is exquisite and the inscription is very touching.' Under Sarah and Robert's names and the date had been engraved 'From all your devoted household.'

'Thank you, my Lady, I will pass on your message.'

Dinner had come to an end and the guests were assembled in the big drawing room with coffee and liqueurs. Robert deprecated the division of the sexes at the end of the meal and had rejected such an antiquated, outdated idea.

Alexandra had enjoyed her meal as much as anyone, she had retained her healthy appetite after an initial bout of nausea in the early days and was now sitting among the rest of the guests with Robbie in close attendance. Lauren and Sarah had both been keeping a watchful eye on her, but at that moment were having a quiet conversation between themselves.

Robbie came over and informed them very quietly that he was going to take Alexandra back to their own home.

'Don't worry, Mother, Lauren. Philip and Mary are coming back with us and he says the fewer people at this stage, the better.' Philip Harfield was their comparatively young physician and his wife, Mary, was also a doctor practising as a gynaecologist specialising in obstetrics.

Sarah and Lauren exchanged concerned glances but both acknowledged the wisdom of keeping out of the way until being told otherwise.

No one apart from Robert and Adrienne seemed to have noticed anything unusual and Sarah, Robert, Lauren and Adrienne tried to concentrate on entertaining the guests. Sarah recollected Robert's saying, 'I wonder if the baby will upstage our Silver Wedding?' They didn't know then that it would be two babies arriving and it seemed that they had done just that. Sarah didn't

231

mind in the slightest but she couldn't help being on edge for her lovely Alexandra. She was a very healthy young woman and there was no real reason to worry but it was hard to give her full attention to being the perfect hostess in the circumstances and she knew that Lauren was feeling the same. Even Adrienne was not immune from the anxiety – Alexandra was almost like a daughter to her, too.

The time seemed to drag by but when Sarah looked at the clock, less than an hour had gone. A first pregnancy always took longer than subsequent ones, she must try and think of something else. The minutes continued to pass on leaden feet as she attended to the needs of her guests. She could feel that Lauren was as tense as she.

What seemed like hours later, the telephone rang and as she rushed to answer it, Robbie's jubilant voice enquired, 'Does anyone want to come and see their new grandson and granddaughter?'

Sarah did not know whether to laugh or cry with relief, 'Robbie, oh, Robbie! Have you really got one of each?'

Robbie's voice sounded triumphant as he said, 'We certainly have and even allowing for being biased, they are rather good-looking.'

'Are they all right, darling, – and Alexandra?' Sarah asked anxiously.

'Absolutely blooming, as you will see for yourself,' Robbie told her reassuringly.

'We will come straightaway, darling. Congratulations from us all.'

'Thank you. See you in a few minutes.'

Sarah replaced the telephone with a hand that trembled slightly. It was over and they were all well, thank God. She relayed the news to Robert, Lauren, Tom and Adrienne, rather superfluously as it happened, as they had been hanging on every word.

While Adrienne stayed behind to stand in as temporary hostess, the others slipped out and hurried to the Dower House.

They found Alexandra sitting up in bed looking unexpectedly radiant and beautiful for a woman who had just produced twins and Robbie looked ready to burst with pride. Philip and Mary, with the help of the local district nurse whom they had called in, had restored everything to perfect order and the new additions to the Falconbridge family were sleeping peacefully in their cots.

232

Lauren, Sarah and Tom just gazed and gazed in silent awe while Robert spoke for all of them.

'As you say, Robbie, even allowing for being biased they are rather good-looking,' and turning to Alexandra he said, 'Congratulations, young lady, you have made us all very happy.'

Alexandra beamed at him, 'Thank you, Father, they wouldn't dare arrive without the Falconbridge quota of good looks, would they?' unknowingly repeating almost word for word what Sophie had said when Robbie was born.

The two small recipients of all the admiration continued to sleep and Sarah wondered briefly if either of them had inherited the wonderful Falconbridge eyes like Robert and Robbie, but only time would tell, it was early days yet before they would develop their final colour.

Robbie announced, 'Let me introduce you to them, ladies first, please meet Lauren Alexandra Estelle and her younger brother by ten minutes, Richard Robert.'

Sarah and Lauren were so happy that they were close to tears and after congratulating both the new young parents, Sarah suggested that she and Robert should return to Heronshurst, leaving Alexandra to the special pleasure of sharing her new joy with her mother and father.

'Yes, you have deserted your guests, haven't you?' Robbie said. 'I will see you out. What a really memorable day – your Silver Wedding and two new additions to the family,' but at that moment, he was not aware of just how memorable.

He stood at the door, watching his parents walking arm-in-arm along the path to rejoin their guests, their backs still straight and erect. How proud he was of them! and what a happy life they had given him. He silently sent them all his love and thanks.

As they passed through the shade of some trees, the hem of his mother's dress caught the light from the external lamps around Heronshurst and shone with a golden gleam. How strange, Robbie thought, I could have sworn her dress was a soft turquoise blue.

The figures emerged fully from the shadows and Robbie found himself looking at a young girl in a gold satin dress, her dark brown hair was piled high on the top of her head at the front and sides, with ringlets at the back. She was accompanied by a tall, young cavalry officer in full dress uniform, who had his arm protectingly round her waist. As Robbie stared in wonderment, they turned and waved to him and even from where he was standing, Robbie could see that they were smiling. He waved in response and as they continued on their way, the two figures gradually re-emerged as his parents.

Robbie stood bemused for several moments, deep in thought, so that was how the legend evolved. He felt very awed and privileged to be granted the sight he had just witnessed and stood for a moment longer, aware that he, too, had been the final link in the legend that had come true despite the odds against it.

He returned to his lovely wife and new family to tell her of his experience, giving her as matter-of-fact an account as he could, finishing, 'So Estelle did find her way back to Heronshurst and her Robert and they lived their life again on earth and brought up their son, as Estelle had predicted, through Father and Mother. It was said that the reason Estelle had never been seen at Heronshurst was because her spirit went wandering to find Robert and that if ever she was seen here it would be because her search had ended with her finding him and her spirit was at rest. They are happy now, united forever, their Destiny fulfilled.'

THE END